# RIVERRUN
BEYOND THE FIVE SENSES

# ABOUT
# EDWARD BURLEY

Edward Burley has always been fascinated by human behaviour. What makes people do what they do? He could think of no better place to explore this question than in the world of crime fiction.

Edward lives in the West Country with his wife, two children and healthy guitar collection.

For the fallen

EDWARD BURLEY
# BLAME

FORESHORE PUBLISHING
London

Published by Foreshore Publishing 2022.
The home of quality short fiction.

Copyright © Edward Burley 2022

This book is sold subject to the condition that it shall not, by way of trade or otherwise, be lent, re-sold, hired out, or otherwise circulated without the publisher's prior consent in any form of binding or cover other than that in which it is published and without a similar condition, including this condition, being imposed on the subsequent purchaser
Foreshore Publishing

The Forge 397-411 Westferry Road,
Isle of Dogs, London, E14 3AE

Foreshore Publishing Limited Reg. No. 13358650

ISBN 978-1-7395930-3-2

www.foreshorepublishing.com

# PROLOGUE

The rain tapped on the living room window as if asking for permission to enter. The young boy looking out of the window wished that he was anywhere but here. His head hurt. His tears had run dry. 'I don't ever want to feel like this again,' he said out loud before feeling the familiar hand of his Aunt Mary touching his shoulder.

'You're the man of the house now' she said, squeezing slightly. 'With great responsibility. Honor thy mother and father.'

*What does that even mean?* the boy thought to himself.

'Your Dad needs you to step up, be strong and look after your mother now he's gone. Come on.'

Mary took him by the hand, gently ushering him back into the room.

A sea of people dressed in black, sipping from his parents' China cups and chatting amongst themselves greeted him. To the right of the room, along the back wall was a decorating table dressed in white. Upon it were triangular shaped sandwiches, miniature sausage rolls, slices of quiche, cakes, and a selection of fruit. He could overhear the various conversations of those in the room.

'I'm just going outside for a cigarette,' he heard one man saying. 'I'd pass them out, but I think some of us in the congregation are a little underage'. He looked over at the boy, staring back at him with a glazed expression. His aunt had left him. She was now mingling with some of his mother's teaching colleagues making small talk.

*Why can't they all just leave us alone?* he thought to himself, trying to block out the noise of the room. 'Well, we had planned to go down to Beer this summer, but unfortunately, we couldn't find the time.

My husband Craig was unable to take time off from his work,' said Janet Leech.

'Pardon my ignorance, but where exactly is Beer?' asked Sheila Judd, holding her paper plate in her left hand and examining the contents of a rectangular sandwich with her right.

'It's a little finishing village in East Devon,' replied Janet. 'A very quaint little place. Streams flow down the Main Street between the pavement and the road. My Sister owns a fixed caravan at the caravan park on top of a steep hill overlooking the bay. It really is a beautiful place.'

'Sounds idyllic,' replied Shelia.

The boy wondered around another group of adults talking amongst themselves, desperately trying to find his mother having been abandoned by his aunt. His eyes eventually fell upon her in the corner of the room, sat down on a chair next to one of his older cousins. As he began to make his way towards them, a man stepped out in front of him.

'Hello Joseph.'

The boy looked up into the smiling face of Shane Fox, one of his father's colleagues from his driving school.

'I'm so sorry son. Your father really was a truly nice man.'

Joe could feel the emotion in him begin to rise. He tensed his body.

'He loved you very much. Talked about you all the time. He was very proud of you.'

Joe tried to say thank you, but all he could manage was an awkward smile. All he wanted to do was shut himself away and disappear into a world of fantasy. The woods or the seas of Narnia would be a welcome refuge from this.

'It's true,' came another voice, female this time. 'He had a picture of you and your mother he kept tucked up in his sun visor.'

Cheryl Levitt walked over to both Joe and Shane before crouching down in front of him, her eyes level with his.

'Your father was the second driving instructor I had. During one lesson I ended up crashing into another car at a busy junction. I thought he would be extremely angry as I had written off the vehicle, but he was far more worried about me.'

Joe shuffled his feet uncomfortably.

'Anyway, I sustained an injury during the crash and couldn't drive for a while,' Cheryl continued. 'But every day, your father phoned my parents to check on how I was regardless. That's the kind of man he was.' She paused for a moment and took a deep breath, trying not to let her emotion get the better of her. 'He helped me to overcome my fear and get back behind the wheel of a car, something I never thought I would do. But he knew. He knew how important a skill it would be for my future career. I'm so sorry.'.

Starting to sob now, Cheryl stood up and disappeared back into the other mourners in them room.

*How do I even begin to live up to my father?* Joe thought to himself as he turned and ran back towards his quiet space by the window.

\*\*\*

'Knife. knife!' exclaimed Connie Betton, running through the main doors that led into the sixth form common room. 'There's a knife on the school grounds!'

Several of the students sat nearest the door looked up at her and laughed, but most of her peers didn't hear her over the loud music coming from the stereo at the far end of the room. It wasn't until Doug Charles, the head of the sixth form walked in purposefully behind Connie that the mood in the room changed. 'Can I have your attention please. It is believed that someone is carrying a knife on the school premises,' he said. 'I've locked the doors. The Police are on their way. We are all to remain inside until they give us all clear.'

Several of the students still didn't hear him over the music.

'Oh, for heaven's sake!' Doug exclaimed.

He made his way over towards the far end of the room. Josh Wyman was sat on the back of the chair nearest the stereo, singing along to every word. Rather than try and get his students attention again, he walked straight up to the stereo and pressed the off button. The music abruptly stopped. Doug now had everyone's attention.

'Err. Sorry Sir,' said Josh timidly having seen the look of exasperation on his teachers face.

'Now, as I was trying to say over the noise, we're all staying here until we're told otherwise. It is believed there is someone carrying a knife on site.'

Having heard him this time, several students sat next to the large rectangular windows now span round in their seats and pressed their heads against the glass, scanning in both directions. Others stood up behind them, trying to catch a glimpse of any movement outside of the common room.

'Any ideas where they've been spotted Sir?' asked one student.

'Down by our sports centre, heading up this way John,' he replied.

Another sixth form teacher, Evelyn Gray appeared from behind the double doors that led to the centre's classrooms.

'What's going on Doug?' she asked quizzically as she walked towards him past the rows of cushioned green chairs.

'Some idiot brought a knife onto school grounds Evelyn,' he replied. 'Why they built the school around an old public footpath in the first place is beyond me!'

'You mean it's not a student?' Evelyn asked.

'I don't know,' Doug replied. 'Let's just hope it's a false alarm.'

'Is that the office phone I can hear ringing?' asked Evelyn, nodding in the direction of the common room entrance.

'Yes. Excuse me!' said Doug, walking hastily back towards the front of the room.

In the amongst the groups of students chatting amongst themselves as to who the culprit could be sat a solitary figure with his head in a sociology book. 'Joe,' whispered a voice suddenly next to him.

'What a way to get people's attention.'

On hearing this remark, Joe lifted his head from his book and stared at Ross Barry. Ross slipped his backpack off his right shoulder before sitting in the seat next to him.

'Surely we have evolved socially and linguistically to not need to use the threat of violence for our own means don't you think?' Joe asked.

Ross laughed.

'Violence is a part of nature, as are we humans. In the right circumstances it could be anyone out there with the blade Joe.'

Joe thought about this last statement for a moment.

'You're right,' he said finally. 'I pity them.'

# 1.

The New Start charity shop was busy. Since they had moved to their new premises in the main high street, the staff had seen a dramatic increase in customers coming through its doors. Not only that, but the general public's attitude towards the shop had completely changed since it first opened in its previous location ten years ago. To salvage an item barely used at a bargain price was now considered sensible shopping, and its customers were not short of options.

There were several people in the shop this afternoon, casting their eyes over the various clothes racks, bookcases and even jewellery on display. One member of staff was currently attempting to climb into the window display to remove a jacket from a mannequin.

'It was this one wasn't it dear?' she asked, having finally got herself within reaching distance.

'No, the other one,' came the reply. 'Sorry.'

'That's Ok,' the staff member replied. 'Give me a moment.'

On the other side of the shop, a man was approaching the till with several items. He was carrying amongst these a man's coat, a high visibility jacket, a baseball cap, and a large backpack. Beneath these items was a radio-controlled car. He surveyed the shop, trying to find the nearest free member of staff that would be able to serve him when he arrived at the desk. Just as he placed his items down ready for the cashier to scan, a woman stood up from behind the counter. She had been crouched down re-stocking the carrier bags just out of sight.

'Good afternoon,' she said to the man in front of her. She picked up the radio-controlled car and turned it over, looking for its barcode.

'That's a real bargain,' she said having scanned the item. 'Looks practically new.'

The man at the counter smiled.

'Yes,' he replied. 'Perfect for the Kids! It's the next thing, next thing, next thing, next thing; Then eight weeks later it's shoved in the bottom of the wardrobe. No point in spending a fortune.'

'Very sensible,' the cashier replied, continuing to ring up the rest of the man's items. 'Off anywhere nice?' she asked whilst scanning the backpack.

'Not imminently, but that price is too good to ignore. I paid a lot more for my current one and it's looking a little old and battered now.'

'That'll be nine pounds please,' the lady replied having rung up all the items. 'Do you need a bag?'

'No thanks,' came the reply.

'Are you paying by cash or card today?' the cashier asked, 'Only this reader takes a moment to warm up.'

'Cash' said the man, handing over a ten-pound note.

The lady behind the counter smiled at him whilst giving him his change and receipt.

'Have a good afternoon,' she said as he collected his items and strolled towards the exit.

'I will try' he replied.

After exiting the shop, he took the half dozen paces across the pavement towards the road where his car was parked. Having unlocked the vehicle, he headed round to the rear and opened the boot. Most of its room was already occupied by an archive box, but with a little manipulation he managed to get everything in and successfully close it again. Heading back round to the front of the car, he waited for a gap in the traffic before opening the driver door and climbing into its seat. He placed and turned the key in the ignition before flicking on his right indicator. Having ascended the gears, he removed one hand from the steering wheel and pushed the button on his car stereo.

Joseph Darby had been a sociology of culture lecturer for twenty years now, witnessing first-hand what he believed to be the cultural devolution of societies youth. Extreme action was now needed to put all the people he was trying to reach back on the right path. Today's little shopping trip was the final piece of a puzzle in a plan two years in the making.

He had been ciphering chemicals from the university's chemistry laboratory millimetres at a time to not arouse suspicion over the last twenty- four months. His arsenal would be low cost, easy to plant and highly effective based on the statistics he had found. They could also be concealed in anything from a shoe to a truck, so a bigger vehicle than the one he was currently driving had been bought and modified. To avoid a large purchase showing up on any bank statement, Joe had paid the seller in cash by making weekly withdraws from a cash point and stockpiling the money at home.

Everything was now in place. He had the items to disguise both himself and his true intentions. It was time to visit to his father.

\*\*\*

Having parked his car at the front gate, Joe entered the churches grounds and followed the gravel pathway to the left. He scanned the gravestones until he came to his fathers, George Darby.

Dead, wilted flowers protruded from the flower holder. The grass was still wet from the previous night's rain.

Bending down, he removed them before throwing them under the bushes directly behind him.

'Hi Dad.'

As a child he would spend hours talking to the gravestone that marked his father's final resting place. 'I would have brought you some fresh flowers, but the daffodils are way out of season,' he said standing up. He stood silently in thought, struggling to find his words. 'I know you would strongly disapprove of what I'm about to do Dad, but there is no alternative. Mother has Mark now; she doesn't need me. This is something I must do, and not just for myself.'

He heard footsteps on the path behind him and glanced over his shoulder. A couple were making their way into the yard with a fresh bunch of flowers, gardening gloves and an empty carrier bag ready to tend to their loved one's grave.

'Goodbye father. See you on the other side.'

\*\*\*

Sally Raymore had just arrived at St Peters Church pre-school to collect her son Connor.

She was stood congregated in a glass lobby with the other children's parents, guardians and grandchildren between the churches main entrance and its separate preschool building.

Everyone watched as Kim, one of the preschool teachers came to open the locked door to allow them access into the building. Sally followed the other parents down a long corridor and into main room of the school, passing the parish office, a vacant classroom, and toilets.

All the children were sat ready for collection on a mat with different coloured squares.

'Mum!' yelled Connor over the sounds of the other children. Sally was stood searching for his signing in and signing out card as he ran over to her. Once she had found it, Sally quickly wrote her initials and the time of collection using one of the pens dotted amongst the cards.

'Mum let's go!' said Connor. He seemed to be filled with the same amount of energy this afternoon as he did earlier in the morning when Sally had dropped him off.

'Connor,' she called after him as he headed towards the doors. 'Don't forget your lunchbox.'

'Oops, sorry Mummy,' Connor replied.

He walked over and collected his lunch box from a wooden trolley before re-joining his mum stood by the door with two of his teachers.

'Bye Connor,' smiled Janet as they walked through the door. 'Have a good afternoon.'

Sally smiled at the teacher. 'Thank you. See you soon.'

'Bye' called Connor, already halfway down the corridor.

'Wait please Connor,' Sally called after him. 'Stop.'

Connor stopped in the middle of the corridor. 'Make sure your coats done up properly please young man,' said Sally catching up with him. 'The wind is picking up based on the looks of that tree. Thankfully we don't have far to walk.'

Once Connor had zipped up his jacket, the continued along the corridor and out into the foyer. Sally held the outside door open, and they stepped outside into the wind.

'Burr!' he exclaimed as they made their way towards home.

'Did you have a good day then?' Sally asked as they walked along the pavement.

'I was playing outside in garden with Alex,' Connor replied, stretching out his left arm and running his fingers through the leaves of the trees at the bottom of the gardens they were passing. Several cars passed them with his friends waving at him, but Connor was too distracted to see them.

'I've got mud on me,' he said proudly.

'Yes, I can see that' replied Sally smiling. 'Not to worry though. You can change when we get home.'

They walked past the parking area and fenced off communal garden area at the back of the block of flats they lived in. Sally pressed the tradesman button at the bottom of the doorbell and intercom system. The door swung open on its electric hinge, and they entered the communal hallway. Sally took her house keys from her handbag and unlocked their front door. As soon as the gap was wide enough for him to fit, Connor slipped through. Sally could hear his footsteps as he ran down their hallway toward his bedroom.

'Shoes young man!' Sally called after him as she bent down to pick up the post. "I don't want mud everywhere.'

Connor appeared from his bedroom at the far end of the hallway. He took off his school bag and sat on the floor to undo his shoes. Once his shoes were off, he stood up again, undid his coat and let it slide down his arms and onto the floor.

'Pick that up please Connor,' said Sally, flicking through the pile of letters and junk mail that made up today's post.

Connor did as he was instructed.

'Sorry Mum,' he said before running back down the corridor to his room.

'Kids!' Sally exclaimed out loud.

She turned left and entered their living room, throwing the junk mail into her wastepaper basket as she headed towards the sofa. Sitting down, she turned over the remaining envelope in her hand and started to open it. Hopefully this was what she had spent the last few days waiting for. She could hear Connor is his bedroom playing with his favourite action figures as she removed the contents of the envelope. Inside were two timed tickets for the exhibition at the city's bay centre tomorrow morning. She had deliberately not told Connor, hoping to surprise him. He was currently playing with the figures from the popular series that was the subject of the exhibition. Smiling, Sally stood up and exited the living room heading towards the kitchen. Connor could still be heard playing as she placed the tickets into the large pocket at the bottom of her family planning calendar that hung on the wall before picking up the kettle.

To the sounds of intergalactic trouble, she refilled the kettle and placed it back on its stand before flicking the on bottom. She smiled. Connors face in the morning would be a picture.

# 2.

Later that evening having changed clothes, Joe placed a tablet into the dishwasher's door compartment and shut it. He turned the dial to the right until it reached the Clean and Shine cycle. After pushing the on button, he folded up the tea towel that was abandoned on the side and hung it over the upper handle of the oven.

He turned and walked over to the fridge and opened the door. The shelves were well stocked with plenty of foods for a few days, but that didn't matter to him. He was accessing what he could get away with buying that would necessitate his leaving the house under normal pretences.

*Milk*, he thought to himself. *A cucumber, and baby leaf salad.* He picked up and shook the salad dressing bottle.

Dressing too.

He shut the fridge and headed out of the kitchen, down the house's hallway towards the front door and into the sitting room. His wife Claire was sat on the rug in the middle of the sitting room in front of the sofa. On the coffee table in front of her was a textbook and a pile of papers that had been handed in by her chemistry students she had taught earlier that day. Joe couldn't help but notice the glass of red wine also on the table. She was currently using the TV remote, flicking through the channels trying to find something to watch.

'I have to nip out for some fresh salad supplies,' he said from his position behind the sofa. 'Do you want anything?'

'No thanks Joe,' replied Claire, her eyes still on the television screen in front of her. 'I just need to crack on with this. See you when you get back.'

'Ok,' he replied and left the room.

He wondered towards the front door and slipped on his shoes before patting his pockets making sure he had both his wallet and car keys. He had placed his newly purchased coat back in his car earlier. Joe opened the front door and shut it behind him, before stepping down from the front doorstep and out into the evening air.

\*\*\*

Joe stood outside the cinema looking at the show times. By his calculations the film in screen two would finish roughly around the same time the trailers started in screen four. *Perfe*ct.

Anthony was sat behind the kiosk inside the foyer twiddling his thumbs. His colleague, Sophie was on her break. Despite only having served six snack deals and dispensing just two tickets, the cinema was busy. The marked-up prices on the items in the cinema shop meant most people now brought their own refreshments in with them. The pre-booked ticketing system meant even less transactions between the staff and customers. By tapping in their surname and scanning their payment cards into one of four available machines in the foyer, people were able to redeem their tickets.

*If it weren't for the need of us checking their tickets, we'd be out of the job,* he thought to himself.

He looked up just as Joe walked in through the entrance and straight up to the kiosk.

'One for screen four please,' he said, glancing from side to side at the stairs to screen one and the doors he had just entered.

'£4.50 please. Can I get you any snacks or drinks this evening?' Anthony asked him.

Joe glanced at his name tag.

'No thank you Anthony,' he replied.

'Just £4.50 then please,' said Anthony. He took the money and handed Joe his ticket.

'Enjoy the film.'

Ticket in hand, Joe turned and walked through the entrance doors of screen four. He followed the sloping corridor and walked into the small screen room whilst slipping on a pair of skin tone disposable gloves. Walking along the wall to the left side of the theatre, he followed the isle towards the front until he came to the fourth row. D. He edged sideways past the folded-up seats until he reached seat number 11. He took his coat off and placed it over the chair beside him and sat down.

Reaching into the right pocket of his jeans, he fumbled with his house keys before pulling out a battery. He then put his hand into his coat pocket next to him and pulled out a black timer.

He removed the back and inserted the battery as directed by the location of the spring contacts. Thankfully he had already familiarised himself with the timer in better light, as he knew the lower lighting levels in the room would affect his visibility. Having inserted the battery into the timer and replacing its back, he turned it over. Four zeros were now flashing up at him, prompting him to enter a time. He held down the right-hand button below the digits until it read thirty minutes before hitting the start button. He placed the timer back into his coat pocket and closed his eyes.

He could hear the people coming in after him, the chatter of couples and groups finding their seats, a few already skimming and crunching the top popcorn from its cardboard containers. He opened his eyes. The rows in front of him were also now filling up, with the odd chair free between the various groups of people.

Joe took a deep breath. He had arrived. All those months of preplanning had led up to this moment. Now he had only two choices in front of him. He could back out, or he could proceed.

He looked around and stood up, before edging his way back along the row quickly, this time passing people occupying the seats that were previously folded up before walking swiftly back towards the entrance.

'That guy left his coat!' said a man to his wife who had sat in the seats directly behind him. He glanced behind him hoping to catch Joe's attention, but he'd already left the screen room.

'Don't worry Tom,' replied his wife. 'I'm sure he's just gone to use the gents quickly before the movie starts. He'll be back. Try the popcorn, it's still warm.'

'I guess so…' Tom replied.

Joe was stood just inside the doors of the screen room. He paused, waiting to make sure that there was enough of a crowd exiting screen two to shield him from the view of the counter opposite. He spotted his moment, opened the screen door, and exited the building amongst them.

*Phase one, part one complete,* he thought to himself as he headed off in the direction of the nearest supermarket.

\*\*\*

Sophie was about to start cleaning the popcorn she had spotted on the foyers floor when she heard a loud bang followed by screaming coming from inside screen four.

'Did you hear that?' she asked Anthony.

'Would've been hard to miss!' Anthony replied, looking up from his copy of the cinemas preview magazine he had borrowed from a rack. 'Although the sound design must be awful! I've never heard any film out here before.'

But the screams appeared to be getting louder and closer.

Sophie stood up, just as the double doors to screen four were flung open by thirty people, all trying to push past one another in a stampede towards the exit.

'Bomb! Bomb!' yelled one student over the deafening noise of screams and crying that now filled the foyer. 'Bomb!'

Anthony caught sight of two girls in amongst the crowd. They were crying uncontrollably in each other's arms as they walked. Blood was all over their clothes, and the pair both had cuts to their arms and foreheads. Sophie and Anthony looked at each other, both with panic attack in their eyes.

'What do we do? What do we do?' Sophie exclaimed.

Anthony hit the main fire alarm.

'That will alert the emergency services and prompt the evacuation of anyone else still in the building' he said, having to raise his voice to be heard. 'We need to make sure everybody is out. You follow these people, Sophie. Try to keep them all in one place.'

His colleague didn't reply.

'Sophie? Did you hear me?' he asked.

Sophie had gone into shock. Her skin was the colour of ash. She was inhaling and exhaling rapidly, holding onto the desk in front of her. Anthony touched her hand and she looked up at him.

'Sophie' he said. 'Get yourself out! I'll be there once I'm sure the building is clear.'

Using the top of the kiosk to help keep herself upright, Sophie moved until she was standing directly opposite the main doors. Tucking her hands up around her neck, she made her way shakily across the foyer floor, battling to stay upright as if on a ship in a high sea. She had barely made it out of the building before she collapsed into the arms of a waiting paramedic.

\*\*\*

All was quiet in the police station offices. Officer Hughes had just made himself a coffee, leisurely walking back to his desk to continue his work. Having reached his desk, he pulled out his chair, but just as he was about to sit down the phone went. He swapped his cup between his hands before pressing the phones speakerphone button.

'Hughes.'

'Sir. There's been an explosion at the cinema two minutes ago. The switchboard lit up!' came the voice at the other end of the line. 'Four of our units are already there with the fire and Ambulances services. Bomb squad are on their way.'

'Holy Christ!' Hughes replied. 'I'll have Mills and Dee head to the scene as soon as I can.'

He hung up before yelling into the room. 'Sergeant Donavon.'

'Yes?'

The voice from right behind him made him jump. 'Jesus! Don't do that again!' he said. 'There's been...'

'A bombing at the cinema,' said Donovan, interrupting him. 'Yes, I know. I heard it on the radio. 'What do you need me to do?'

'Stay here by the phone in case anyone calls with any further information or claiming responsibility. I need to attend the scene and coordinate our officers already there so Mills and Dee can do their job once they arrive. Also, make sure we have other uniforms out that can deal with any other problems whilst we concentrate on this.'

'Yes sir,' the sergeant replied.

\*\*\*

Sophie could feel herself being gently assisted to the floor.

'It's ok. We've got you, your safe,' came a calm and motherly voice. 'We're just going to help you safely to the ground, just relax. Mick if you could assist please.'

The paramedics laid Sophie down and placed her legs up on a small bag elevating them slightly.

'Hello sweetheart. My names Carenza, and this is my colleague Mick. What's your name?'

'Sophie' came a faint reply. 'Sophie Townsend. Why am I laying down?'

'Just a precautionary measure,' said Mick reassuringly. 'Your clearly in shock over what's happened. I will remain with you for the moment whilst Carenza helps some of these other folks out here. Let's get you under a blanket.'

Mick rolled out a grey blanket over Sophie. 'Comfy?' he asked.

'As much as I can be led on a pavement,' came the reply.

'Just need to check your pulse rate a second,' said Mick, reaching for some equipment.

As Sophie watched the paramedic preparing beside her, she was aware of a figure standing next to her head. She glanced round to see Anthony, stood staring at the scene in front of him with the look of utter disbelief on his face.

'Anthony' Sophie called up to him. 'Anthony! Sit down next to me before you fall down!'

\*\*\*

Joe really didn't mind grocery shopping in the evenings. There were far less people about. You didn't have to play dodge the trolley or fight to access certain produce. At this time of day, you had your pick. The competition was elsewhere.

He'd already collected the fresh produce he needed. As he exited the isle, he spotted some discounted cakes and high-end biscuits on the shelf directly in front of him. It had been an extremely long time since he had bought anything on impulse. At the beginning of his relationship with Claire, he thought nothing of turning up with such items all the time. Back then it used to delight her, but now she had become far more sceptical as to why he'd done it. What had he done? What was he after?

With that in mind he walked straight past the items heading to the far end of the shop to collect some milk. *Best not arouse suspicion* he thought.

He collected the milk and walked briskly past the wine isle on his way towards to the check outs. His barely half full basket meant that he could use the self-service checkouts rather than having to face a cashier. Although it was part of their job, he thought he would save them and himself from the scripted small talk that was often more painful than courteous. After scanning all the items for himself at a self-service till, he hit the finish and pay button and paused for a moment. *Pay by card. Leave a trail* he thought to himself, removing his debit card from his wallet.

## Blame

Having paid, Joe picked up his shopping bag and flung it over his right shoulder as he walked out of the self-service area back towards the exit.

# 3.

Detective Chief Inspector Colin Mills stopped Detective Inspector Kate Dee outside the entrance of screen four just as they were about to enter. 'Kate' he said, turning to address her. 'Based on what we have already seen outside, I am extremely apprehensive as to what we shall find in here.'

'You're not the only one,' Dee replied. 'But don't worry. I know we are here to do a job. I promise I will remain professional and objective.'

'And I shall endeavour to do the same,' Mills replied, taking a deep breath. 'Ready?'

'No' Dee replied. 'But let's go.'

They had barely opened the door when they were greeted by two men in full body armour.

'There's not a lot to see down there. The forensics team are currently combing through what's left of the room,' said the first man. 'I'm Officer William and this is Officer Rhys, joint heads of the bomb squad.'

'Good evening. I'm DCI Colin Mills, and this is DI Kate Dee,' Mills responded.

'Do we know if anyone has claimed responsibility yet?' Rhys asked.

'Not that we have been made aware of.,' replied Dee.

'Well, we might not be able to tell you the identity of the bomber, but we can tell you how the device itself was made.'

'Please,' said Mills, already looking uneasy.

'Watch your feet when we enter,' said Rhys, turning on a torchlight.

'We appreciate the caution,' replied Mills. 'As a crime scene we know that none of the articles on the floor are allowed to be removed. It's a wonder the last people out were able to make it without tripping over everything.'

Rhys and William led Mills and Dee by torchlight to the back of the screen room where they had erected a portable table with the remains of the device upon it. Dee glanced behind her. The forensics team had erected a tent and lights around what remained of the seating at the front portion of the room.

'Based on what we found after making sure the building was secure, we are certain that the bomb was sewn into the bombers coat and deliberately left on the seats,' continued Rhys.

'Clever,' said Mills. 'No one would question as to why anyone coming to a late night showing of a film was wearing a coat.'

'Risky though,' replied William. 'Especially considering this was an Improvised Explosive Device.'

'Improvised explosive device?' said Dee in a questioning tone.

'Yes ma'am,' said William.

'We refer to them as I.E. Ds for short. In this case the bomber sewed pipe bombs into the lining of the coat,' added Rhys. 'As the name suggests, they are made using metal water pipes, packed with explosive material, and sealed at both ends. An electrical fuse is then drilled into a hole at one end and connected to a timer which, when it goes off, sends an electrical impulse down the fuse, and ignites the bomb.'

'We're still trying to ascertain what was used as the explosive,' said William. 'But my guess would be Triacetone Triperoxide, or T.A.T.P for short. That's the most commonly used explosive in these types of devices. It can be easily manufactured with access to the correct chemicals.'

'I see,' replied Mills, surveying his surroundings not really knowing where to start.

'Do we think this is the work of anyone experienced in the manufacturing of devices of this kind?' asked Dee.

'No.' replied Rhys. 'The evidence doesn't suggest that. I'd say based on the relatively small devices and the way it was snuck into the venue that this is most likely the first time the person responsible has done this.'

'Another odd thing is it appears that no additional shrapnel has been added to the device,' added William. 'We'd usually expect to find nails or other such objects, but not in this case.'

'Didn't I read somewhere that historically, those responsible for using devices without shrapnel inside have often turned out to be driven by making a statement as opposed to mass murder?' asked Dee.

'Yes,' replied Rhys, smiling at her. 'I'm impressed Detective!'

'But,' William interjected. 'It's also worth noting that the average blast radius of this type of bomb is still twenty-one metres. They meant to kill someone.'

'Thank you, Gentlemen,' said Mills. He turned to face Dee.

'I need to find Hughes. Hopefully someone will have some information that will help us identify the person responsible. It may also be worth interviewing the projectionist.'

'Is that you Mills?' came a questioning voice from the other side of the room. 'Movie theatres are synonymous with dim lighting. It's great for the cinema experience, but a nightmare for us to do our jobs!'

The figure then made its way around the chairs towards them. He was dressed in a coverall suit and gloves, having temporarily removed his mask to talk to his colleagues. 'The explosion has somehow affected the buildings generator, so we're having to use our portable lights as you can see.'

'Have you met DC Kate Dee?' Mills asked him.

'No, I don't believe I have,' said the man, smiling and nodding at her. 'It's a pleasure.'

'Dee, this is Buckland, head of our forensics department,' said Mills.

'Hi,' replied Dee.

'Is there any CCTV in here?' asked Mills, scanning the upper corners of the room in search of cameras.

'No. I'm afraid not,' Buckland replied. 'The film studios copyright laws don't allow it. I'll let you know if we find anything significant that will help us identify who's responsible. We are currently concentrating on the deceased.'

'I need to find Hughes,' repeated Mills. Any chance we could use your assistance in illuminating our way back out please Officer Rhys?'

Rhys had returned to the table with William who was sketching into a pad, looking up intermittently at the table in front of him.

'Officer Rhys,' Mills called. 'May we borrow your light again?'

'One moment,' Rhys replied. 'I'll be right with you.'

'God, I hope the press hasn't arrived,' grumbled Mills as he began to pace impatiently.

Dee looked at him quizzically. *Where did that come from?*

\*\*\*

Claire had finally finished her marking for the evening. She shut the book in front of her, before placing the last paper on the top of the pile.

*Done*, she thought to herself. *Time for a bath, followed by a top up.*

She stood up and was about to pick up her wine glass from the coffee table when the phone went. She sighed and sat back down before lifting the receiver.

'Hello?'

She instantly recognised the voice at the other end of the phone. It belonged to her best friend.

'Oh. Hi Holly,' she said, leaning forwards on the sofa to pick up one of the papers that had fallen off the edge of the table. 'No, I'm not watching it, why?'

She placed the paper with the others whilst listening to her friend.

'Jesus Christ!' she exclaimed, leaning over the arm of the sofa and grabbing the television remote.

'Ok. I'm turning it on now,' she said into the phone.

'And for those who have just joined us tonight, let me repeat our main headline,' came the voice of the news correspondent. 'We are live from outside the city's biggest cinema, where just a few hours ago a bomb exploded in screen room four. As you can see, there's still a strong police presence here tonight. Already six people are confirmed to have died, including a couple in their fifties and students from the university.'

'Oh God!' exclaimed Claire as she heard the front door open and close. 'I've got to Holly. Joe's just walked in. I'll check in with you tomorrow. Bye.'

She put the phone down, picked up her wine glass and headed across the hallway and into the kitchen. Joe was casually restocking the fridge shelves when Claire appeared behind him.

'Have you heard Joe?' she exclaimed. 'There's been an explosion at the cinema. Apparently, the reports are saying that a bomb was detonated in one of the smaller screens. I hope to God none of my students were in there.'

Joe said nothing. He shut the fridge door before bending down to take his shoes off.

'Did you not hear me?' Claire repeated. 'A bomb in the cinema! It's all over the news.'

Joe remained silent as he folded the shopping bag and placed it in the cupboard under the sink with the others.

'I'll find out tomorrow,' he said dismissively as he left the room. 'I've got marking to do.'

*Unbelievable!* Claire thought to herself as she heard her husband ascend the stairs.

Who the hell did I marry?

# Blame

\*\*\*

Girard Reeves, Patrick Bateman and Robert Watts were all first-year students at the city university. Having spent another night drinking and dancing in the student's union, Robert was eager for the three friends to catch the last free bus back to their student union halls a mile away. It was either that or face losing at least another hour of the night getting back by foot. Girard was likely to need assistance, and Patrick was unable to walk and sing at the same time. Having successfully navigated the two sets of concrete stairs outside of the building to the pavement, Robert stepped on board the bus. Chatter from the other students onboard greeted him as he headed towards the back of the vehicle to find a vacant seat.

'I'm afraid I'm going to require assistance Pat,' said Girard as the pair stood outside the bus.

'For heaven's sake!' laughed Patrick. 'It's not as big a gap as your brains telling you it is you drunk!'

'Hurry it up please boys,' said the bus driver growing more impatient as he watched the pair. 'I'm leaving in one minute, are you getting on or not?'

'Ok. After three,' said Patrick to Girard. He grabbed hold of his friend by his jacket.

'One. Two. Three'.

The two stepped over the gap between the pavement and the bus.

'Not even the Grand Canyon can stop us!' beamed Girard as Patrick began to pull him up the isle just as the bus engine started.

They found Robert sat at the very back of the bus. Patrick pushed Girard into the seat next to him and shuffled sideways past Robert to the vacant seat by the window.

'Another interesting night,' he said.

'Something like that,' replied Robert.

He looked over at Girard, who had already fallen asleep in the seat next to him with his head on his shoulder.

'Did you hear about the second-year students enrolment cock up?' he asked Patrick.

'No! Too busy taking care of his royal drunkenness there!' came the reply.

'Over the summer, the university installed a new computer system, but they neglected to put half of the second-year students back on the system.'

'Oops!' said Patrick, starting to giggle.

'So not only did a bunch of them have to go down and have photographs taken for new student cards, but they also haven't received their student loans yet!'

'For some people that wouldn't necessarily a bad thing,' replied Patrick, leaning round Robert and looking at Girard.

Just then they heard screaming voices from upstairs. Other voices then started to cry out before footsteps could be heard coming down the stairs.

'Have any of you heard?' exclaimed Anne, stopping halfway down the stairs gripping both handrails tightly to prevent herself falling. 'There's been an explosion at the cinema! People have died!'

\*\*\*

Sara and Scott Paige had been watching the well-worn DVD of their favourite programme curled up on the sofa together until they had both fallen asleep. Sara had stretched out, placing her legs over Scott's lap. She almost always felt the cold at night, so they had draped a blanket over themselves.

Sara woke suddenly. The end credits to the programme ascending the white names of those involved in its creation were on the screen. Scott was still asleep, his head titled backwards leaning against the cushion he had deliberately placed behind him.

'Scott,' Sara whispered, sitting up and poking him in the arm. 'Scott!'

'What?' he said sleepily, rubbing his face before opening his eyes and looking over at his wife.

'I think it's bedtime,' Sara replied. She stood up and wrapped the blanket around her.

'It was your idea to watch your favourite episode before the trip tomorrow,' said Scott, standing up and picking up his empty glass from the floor in front of him. 'I would've gone to bed an hour ago.'

'I'm going for a wee, I'll meet you in our room,' said Sara heading towards the doorway. 'Don't forget to turn the television off.'

'I won't,' replied Scott yawning. He wondered over and turned off the television at the side. *Sod it!* he thought, as he placed his empty glass on the coaster at the front of the stand, *I'll deal with that in the morning.*

He flipped the light switch as he exited the room, heading down the flats darkened corridor. His plan was to linger there and surprise Sara as she left the bathroom.

'I know your there Scott!' said Sara from inside the room. 'Could you please remember to put the toilet seat down next time you use it. I didn't check.'

'Your being very toiletarily territorial for this time of night dear,' replied Scott cheekily.

He heard the toilet flush, followed by the sound of the boiler. After a moment, Sara emerged from the bathroom.

'I shouldn't have fallen asleep. I'm more awake now,' she said.

'And you've remembered what we're doing tomorrow haven't you?' said Scott as they headed towards their bedroom at the end of the hallway.

'Yes,' replied Sara. 'That too.'

# 4.

Joe had a few hours free until he was needed at work. By the time he had come downstairs, Claire had already left for the university. She hadn't said a word to him since his aloof response to her trying to tell him about the cinema bombing last night.

After a moment debating with himself over whether to have breakfast, Joe had decided against it. He put his shoes on and left the house. Most mornings he would have followed his all too familiar route driving in the direction of the university, but today was different.

He was headed towards the cities bay.

Joe watched as the scenery where they lived on the outskirts of the city slowly morphed and changed from high rise buildings, shops, offices, and restaurants into building sites as he drove. The city had started a long-term regeneration project a few years ago to make better use of its old spaces. These areas were currently home to derelict buildings in various stages of disrepair, or empty spaces fenced off by railings. Work had started in the center of the city and had yet to reach this area. In place of the bricks, mortar and iron was a lot more open space, with the sea becoming increasingly visible in the distance the nearer he got to his destination.

Deliberately driving past the large car park outside the target on his left, Joe turned right into an industrial estate. Coming to the end of the first group of units that made up the site, he reversed back into the parking area between them, bringing the car as close to the wall of the first unit as he could before stopping and surveying his surroundings.

There was already a sizeable queue outside the bakers directly opposite him that he hadn't noticed driving past just moments ago. A steady procession of lorry drivers and curriers were re-emerging from the building. Each was carrying a disposable cup of either hot tea or coffee, and a small white paper bag containing their freshly made hot breakfast to be enjoyed before the start of the morning commute. One such person was placing his items into his lorry's cab with the name Lilith in large letters above the windscreen. Joe surmised that this might have been the name of either the driver's mother, daughter, or wife as he watched them climb into the cab and rearranged his breakfast items.

He turned the car's engine off and breathed a sigh of relief. Despite the uneven road surfaces and speed bumps he had driven over on his way, the fragile contents of his boot had not been affected. It had been a calculated risk, but Joe believed it to be the right one. If the package he presented appeared to have been tampered with, it might have brought far greater problems. With his hand hovering over the car's door handle, he watched and waited as the driver opposite fired up his juggernaut and pulled away before exiting the car. Heading around to the back of the car, he opened the boot before putting on another pair of skin tone disposable gloves, the cap, and the high visibility vest he had purchased yesterday. *These things seem synonymous with delivery drivers these days,* he thought to himself, before opening the cardboard archive box in the boot and picking up the separate, smaller pre-sealed package from inside. He replaced the box lid and shut the boot. Having locked the vehicle, Joe started walking back past the industrial units carrying the package.

The last unit he passed before reaching the main road was called City Motorcycles. A sign reading Proof of CBT before sale was boldly displayed in its window. *Our generation were all about four wheels,* he thought to himself. *At fourteen, those of us who were into our cars were all about the Aston Martin V8. Nothing like our father's Morris Marina's.*

With no pedestrian crossing in the area, Joe had to stand at the edge of the curb waiting for a sizeable gap in the traffic. He was starting to feel the weight of what he was carrying in his forearms.

'Come on, come on!' he exclaimed out loud with growing impatience.

To his relief a gap appeared. He crossed the road and headed left, back towards the large car park he had driven past earlier. As he approached the empty car park, he had two choices. He could either cut straight through the middle of it or walk around it. He was sure this was the place he heard them talking about on the way out of his lecture, an exhibition in the centre by the Bay.

Conscious that there may be security cameras covering the car park, Joe headed straight down the far right of the area and along the outside of the building towards its entrance.

On entering the lobby, he couldn't help noticing how the big bay windows created the illusion of space when combined with the morning's sunlight. The buildings unusual L shaped floor plan meant he need to head for the back left of the venue. For a split second he wondered whether he should take his package into the bowling alley on his right but decided to stick to his original plan.

Heading towards the back of the venue he passed a coffee shop, catching a glimpse of employees restocking the chillers in front of the counter ready for the day's trade ahead. A few people were already milling around waiting, eager to get their first caffeine hit of the day.

A sign suspended from the ceiling confirmed the location of the exhibitions entrance and shortly after rounding the corner, Joe found himself stood looking at it.

There were two doors. The entrance to the exhibit on the left and the exit on the right, both with their respective signs over them. Between the two doors along the back wall was a manned ticketing booth with a till. The space in and around the area also doubled as the exhibits gift shop, with various shelves and tables arranged with everything from T-shirts to stationary.

He walked up to the ticketing booth.

'Good morning. Another box of your bestselling souvenirs, judging by the size and weight of this thing!' he said.

Teresa, the girl behind the counter looked up at him and smiled.

'That'll be the wristbands and replica toys then. People are buying them two at a time claiming they are for their nieces or nephews, but my moneys on the dad's keeping them for themselves.'

'Boys and their toys!' replied Joe. 'Have a good day.'

'You too,' smiled Teresa.

After watching the capped currier with his high vis vest wonder off towards the exit having delivered his package, Teresa took the box over to where the wristbands were displayed and glanced over at the toys.

*No need for a refill just yet* she thought to herself as she slipped the box under the shelving unit, carefully pushing it back amongst the others with her foot.

\*\*\*

Scott and Sara were sat in the centre's cafe finishing up their drinks. The exhibition was using a timed ticketing system as a method of reducing lines and overcrowding in anticipation of its popularity.

'How is it?' he asked her.

'Grainy,' she replied, taking another sip.

'Well, that's disappointing,' Scott said, stating over her shoulder.

'Stop it!' Sara exclaimed, having just placed her mug back on the table after another mouthful.

'Stop what?' asked Scott.

'Staring at people, and it's not like you're being discreet either.'

'It's fascinating,' Scott replied, watching a group of people clearly struggling to decide what they wanted to do. As soon as they seemed to have come to a decision and started walking in the direction of their choice, one of their party would stop and the process would start all over again.

'Please stop it!' Sara repeated, her voice becoming exasperated.

Scott sighed.

'Well, it wasn't my idea to leave home so early, was it? How much longer have we got left?' he asked.

Sara looked at her watch. 'About 45 minutes,' she replied.

'We should've seen if there was a pool table free in the bowling alley and just ordered two pints of coke,' said Scott disappointedly. 'Probably would've been cheaper too!'

'Did I tell you about the dream I had last night when we eventually fell asleep?' asked Sara.

'No. I don't think so,' said Scott before taking a sip from his cup.

'Very strange,' said Sara.

'What was it about?' Scott asked, pressing his wife for more detail. He glanced at his watch. A conversation on any subject remotely interesting that would kill some time was most welcome to him at this point.

'Well, we were trying to walk our usual route into the city centre,' said Sara, running her finger around the top of her coffee mug. 'But both of the roads we'd usually go down were cordoned off by metal fences and traffic cones as they were being dug up.'

'How inconvenient!' exclaimed Scott.

'It was. But what made it weirder was that the new road surface was fake,' continued Sara. 'It was suspended in the air like a slide. A child even slid down it, picked up speed as it rounded the corner and crashed into a house opposite.'

'That's a little strange. Was the kid alright?' Scott asked.

'A little surprised and stunned,' said Sara. 'But they got back up and ran off back to their father.'

'I'm presuming you checked your dream book this morning?' asked Scott, looking down at his watch again.

'I certainly did,' Sara replied.

'And?' asked Scott. 'What does it mean?'

'Well, according to the book, it's all about the idea of transformation,' said Sara. 'Yes, there may be problems or accidents along the way as represented by the child, but it all seems to point to a possible change.'

'There's still time to change the road you're on,' said Scott smiling.

'What is that?' asked Sara. 'It's incredibly familiar.'
'That is Led Zeppelin my dear!' Scott replied still smiling. 'Usually I don't dream, or if I do, I don't remember them.'

Sara could see Scott's eyes start to wonder from their table and onto another group of people.

'So, what do you think will be in the exhibit?' Sara asked, eager to try and reengage her husband.

'Bound to be costumes, props, those giants blown up photographs,' he replied.

'It will be interesting to see how far they go back in its history,' Sara said thoughtfully. 'Aren't origin stories extremely popular right now?'

'On the page and up on the screen definitely,' said Scott. 'But we are talking about a tv show here. They usually focus on the time it was most popular.'

Sara stood up.

'I just need to visit the girl's room a moment,' she said.

'Excited tummy?' Scott asked.

'Yes. As always,' came the reply. 'I'll be as quick as I can.'

'No probs sweetheart,' Scott replied sympathetically. 'I'll be here.'

\*\*\*

Connor could not sit still. He was sat on the bus in a seat by the window with Sally sat next to him. They were nearing their destination.

'Connor. You need to sit down and calm down please! You've already kicked the seat in front of you three times. We're just lucky that the man sat in front of you was so understanding before he got off,' said Sally.

A moment later she breathed a sigh of relief as they passed the road sign for the centre.

The bus driver followed the road and came to a stop, just a few yards shy of the main entrance.

'Have you made sure you have everything before we get off Connor?' Sally asked. 'If we leave it on here, we might not get it back.'

'Do you think they'll have the bots? And the costumes?' Connor asked as they got off the bus and started walking towards the entrance of the building. 'And what about the worlds? And the sets?'

Sally didn't reply. She was busy rummaging in her purse trying to find their exhibition tickets, whilst at the same time trying to keep one eye on her son.

'What about the characters?' Connor continued. 'And the weapons? And the scooter?'

'Connor sweetheart,' said Sally finally. 'I know you're over excited, but I know as much as you do. I've found our tickets, and the entrance to the exhibition should be signposted once we get inside.'

'Hurry up then mum!' Connor exclaimed, grabbing her by the hand and pulling her towards the centre's door.

'Slow down Connor! Just listen for a moment please.' She kept holding his hand, but slowed down her walking pace, forcing her son to do the same. Connor stopped walking and turned to face his mother. She crouched down next to him and smiled. 'Our ticket is timed, which means we must wait until the time printed on our tickets before we are allowed to go into the exhibition. We will head into the Centre now and find something to do in the meantime. Do you understand?'

Connor nodded.

'Yes Mum,' he replied.

'What do you want to do until then?' Sally asked.

'Have a Coffee?' her son asked, looking up at her pleadingly.

Sally laughed.

'Me? yes! I'll need it to keep up with you today,' she smiled. 'You on the other hand mister, definitely not. What about a hot milk?'

'Can I have some of those wafer biscuits I like for dunking into the milk too Mum?' Connor asked.

'I don't see why not,' Sally replied, smiling at her son.

'Then yes please!' Connor said smiling back at her.

'Great. And by the time you finish that, it should be our time to go and see the exhibition.'

\*\*\*

Despite it being the last thing that he wanted to do; Joe knew that a quick visit to his parents would be worth it. An alibi. Not only that, but today he had the excuse to leave quickly as he would be teaching.

Joe's Mother was a retired teacher like his grandmother had been. Teaching, you might say, was in the blood. His mother hadn't met his stepfather Mark until she was in her mid-fifties, by which time Joe had moved out and met Claire. Their little flat overlooking the bay was to be their home to enjoy their retirement. It also meant that they would have equity saved should either of them need the capital to pay for care.

Joe pulled into the private car park at the bottom of the block of flats. He exited his car and headed round to the boot. He opened it, took off the cap and placed it back inside the empty archive box along with the high vis vest that had been sat on the passenger seat since he left the Centre. As he locked the car and walked towards the entrance to the building, he thought about the types of pupils his mother and grandmother would have had.

*I bet they never encountered pupils quite like mine,* he thought to himself, *especially not Grandma.*

Joe's Grandmother had taught at a grammar school for the more academic pupils who had been separated from their not so academic peers by the eleven plus exam.

*Bring back the Tripartite school system,* he thought. *That would have a positive impact on the calibre of students from the bottom up!*

He entered the lift to the left of the entrance and pushed the button for the second floor.

Glancing at his watch as the lift ascended, Joe stepped out of the lift once its doors had opened and walked towards their front door. After pressing the doorbell, Joe looked out of the full-length window at the bay whilst waiting for someone to answer.

*No wonder this place was so expensive*, he said to himself as the front door began to open.

'Joseph!' exclaimed Mark as his stepson came into view as he opened the front door. 'This is a nice surprise.'

'Hello Mark', Joe replied as both men leant in to give each other a loose hug. 'Is mother here?'

'Yes, she is, and she'll be very happy to see you,' replied Mark with a smile. 'Is Claire not with you?'

'No. She's in the laboratory as always, but I was passing the area on my travels and thought I'd drop in,' said Joe as he stepped through the doorway.

'Excellent,' said Mark as the two men entered the hallway. 'Can I get you some Tea? I was just about to put the kettle on for your mother.'

Joe rubbed his eyes as they entered the hallway. 'A Coffee would be great if you have some please,' he said.

'Coffee it is then,' replied Mark. 'You'll find your mother out on the balcony.'

Joe glanced up at the wall on his right as he walked down the hallway. Hung in various sized frames all along the wall were several pictures. Included amongst them was old school photographs which tracked his time from reception to year six. Another collage included his graduation portrait, and a picture outside of the house he had rented during his time at university.

Also on the wall was an old picture of Joe as a boy, sat with his father in the dual controlled car he would spend all day in with his driving students.

He remembered being sat on his dad's lap, holding the steering wheel and driving along a beach one summer. They had gone up and back on the same stretch of sand that was used for parking during the summer season dozens of times. Joe couldn't have been older than five at the time. Other pictures, including those from his mother's wedding to Mark were there, along with pictures of Joe and Claire's big day. A simple affair with a few of her close friends.

No sooner had he brought her home than the questions had started.

'So, Joseph. What are your intentions?' His mother had asked him one afternoon. 'You can't string her along, she's too good for that. How long has it been?'

He couldn't remember the last time he had seen, let alone spoken to his best man as he carried on past the pictures and into the living room.

He had to walk around his parents living room furniture to get out onto the balcony that overlooked the bay. The sudden change in light made him wish he'd brought his sunglasses as he stepped outside. Just in front of him his mother was watering one of three hanging boxes facing inwards on the balcony railings with her cream-coloured watering can.

'I thought I heard your dulcet tones Joseph,' said Faye as she finished watering the box she was on and placed the watering can on the floor. She turned and smiled whilst walking towards him. 'It's great to see you son.'

The two embraced.

'What have you done with Mark?' she asked.

'He's in the kitchen making drinks,' Joe replied.

'Shall we go in and sit?' asked his mother, wondering back in through the open French windows and prompting Joe to follow her.

They entered the living room area. Joe sat down with his back to the patio doors on one sofa, and his mother sat on another sofa directly in front of him. To the left of them was the television set, and between the two was a rectangular shaped wooden coffee table. In the other corner facing into the room was a writing desk.

'I was just taking a break from writing my next letter to my old friends who I went to university with. Most of them are grandparents now,' said Faye, pausing and looking up at Joe.

He rolled his eyes at her. *You can never resist mentioning that!* he thought.

'We could all email each other, but there's nothing like receiving a handwritten letter by post.'

'How's Claire Joe?' asked Mark, placing the tray of drinks in the middle of the coffee table before sitting down next to his wife.

'Good thanks Mark,' replied Joe. 'Busy as always.'

'Are you still playing with cars and deafening the neighbours?' Mark asked with a smile.

'When I have the time,' Joe responded.

'Don't neglect your priorities son!' his mother snapped. 'Especially Claire. She's the best thing that's ever happened to you!'

'They are allowed some time apart Faye,' Mark replied. 'My first wife and I suffocated each other.'

'Can you get Claire to phone me please?' Faye asked looking at Joe. 'I miss her.'

Joe took a big sip of his drink before staring into his cup.

'So, what's on your agenda for today?' asked Mark, leaning forward to put his cup back on the tray in front of him.

'Not much,' Joe replied. 'I'm teaching in less than an hour, but I thought I'd best drop in. I don't know when I'll be able to see you next.'

'Well, we appreciate you coming,' said Mark. 'Don't we Faye?'

Joe looked at his mother. She seemed lost in thought.

'What?' she asked. 'Sorry. I've been thinking about what to put in my letter next. I certainly won't be focusing on that cinema bombing. Shocking that is. I've lived here in this city since before you were born, and nothing remotely like this has ever happened before.'

'It's bloody awful, isn't it?' said Mark.

'Was anyone you know affected by it Joseph?' his mother asked.

Joe didn't reply. He stood up and placed his coffee cop on the tray. He did not want to give the current topic of conversation more time to snowball.

'I best be off,' he said. 'All it will take is some traffic congestion somewhere on my route and I'll be late, especially as they've decided to dig up all the roads at the same time it would seem.'

'Well, it was great to see you,' said Mark standing up.

'Mark. Please. Take a seat,' Joe said, pointing to the chair behind him. 'I'm a big boy. I can let myself out.'

Mark sat back down as Joe looked at his mother. 'Bye Mum,' he said. 'I'll get Claire to phone you when she can.'

Faye looked up at Joe and smiled at him.

'Did you know that the name Joseph comes from Hebrew and means he will add?' she asked.

'Yes. You've told me hundreds of times,' Joe replied.

'Probably started before you were born,' said Mark smiling.

'Well for your late Fathers sake, please be sure to keep adding to the world rather than diminishing from it,' said Faye.

'I'm working on it,' Joe said, looking at her with a serious look on his face.

'We love you,' replied Faye. 'Love to Claire.'

As Joe shut the front door behind him, he had already decided to walk down the stairway rather than take the lift back to the bottom of the building. The warmth and light of the sun hit him again as he walked back towards his car.

\*\*\*

Sara and Scott, having looked around the exhibition, had emerged from its exit door and into its shop. Scott had immediately left his wife's side and was pouring over the higher priced memorabilia that was on sale. Sara had watched her husband in amusement at first but had grown impatient. He kept picking things up and turning round to show her, whilst rubbing his thumb and middle finger with his free hand, mouthing various numbers through his grin.

'What's the point of buying it if you're just planning to sell it on eBay?' asked Sara as she approached him with a puzzled look on her face.

'With the right buyer I could triple my money,' replied Scott.

Sara rolled her eyes at him.

'Look. I'll go and buy our official souvenir photograph, and you behave yourself! Pick up a keyring or something.'

'It'll cost more to post them in the long run!' replied Scott laughing.

Sara hit him playfully.

'Will you stop it! Us coming here wasn't about making a profit. This was about us and our shared loved of something. I love you to bits, but you're not half weird!'

Scott laughed again.

'I'll see you in a second,' said Sara, wondering over in the direction of the kiosk.

Scott frowned as he placed the item back on the shelf. There was no use arguing with his wife. He turned and surveyed the rest of the shop, his eyes falling upon a child trying to bribe their parent out of anything and everything they could get their hands on.

'Oh, please Mummy. I'll play with it every single moment I am not at school!' said Connor from beside the play sets.

'At seventy pounds it will remain on the shelf Connor Raymore!' Sally replied firmly. 'There are plenty of other things to choose from that won't bankrupt us. Please keep looking.'

'Can I have it for my birthday then?' came the reply.

'Nice try mister, but your birthday isn't for ten months. I'm not saying you can't have anything else, but I'm not getting anything that expensive,' said Sally.

'You can't play with a keyring or T-shirt though…' Connor replied sulkily.

'That's not the point son. You already have all the action figures at home. That's probably more than most children have.'

'Oh alright…' said Connor backing down. He knew he wasn't about to change his mother's mind. 'I'll have another look.'

'Thank you,' Sally replied.

Connor started wondering over to another stand, but he never got the chance to look again. The last thing that he heard was his mother screaming his name.

# 5.

With the bomb squad having done their job, the forensic and other teams had already entered the centre. Mills and Dee had made their way through the emergency vehicles and personnel outside, surrounded by the centre's employees and public.

'I have a nagging sense of Deja vu,' said Dee as the detectives entered the venue.

'Yes, and I fear the mobile television vans will be outside any minute. They dropped the ball yesterday evening and won't want to repeat their error,' said Mills.

'That's the last of our worries Colin,' replied Dee. 'We've barely finished dealing with last night!'

'I'm trying not to ruminate on that,' came the reply.

Dee pointed upwards towards the exhibition sign as the two detectives silently passed the coffee shop. The scene as they approached the area of the exhibition looked like a horror film only worse. These victims were real people, blood staining the once blue floor dark red.

It was in situations like this that Mills always questioned himself why? Not only why would someone commit such crimes against their fellow human beings, but why he had chosen to subject himself to such sights. Yes, it was his job to do it, but there were plenty of other jobs within the force that didn't require you to survey scenes of such devastation and loss of life. He made his way over to the forensics team, who along with the bomb squad were studying what was left of the device.

'Hello again all,' he grumbled. 'My first obvious question is have you had time to figure out if this device has been manufactured in the same way as the one used in the cinema bombing?'

'Yes,' replied Rhys. 'Well, it's another chemical based IED just like before with the same components to it. The only difference is they used a lot more explosive charge in the box this time.'

'Do you think it could be a copycat?' Mills asked. 'No, I don't think so,' replied Rhys. 'We're ninety nine percent certain that this device is identical to that used at the cinema. It appears to have been made using the exact same methods and components, except it was concealed in a box rather than in the lining of a coat.'

'Also, no additional shrapnel was added again,' added William.

'Did you find any other devices on your search of the premises?' asked Mills,

'No,' replied William.

'Once again consistent with the cinema,' added Rhys.

DI Dee was with police officers Jons and Wood, who had congregated by the cafe.

Several people had attempted to re-enter the building, heading towards the exhibition area in a desperate attempt to find their missing family. Jons and Wood's job had been to prevent them from getting any further and confronting the scene just around the corner. It was bad enough having to watch as the coroner and his team had arrived and started to remove bodies.

'I know you guys have been stationed in this position but has anyone reported anything out of the ordinary to you?' she asked. 'Someone acting suspicious perhaps?'

'According to everyone we've heard from it was a normal day. Well, that is until a bomb exploded, and all hell broke loose!' said Jons.

'I'll have security pull CCTV for the last few days to go over back at the station. Hopefully it caught whoever is responsible walking in with the device,' Wood added.

'Good,' Dee replied. 'Fingers crossed it'll give us a better chance of identifying the bomber this time.'

Mills approached the group.

'Based on what has been found, Rhys, William and Buckland are almost certain this was done by the same person who targeted the cinema.'

'Oh God,' replied Dee. 'I hope to hell we get something from the tapes this time. Wood has already volunteered his services to retrieve them.'

'Good,' said Mills. 'Speaking of which, have the camera crews turned up yet?'

'No,' said Dee. 'Thankfully someone took the initiative and stopped any vehicle apart from the emergency services entering or exiting the car park, and I am yet to hear the sound of a helicopter.'

'Good. I'll dictate our police statement down the phone on the way back in the car once we have obtained the CCTV footage,' said Mills. 'We can't afford to have the press clogging up the switch board or taking up any more time than is necessary.'

\*\*\*

Matt Clemence was in his Halls of residence kitchen preparing a late breakfast. He had turned on the communal TV but muted its sound to not disturb his flatmates. Having finished buttering his toast, he took a bite before looking up at the screen. There in front of him were live images of the centre from a distance, alternating with still pictures from the interior of the building. The scrolling text at the bottom of the screen that gave viewers live updates then confirmed the death of a mother and child but did not name them.

Grabbing his orange juice off the side and picking up his plate with his other uneaten toast, Matt made his way over to the table and chairs and sat down. His flat mate Toby Gideon then wondered into the room, dressed in what Matt recognised as the same t-shirt and boxer shorts he had seen him in yesterday.

'Can you believe that Toby?' Matt asked pointing up at the screen. 'A kid. Unbelievable!'

'I'm still processing the fact Skip got killed in the cinema bombing last night mate,' came the reply from Toby, with his head inside the fridge. 'My head is banging.'

'The Police haven't confirmed it's him yet though T,' replied Matt. 'There's a chance it wasn't him.'

'But I know it was,' replied Toby solemnly. He removed the milk and closed the fridge door before opening the carton and taking a giant swig. 'I was there when he bolted out the door yelling that he was off to watch a film. The last thing he said to me was he'd see me in a bit.'

Jesus!' exclaimed Matt. 'That milk is yours, isn't it?'

'Don't know, don't care,' Toby replied, taking another swig. 'I'll get some more later.'

He sat down opposite his flat mate at the table. 'I swear to God. If the police don't do anything and this happens again, we shall take matters into our own hands! I'm not about to be shepherded and curfewed because they can't do their jobs.'

'What about your dad T? Can't he do anything?' Matt asked.

Toby wiped his mouth to stop milk running further down his chin and laughed.

'You're joking, right? His working life is a popularity contest full of empty promises, much like his role as my so-called father is. No doubt this tragedy will be exploited for political gain.'

Neither Matt nor Toby had noticed their other flat mate Yichen Li enter the kitchen until they heard the water filling up the kettle.

'Hey Li. I bet this type of nonsense would never happen in your country, would it?' said Matt.

Li smiled.

'I don't know to be honest with you. Growing up where I did, police officers knew all the families in the area personally. That and the police carrying a gun was all the deterrent one needed.'

'I didn't know Chinese police officers were armed,' said Matt. 'What about your laws on crime?' he asked quizzically.

'Chinese law around murder or terrorism is very similar to what you have here,' Li replied. 'With a minimum sentence of ten years for murder.'

'I bet you guys are far more competent at it though,' added Toby.

Li smiled at him.

'I would not like to comment. All I know is that according to my father, English is the language of business.'

'And bullshit!' exclaimed Toby, making all three of them laugh.

'Turn the TV up can you please Li?' Matt asked.

'Of course,' Li replied, feeling along the left-hand side of the television before finding and pressing the volume button.

'Whilst the police are yet to release an official statement at this time, we can indeed confirm that a mother and child are thought to be amongst the dead in the second explosion in the city within twenty-four hours,' said the News reporter. 'As you can see, police vehicles are currently controlling access to the site so this is as close as we can get. We will remain with you on air and give you immediate updates as and when we receive them. The first minister is said to be making a statement shortly, so do stay with us. This is Gavin Jordan. City News.'

***

Liam Mason had driven himself and his wife Kelly to the city coroner's office.

Having parked and turned off the engine, he pulled the car's hand brake up firmly before undoing his seatbelt.

'Why are we here? What did we do?' he asked out loud, staring at the limestone cladded building in front of him. A sign on the left of building read Staff Only Car Park.

Kelly remained silent in the passenger seat.

'I guess we go in through that porch way with the pyramid roof then,' said Liam.

Huffing loudly, Kelly undid her seatbelt and got out of the car, slamming the door behind her as hard as she could.

*She didn't have to come*, Liam thought to himself as he got out of the car. *Only one of us needs to provide them with what they want.*

Silently, the couple made their way over to the entrance. With Liam holding the door open for his wife, they stepped into the entrance lobby. Directly to their left was a staircase leading up to the second floor, with the reception desk just beyond it.

Apprehensively the couple walked towards it. 'Mr and Mrs Mason,' said Liam before they had even reached the desk.

'Please, do take a seat,' replied the receptionist. She pointed to a row of chairs laid out along the wall directly opposite the reception area. 'I'll let Dr Myers know you've arrived.'

Liam caught sight of a sign suspended from the ceiling showing the location of the morgue and autopsy rooms. According to the sign they were located behind the wall where they were sat. He shuddered. Just then he felt his wife's hand taking hold of his. He turned to look at her, but before the couple had a chance to say a word to each other a figure appeared in front of them.

'Mr and Mrs Mason I presume?'

Liam stood up.

'Yes. Please call me Liam,' he replied, offering his hand.

'Doctor Nick Myers,' came the reply accompanied with a firm handshake. 'Please follow me.'

He led the couple back towards the staircase. Liam couldn't help noticing the oak banister as Kelly slid her hand over it on the way up the stairs.

'This place is like a modern hospital housed in an old shell,' he said out loud.

'A grade two listed Tudor shell to be precise,' Myers replied as they reached the top of the stairs. "It's just over here.'

They crossed the landing and entered a rectangular shaped laboratory.

'I apologise for the lack of comfy furniture, but a clinical environment is essential,' said Myers, ushering the couple to sit in two laboratory chairs opposite a third and a table which housed a computer and various implements. 'As you know. You are here today to help us conclusively identify the body we believe to be that of your son Shaun.'

Kelly took hold of her husband's hand again and squeezed.

'As it is, due to the circumstances surrounding Shaun's death we are unable to use our usual methods of identification. The use of supportive documents, fingerprints or dental records is normally sufficient to help us correctly identify a body.'

Kelly started to sob. Liam just stared blankly at the forensic scientist.

'Although I'm sure this comes as no consolation at all to either of you, Shaun would not have been in any pain,' said Dr Myers.

Liam put his arm around his wife.

'It's very uncommon not to find the deceased carrying anything that would help us identify them,' Myers continued. 'If this is your son as we believe it is, only a solitary key and several coins were found on him.'

'That's our Shaun,' Liam replied. 'Everything spur of the moment. We could never reach him, always losing or forgetting his phone. Putting down one thing he needed whilst picking up the other thing. I've no idea what was swimming in his mind half the time to be that forgetful, but I was always intrigued...'

Kelly's sobs had become louder now. Dr Myers swivelled round in his chair and picked up a box of tissues. Turning back to face the couple, he held out the box towards her.

She took one from the box and began to wipe her eyes.

'Thank you,' she said, looking up at the doctor properly for the first time since they had met downstairs. He smiled back at her.

'So today we need to obtain a sample of DNA from either of you to carry out a process called DNA fingerprinting,' continued Myles. 'We compare your sample to the one we have already taken from the deceased, looking for the same markers within them. If they are a match, then we know conclusively that it is Shaun.'

Liam took a deep breath.

Dr Myers turned back towards his desk.

'Which of you is providing the sample today please?' he asked, putting on a pair of latex gloves.

'That would be me,' said Liam apprehensively.

'Ok Mr Mason,' replied the Doctor. 'We will be doing a simple mouth swab. I have all the necessary equipment ready for us here if you are happy to proceed?'

Liam remained silent as he watched the doctor open the pre-labelled vial on his desk and unwrap a long sterile swab.

'I will take the sample by rubbing this swap on the soft tissue of your cheek just inside your mouth,' Myers explained, moving his wheeled chair forward towards Liam. 'Are you still happy to proceed?' he asked again.

Liam nodded before tipping his head backwards slightly and opening his mouth. Myers inserted the swab and ran it up and down his left cheek rotating the tip as he did so. He then removed it. Turning back towards his desk and using his legs to propel him over to it, he placed the swab straight into the vial.

'It's a strange sensation, isn't it?' he said to Liam as he watched him seal the top of the vial before placing it into a labelled sample bag.

'Not as invasive as I was expecting to be honest,' said Liam. Kelly was staring at her husband in gratitude. She squeezed his hand again.

'It could take up to eight hours for us to fully process the sample, but due to the significance of the circumstances I expect it to be much sooner,' said Myers turning back towards the couple.

'So be it,' replied Liam.

'I shall have our receptionist contact you as soon as possible. Once his identity is confirmed, we can begin the process to get his body released to you for you to start making funeral arrangements,' said Myers.

'Thank you,' said Liam solemnly. 'We're not going very far.'

'Allow me to see you to the top of the stairs,' said Dr Myers standing up.

Kelly and Liam followed his lead. Hand in hand they exited the laboratory. Opposite them was the buildings archive room and Dr Myers office.

'Thank you for coming,' said Dr Myers as they reached the top of the stairs. We will see you presently as soon as we have the results.'

Kelly could feel her legs starting to give way as they descended the stairs under the watchful gaze of the doctor. Liam held the buildings door open for his wife again as they exited and stood helplessly as she collapsed onto its porch floor, overcome by her grief.

# 6.

Joe was stood in his office in the university social sciences building collecting the necessary slides and handouts he needed. He had deliberately kept a low profile in a desperate attempt not to be drawn into the only topic of conversation currently circulating between everyone on campus but hadn't even got out of his car before someone started calling to him.

'Oh my God Joe, have you heard?' asked Julie, another of the social science lecturers who had returned to her car briefly to pick up her purse.

'Yes, yes I heard,' Joe had replied, shaking his head as he locked his car.

Thankfully the social science department had ample office room for staff to have their own private areas. The building had been there since nineteen sixteen. It's high ceilings and carved oak furnishings a nod to its heritage as an establishment to higher education.

*Not that any of the students nowadays even notice* Joe thought to himself as he left his office on his walk to the lecture theatre.

He opened and closed his office door behind him. Having taken several large strides down the corridor he stopped and turned, realising he had left the resources he would require on his desk. Odd. This had never happened previously.

As he made his way back to his office, he now had to dodge students pouring into the building from the opposite direction, following the only route down to the lecture theatre he would soon be teaching in. Not one of the students noticed him as he placed himself again the far wall and skimmed past them back to his office; they were too busy with their own conversations between each other or lost in their own little world, soundtracked with the music from their headphones.

All the offices were located down a corridor to the right of the building. He opened the door and headed back over to his desk, picked up what he had meant to take on leaving the first time, and exited the room again. He pushed the door behind him, but this time it did not shut completely, and continued in the direction he had first set off in, walking past a round oval office heading to the left. This room was never used for general teaching, its shape impractical for anything other than a long oak desk that was used for meetings, although it had just recently been used by a film crew as an interior for an on-going series.

Having got further than his first attempt, he was now entering what was clearly an extension to the original building that had been added at some point in correlation to the university's expansion. A slight ramp led him downwards. He entered the first door on his right and entered the first of the buildings two more modern lecture theatres. It was a gradually sloping room with fixed seating and long rectangular desks running the entirety of each row for the students to write. Situated at the front was a large white board with a chair, table, and overhead projector. Several of the rows were already full, with students still arriving after him.

Joe glanced at his watch. Despite his misstep with the paperwork, he was still two minutes early. He put his bag on the chair and placed the lesson plan on the table in front of him.

Thumbing through the pile he had brought with him; he found the handout documents ready to give to his students at the appropriate time and placed them separately at the left of the desk.

He glanced at his watch again. Time to begin.

'Good morning,' he said. 'Now. I know recent events have left you all feeling on edge, but we must try and remain focused. Welcome to part two of migration and ethnic relations.'

He placed the first of several transparency sheets on the overhead projector and flipped the button on its side. He blinked as he adjusted the projectors light and position to bring its image into better focus on the screen behind him.

'Let's begin.'

Jay, a student sat at the back of the room, nudged his friend Layton sitting in the seat next to him. He was rummaging in his bag desperately searching for a pen.

'Is that really all he's going to say?'

\*\*\*

Somehow unbeknownst to Joe, his last seminar of the day had over run. There was usually one student who asked a multiple of questions during such sessions, but to his and the rest of the students joy this group had been gifted a second student who also did the same thing.

He left the building on the way to the staff car park, carrying an archive box containing the coursework he had just received. When he had started lecturing at the university, he didn't mind coming in early and staying late if that was what needed to be done. Life was about the work and empowering his students as much as possible. These days work had become an inconvenience to his life.

Joe walked around to the back of his car, opened the boot, and placed the archive box inside before realising Claire was already in the car waiting for him. Usually, he headed over to chemistry department to wait for her. The couple had carpooled for several years to the university. Although they had the option to drive separately, those occasions were rare unless they were unavoidable. Despite it not being the most city friendly vehicle, the couple were conscious of needing to keep a bigger vehicle for sake their parents. It was only a matter of time before they would need more help. Getting rid of their second run around wasn't on the cards either. Joe was convinced that a lack of independence between couples did not help current divorce rates. He often wondered what would have happened to his mother after his father died had she not had her wider network of friends before she met Mark.

There was very little chatter between them on the drive home. Joe turned on the car stereo to fill the silence. The sound of an overdriven guitar crashed out of the speakers.

'Turn that off, it's too loud for me!' Claire exclaimed.

Joe hit the off button.

'Sorry,' Claire said sheepishly. 'I don't know why but I have a headache coming.'

'I'm sure breathing in chemicals all day surrounded by tall children in lab coats doesn't help matters,' he replied.

'It's not like we're hot boxing them!' she said defensively. 'We have zero tolerance in our department for substances, you know that. We can be subjected to a test at any time should suspicion arise.'

Joe didn't reply. It was at that point the cars fuel light illuminated.

'Might as well go get the fuel now…' he grumbled. Ten minutes later, he drove the car onto the garage forecourt and straight through to pump number one.

Turning off the engine, he pressed the button that released the fuel cap cover.

After climbing out and walking around the back of the car to the passenger side, he unscrewed the cap and lifted the nozzle from the pump.

He had just placed the nozzle into the car when Claire wound down the passenger window.

'Joe. Can you grab some milk if they still have any when you go pay, please?' she asked. 'It'll save either of us having to go out later. I plan on having a hot bath before I attack the mountain of papers that need marking and very little else.'

'Ok' he replied dismissively.

He pressed the lever on the fuel gun and stared over the top of the vehicle at the traffic starting to queue on the main road beyond the fence that surrounded the garage. Joe heard and felt the fuel pump stop, indicating that the petrol had reached the nozzles end inside the fuel tank. He put the nozzle back and making note of the pump number, crossed the front of the forecourt and into the garage to pay.

There were two people already being served at the two tills, so he stood in the middle behind them both with two low shelves of confectionery on either side of him. The man on the right till finished serving the customer in front of Joe before standing up. He crossed the space behind the counter and out through the Staff Only door.

Joe exhaled. It was jobs like these, all be it necessary daily life tasks, that made him the most impatient. After the woman in front had been served, he walked up to the vacant cashier on the left.

'Pump number one please.'

The man behind the counter had just accessed the till when he remembered the milk.

He turned and quickly headed over the fridge that ran the length of the back wall, grabbed the nearest green topped milk carton, and quickly returned to the till.

The cashier said nothing. He scanned the milk before hitting the total button on the till.

'Forty-one pounds fifteen please,' he said.

Joe had already fished his bank card from his wallet. He inserted it into the reader and tapped in his PIN number. He removed his card, took his receipt, and picked up the milk to leave. He hadn't noticed it when he entered but located to the right of the doorway was a paper rack.

It was a little early for the usual mid-week newspapers to be released, but clearly the last few days had seen the editors push for early publication to capitalise on the events to use in their headlines. His eyes scanned over them. Second blast claims youngest victim.

Minister calls for patrols on the street. Police getting closer to arrests claimed another.

He exited the garage and got back into the car, passing the milk to Claire, and fastening his seat belt. As he pulled away, he already knew what he had to do. Now was the time to play his decoy.

\*\*\*

Mills, Dee, Wood and Jons crowded round the computer screens about to playback the CCTV footage from the centre. Wood glanced at the name plate on the operator's desk.

'I didn't t know that Alec was your first name, I just presumed it was Justin,' he said.

Justin laughed.

'Few people do. Mind you this is the most people I've had in my little corner of the station before, and I always introduce myself as Justin!'

'Do you not like your first name?' asked Jons.

'No, it's not that. In my house at secondary school, everyone referred to each other by their surnames. After five years it just became the norm,' said Justin.

'Surely you're teachers still addressed you as Alec though?' said Dee.

'Yes, but luckily for me I didn't have to talk to them much!'

After double clicking the video file, Justin tapped the keyboards space bar. Everyone behind him watching the footage eagle eyed.

'There!' shouted Dee. 'Run that back and play it again please Justin.'

The operator did as he was asked. 'That must be him,' she said.

They could see a figure in a high vis vest and baseball cap enter the centre carrying a box, heading in the direction of the exhibition.

'Impressively fast detective,' said Justin as re-ran the footage and time stamped it.

'Can we magnify the footage enough to see his face?' asked Mills

'No sir, I'm afraid not.' replied Justin. 'The position of the cameras and him deliberately wearing that cap mean we will still only see the lower part of his jaw.'

'Dammit!' exclaimed Mills.

'I can't believe the balls on him!' said Wood.

Everyone turned to look at him.

'Skin tone gloves as well. Clever. No-one's going to be paying attention to your hands at that time in the morning,' added Dee.

'The only reason we can see them is due to that fortunate light,' said Mills.

'We may not be able to make a positive ID based on this footage, but at least we've got something we can give to the press,' Justin added.

'No!' said Mills firmly. 'No one is to inform the press of anything specific until I authorise it. Is that clear?'

Justin spun round in his chair and looked at him along with his other colleagues. All of them were confused by Mills comment.

'If we release these images, then every delivery driver who looks like our friend there instantly becomes a target for retaliation,' said Mills. 'We need to keep the details of our suspects identities out of the press as long as we possibly can. With all of us working on this, hopefully we'll get a lead soon.'

'I'll keep running it and see if I can turn up anything else,' Justin said.

'Great,' replied Mills. 'Thank you.'

Everyone exited the room, leaving Justin at his desk preparing to restart the footage again.

'The armed unit chief has arrived Mills,' said Hughes as Mills crossed the room heading towards his office.

'Great. Give me five minutes and I'll be right with him,' Mills replied.

Mills closed his office door and sat down in his spare chair that he usually offered visitors to his office. All he wanted and desperately needed was five minutes peace on his own, before going back out and facing a situation that was escalating at an astonishing rate.

Armed police? What was next? The army? Curfews?

*Heavy is the head that wears the crown. and this head hurts!* he thought to himself.

Just then his phone rang.

'Oh god! Just two more minutes!' he exclaimed out loud before rolling himself forward toward his desk using his feet and the chair wheels. He leaned over his desk and picked up the receiver.

'Yes?'

'Mills? Is that you?'

'Yes Buckland, it's me,' he replied.

'Sorry,' said Buckland. 'I'm so used to hearing you answer by saying Mills first. When you didn't, I thought I better check.'

'That's ok,' Mills replied, picking up a pen on his desk and flicking it between his fingers. 'What is it?'

'Having run all the necessary processes, I can now confirm for certain that it's the same person or persons responsible for the manufacture of both the cinema and centre bombs. I know you've got a meeting in a second, so I thought I'd save you the walk downstairs to tell you.'

'Thank you. I appreciate that,' Mills replied.

'No probs. Bye,' said Buckland before hanging up.

***

*Just the one!* Mills thought to himself as he begrudgingly opened the door to his office, making his way towards the conference room. *A small win.*

Dee was already inside, chatting to the senior members of the Armed police division.

As Mills entered the room, both men turned to greet him.

'Detective Mills,' said the first man offering his hand. 'Sorry we are here.'

'Don't be sorry, I'm grateful for the help.' said Mills, directing both men to sit.

'Forgive us for not introducing ourselves. I am Officer James, and this is Officer Simon, armed police unit. How can we best assist you to protect the public and catch whoever is responsible?'

'I am confident your presence will have a positive effect on proceedings,' replied Mills. 'It's more a question of where best to deploy you. As you can see, we've already mapped the locations of the two incidents on a map of the city. Two completely different locations.'

'Based on the last two incidents, wouldn't public buildings be the best areas to concentrate on?' James asked, surveying the map. 'That's the one thing both previous targets have in common.'

'Yes, I'd presume so,' said Mills. 'Both incidents happened several miles apart from each other as you can see. What concerns me is I know that neither of us have enough resources to cover the whole city.'

'I'd start in the city centre and work outwards,' said Simon. 'We can also team up with your regular patrol personnel, so the firepower is spread over a large area rather than concentrated.'

'That makes the most logical sense,' said Mills. 'Have a word with Officer Hughes, and Sargent Donovan. They will be able to show you where we are currently deployed and how best we can integrate you.'

'Very good,' replied James standing up. 'Best get to it. In the meantime, you concentrate on catching the culprit!'

'We will,' replied Mills. 'And thank you for your assistance.'

\*\*\*

Faye and mark were sat in their car, both regretting their decision to drive into the city.

They were currently in a queue of traffic on approach to the centre with cones filtering two lanes of traffic into a one-way system.

'We may need to look at trading this old girl in for a bus,' said Mark sarcastically. 'At least they can get close to the areas that have now been pedestrianised.'

'I don't think that's the only hold up,' replied

Faye, her head pressed up against her passenger side window. 'Look.'

Mark raised himself up in this chair and leaned over to the left.

They saw the tops of several placards first. 'No. No. No!'

A chant continued to get louder and louder before several hundred protesters filed along the pavement next to them and between the cars with the placards, newspapers, and a few umbrellas they'd written on. UK Not the USA said one. The Bills Big Enough read another.

Another small group within the group had taken the familiar no sign with its striking red line and circle and put a gun in the middle.

'Well, I hope the organisers are satisfied!' huffed Faye.

Another protester marched past their car holding a sign with Nineteen eighty-four it's Not written on it.

'I don't understand it,' replied Mark, watching out of his driver side window in bewilderment. 'This is for their protection as well as it is everyone else's.'

'A few of them must be grandparents,' commented Faye. 'Of all people!'

Mark shook his head. 'It's a Mad world.'

A few steps behind the protesters, Zoe Lee and two fellow police officers were following them.

'As long as they remain peaceful, we won't have to arrest anyone,' she said to her colleagues as they walked together in unison. 'Any idea where they might be headed?'

'Well, the city news studio is about one hundred yards further down the road to the right,' said her fellow officer Paul King, keeping his eye on a few protestors who seemed to have broken away from the crowd. 'My guess is they're heading for the lawn outside.'

'Fabulous!' replied Zoe, rolling her eyes. 'Part of me hopes that's their destination, but the other part hopes they continue up the road and into the park. Either way, I'm loathed to call for backup whatever happens.'

# 7.

Michelle and Russell Gilmore were at the head of the procession of protestors. All were waving their banners and shouting at the bewildered faces of pedestrians and motorists as they passed them.

'So, is the plan still the plan sweetheart?' Michelle asked her husband.

'Yes. You gather everyone on the lawn outside the television centre,' he replied. 'Keep it peaceful though, just chant no repeatedly or something.'

'Don't worry, I'm not about to cause civil unrest,' said Michelle. 'It is only a distraction after all.'

'Yes, it is,' her husband replied with a smile. 'Are you ready Conrad?'

'I am,' replied Conrad Set, walking directly behind the couple. 'I hope your feeling strong Russ!'

Russell let go of his wife's hand and handed her the placard he was carrying. Michelle then began to lead the other protesters onto the grass outside the studio. Russell remained on the pavement with Conrad, waiting.

'Good luck,' said Harry Reid as he passed the men with his wife Geraldine.

Russell smiled at the couple.

'Keep waving your banners high!' he replied. 'You guys haven't seen Dave Mayatt, have you?'

'I'm here you madman!' chuckled David. He was walking almost directly behind Harry and Geraldine. 'The police are still tailing our group,' he said, standing aside with Russell and Conrad to allow those behind him to enter the garden.

'Good,' Conrad replied. 'Hopefully they will remain with our pack of vocal opposition.'

The three men then continued to walk up the road, leaving the group filing into the garden chanting. Deliberately quickening their pace so as not to be spotted by the tailing police officers, they took the first right and proceeded to make their way down the road. The back entrance to the television studio was located just up ahead.

'I hate being right,' said Officer Paul as the police officers were gathered watching the protesters on the lawn waving their banners and chanting in unison.

'This is all about trying to attract the media's attention, isn't it?' replied Zoe, her eyes scanning the group.

'I'd say so,' replied Paul. 'But I can't see a camera crew emerging from those front doors anytime soon.

If they give this group what they want, then they'll have people permanently camped on their doorstep. That and they've already got plenty to fill their programs with these days unfortunately.'

'Sad but true Paul,' replied Zoe. 'Sad but true.'

\*\*\*

Russell, Conrad, and David had reached the back entrance of the studio.

'Time to ditch the placards and coats gents,' said Russell. Both men then leaned their placards against the stone wall before undoing and removing their coats.

'Looking sharp Dave!' said Conrad. All three were now stood in white shirts and black trousers.

'I do scrub up rather well if I do say so myself,' David replied with a grin.

'Let's use that security booth rather than trying to jump the gate,' said Russell, pointing to the left. 'Its roof is flat.'

'Come on then Russ,' said David.

He walked over to the back of the security booth. Bending his legs, he cupped his hands in front of him. Russell approached him and put his left foot in David's hands. He then reached up and grabbed hold of the top of the small concrete roof with his arms as David lifted him. Having got himself on top of the security booth, Russell turned and held his hands out for David.

'You next Dave,' he said. 'If you would please Conrad.'

Conrad repeated David's actions, whilst Russell climbed off the other side of the booth.

He was now stood inside the studio backlot.

'Quick!' said David, turning back towards Conrad and motioning him to grab his hands.

'Don't worry about me Dave,' Conrad replied. 'You guys go!'

David jogged up to Russell, who was looking up at the top of a large signpost in amongst some bushes pointing in the directions of the various studio's locations on the site.

'Which way Russ?' Dave asked.

'We both go left!' Russell replied, already starting to head in that direction. 'You head in towards the television studio, and I'll try and get on the radio.'

A loud shout came from in front of them. 'Hey!'

Both men turned to see a security guard approaching them at growing speed.

'Go!' shouted Russell as the pair ran towards the studios back entrance. Thankfully it was not locked, allowing them to dart straight through the door.

\*\*\*

Jeff Todd, the head of the studios security really didn't know what to do as he entered the building behind Russell and David. Neither man was visible to him. As he couldn't go in both directions at once, he'd have to make a choice. All his years' experience in security, and he'd finally been caught off guard. The more he thought about it, the more it annoyed him. All it had taken was a simple misdirection from those currently occupying the front lawn. Still, he stood by his decision to have most of his team stationed by the entrance. There were a lot of disgruntled people out there, and no protest that he'd ever heard of that had ended in violence had immediately started with violence. Best to remain cautious.

Russell had reached the buildings research room. Trying to remain as casual as he could so as not to draw attention to himself, he sat down at one of the vacant computer desks in amongst a few of the studios research team. To his surprise not one person looked up from their computer screens. *Perfectly pitched clothing,* he thought to himself. *I am now a needle in the haystack.*

The entrance to the radio station itself was at the far end of the room he was in behind a set of locked doors. He stood up and slowly made his way towards it, knowing that he had the option of repositioning himself in another empty chair further into the room if he needed. To his surprise the studio door then opened. He quickened his pace. After quickly standing aside to let the person who had just exited him pass, he caught the door before it closed and resealed itself and stepped through into the radio studio. All he had to do now was get on air.

\*\*\*

Richard Mayhew was sat trying to arrange the various pieces of paper that had accumulated in front of him during his time on air.

'Three minutes Rich,' said the familiar voice of Charles Alice his producer.

'Cheers,' Richard replied through the off-air microphone. 'Just trying to find the next bit in amongst all this.'

With his eyes down scanning the documents in front of him, he did not see the unfamiliar face of Russell enter the room and sit down in the chair opposite him.

'That's sorted that,' he said, tapping the pile of papers on the desk in front of him. It wasn't until he looked up that he caught sight of Russell.

'I didn't know we were expecting guests?' he said, looking at Charles through the glass window between the studio and the control room. He watched as he saw his producer pick up the telephone. *I'm presuming he's placing a call to security*, Richard thought to himself. *At least I hope that's what he's doing!*

'We don't want, need or desire any trouble please,' he said, looking over at Russell.

'Do I look like I'm dressed for trouble?' Russell replied, looking down and straightening his shirt.

'Then do you want?' asked Richard.

'To talk about guns being put out onto our streets,' said Russell. 'I mean, what comes after that?'

'One minute Richard,' said an anxious Charles. 'Security should be here any second!'

'You just want to talk?' said Richard. 'You'd leave without resistance once we're finished?'

'Absolutely,' Russell replied.

Jeff Todd then entered the room, flanked by another member of security.

'I apologise gentlemen,' he said. 'We'll get rid of him.'

'Thirty seconds,' said Charles, pacing up and down the control room in front of the glass.

'Time to go Sir,' said Jeff moving towards Russell.

'Wait!' exclaimed Richard suddenly. 'If you agree that the security can remain in the room with us, and that you promise to not use blasphemy of any kind, I might be willing to put you on air.'

Russell smiled at him.

'Thank you. I always thought you were a reasonable man,' he said.

'There's a set of headphones there just to the left of you, if you'd like to put them on,' Richard replied. He stood up and adjusted the position of the microphone on the desk in front of Russell.

"No!" yelled Charles through the talk back microphone. 'You cannot do this Rich! We'll be thrown off air and out of the building, each of us carrying a cardboard box and a P forty-five!'

'No, we won't,' replied Richard defiantly, looking directly at his producer. 'This unique opportunity could be the making of our broadcasting careers Charles. History.'

'Just hurry up and make a decision please gentlemen,' said Jeff looking at his watch. 'I've got a lawn full of people out front who could potentially turn nasty at any moment.'

# 8.

With Claire now in the bath, Joe had made another excuse to leave the house. Claire had been distracted, and didn't even question what, where or why he was going from the moment he had mentioned his mother.

He had taken a bus into the city, wearing his cap, an unbuttoned shirt, and the backpack. Having deliberately left a few days stubble on his face, he was certain he would not be recognised as he slipped on another pair of gloves as he walked. He glanced at his watch. Quarter to five. Perfect. Evening prayers.

Thankfully the armed police were yet to be deployed in the area as he quietly crossed the road and ascended the stairs of the Mosque, adjusting his cap as he did so. Entering silently, he glanced to his left. On the side were various leaflets. He picked up the nearest one and quickly slipped back out of the same door.

He felt the first few drops of rain as he descended the stairs and headed off in the opposite direction he had approached from. Once he had rounded the corner at the end of the road, he stopped behind a raised flower bed and crouched down.

Joe undid the top pocket of the backpack he was wearing and looked at the community events diary he had just picked up. He placed the leaflet inside the backpack and zipped it back up before carrying on walking towards his next target. Should he run into any questioning officers who wished to stop and search him before entering the building, he had faith that the deliberately placed women's underwear at the top of the bag would cause them to stop investigating further due to becoming embarrassed. Hopefully they had not seen the film that he got it from. With the rain getting progressively heavier, he gradually quickened his pace.

Joe walked along the road deliberately looking around in all directions like he had never been there before. At the other end of the street a voice could be heard being projected over the rest of the noise from a small amplifier.

'Darkness is present in the absence of light. God is light, in Him is no darkness at all.'

*A manic street preacher* Joe thought to himself as he paused a moment to listen. *It's working.*

Just then he spotted one of the first armed patrols on the opposite side of the road. Joe quickly headed further up the road and inside the venue, walking briskly past the signs outside offering drinks at discounted prices for people able to show their student card at the bar. There were many like this around the city. He headed straight over to a long rectangular bar which ran the length of the left-hand side of the venue.

'Just a sec,' said Tom, a tall man attending the bar this afternoon. He placed a pint in-front of another customer who slowly wondered off back to find his table.

'Yes sir,' he asked, walking towards Joe behind the bar. 'What can I get you?'

'Pint of beer and a portion of chips please,' Joe replied, adjusting his cap.

Tom used his key fob to activate the till and tapped in the order.

'Table number?' he asked.

'Don't know what that is, but I plan to sit over there,' Joe replied, pointing to the table directly under the stairs to the upper floor, next to the dance floor and DJ booth.

'Table three. Ok,' replied Tom. 'Anything else?' he asked.

'No thanks,' came the reply.

'That'll be seven ninety-nine please.'

Joe handed over a ten-pound note and waited for his change.

'I'll just grab your drink for you now, and we'll bring your chips over to your table,' said Tom.

Having been served, Joe took his drink and wondered over to table three. He took off his backpack and sat down at the table with his back facing the rest of the bar. A girl wondered over with his basket of chips which she placed on the table in front of him.

'Thanks' he said.

'Sauces are over there to the left of the bar if you would like some,' she said, before retracing her footsteps and returning through the kitchen door to the right of the bar.

Joe sampled a chip before pouring half of his pint into the empty glass on the table next to his. He then grabbed the backpack and stood up. When no-one was watching he walked behind the DJ booth and crouched down. There were two big speakers encased in cabinets either side of the shelf that supported the mixing desk with the table below for a laptop. Below this there was a maintenance hatch. He lifted this up to reveal the hollow space deliberately created to allow for a workman and their tools to reach the electronics housed inside.

He placed the backpack inside this space to the right under the speaker nearest the dance floor, before carefully undoing the zip to the main compartment. He found the timer and placed the battery from his pocket inside just as he had done previously.

*How long?* he mused. *Four hours should suffice.*

He set the timer for two hundred and forty minutes and pressed the start button, before slowly placing the timer back into the bag being careful not to catch his hand in the wires.

Joe shut the hatch again and stood up before returning to where he was sat. He picked up the basket containing the rest of the chips and placed them on the next free table as he walked towards the exit.

\*\*\*

Girard, Robert, and Patrick were on their way into the city for the evening.

'I thought we were supposed to get food after the club?' said Girard.

'I would have eaten there if we had left earlier, but they'll have stopped serving food now.' replied Patrick. 'And besides, that's so cliché.'

'Oh, for god's sakes you too!' snapped Robert. 'There are dozens of eateries on the way in. Patrick can just run in to any one of them and grab something.'

'What's the rush?' asked Patrick to his flat mate. Robert seemed to be trying to speed up the group of friends walking pace.

'I said we'd meet the others at Seven,' Robert replied.

'You mean you said you'd meet him there!' Patrick replied with a grin.

Girard laughed.

'Nothing to do with it!' Robert exclaimed.

'Yeah right!' said Patrick.

'We've known you nearly a year now son!' Girard said. 'We can tell.'

'Your point being?' Robert asked, trying to contemplate what on earth he was on about.

'My point being you can't fool us anymore my friend,' Girard replied.

'I'm going to take you for everything you have next Poker night!' smiled Patrick as the three friends walked along the newly pedestrianised street heading into the city centre.

'Try it!' responded Robert, hitting his friend on the chest playfully.

'Do you not think it would've been far easier for everyone to set this night up in the student union?' Patrick asked.

Robert rolled his eyes.

'Where's the fun in that?' Girard said before Robert could respond. 'We spent the first half of our first year in there before we ventured out into the big city. And besides, tonight we're under the protection of the city's finest.'

He spun around, now walking backwards and put his two thumbs up.

'What are you doing?' Robert asking him, glancing behind his shoulder.

'Thanking the officers covering our rears!' Girard replied.

Robert twisted further.

'Oh, I see. For Gods sakes behave yourself G!' The friends walked down through an underpass, it's wall's a mixture of street art and tags by urban artists trying to perfect their craft.

'We've lost our chaperones,' said Patrick disappointedly, watching as the officers carried on walking in the direction of the road behind them.

'Don't worry Pat,' said Girard. 'Plenty more about.'

They proceeded up the ramp on the other side of the main road that brought traffic into the city. To their left was an old boarded up live music venue, next door to a bank.

'Bet you didn't have to pay over seven quid a pint in there like you do in the arena!' Patrick said as they walked past.

'Cashpoint!' exclaimed Girard suddenly.

He jogged up to the machine outside the bank and pulled his bank card out of his pocket.

'Why does he never bring his whole wallet out with him?' asked Robert as they stood and watched Girard take out his debit card from his jeans pocket.

'Less to lose,' Patrick replied. 'He said you are better off just cancelling one bank card than having to worry about sorting out the entire contents we all keep in our wallets.'

'You know he actually has a point there…,' said Robert. The expression on his face then suddenly changed from casual to surprise. 'I can't believe I just said that!'

Girard returned to his two friends. 'Point about what now?' he asked.

'You not bringing your wallet out with you!' said Robert.

'Oh that. Old news. Far more interesting things going on,' replied Girard. 'Pat look behind you mate' he said.

Patrick span round.

'The perfect eatery for food to go,' Girard smiled. The three students made their way across to a fast-food restaurant on the opposite side of the street. As they approached the entrance the smell grew stronger. Two police officers walked out of the entrance, walking towards them carrying their hot food.

Girard stuck his head in the air and sniffed as they passed him nearby.

'Evening officers' he said.

'Good evening,' replied the policeman nearest him.

'Is it greedy to eat something else having only just eaten?' Girard asked his friends as he watched the officers beginning to unwrap their food. 'Because that smells insanely good!'

Robert reached the entrance to the restaurant first. He opened the door and stood to one side, holding it for his companions to enter before him.

'In you go you two,' he said with a forced smile. 'But hurry up!' he exclaimed, letting go of the door. He glanced at his watch and began to pace around outside, trying to rid himself of nervous energy. Reaching into his shirt pocket he pulled out a packet of cigarettes. He opened it up, took out the lighter that he had placed in the empty space in the box followed by a cigarette which he placed between his lips and lit.

'Every flipping time!' he exclaimed, tilting his head up and exhaling smoke into the air. He watched as the two patrol men headed off in the direction they would soon be headed.

***

'Now that was good eating!' said Gerard as they were approaching their destination.

The bar in question was situated at the far end of a long stretch of road. To reach it they had to walk past a much larger nightclub.

'It's just up here,' said Robert to his friends, pointing further up the road as they walked past the people queuing outside. In amongst the groups of nightclubbers, they could make out the patrol officers on duty. One was clearly relaying instructions to their colleagues nearby via an earpiece. The other did not look impressed at the stream of comments and people who kept coming up to them in various states of intoxication.

As they walked on further up the road, they could hear a girl arguing with one of the bouncers on the door. Judging by the look on his face this was a situation he often encountered, but still found just as annoying as the first time it had happened.

'A fiver entrance free? Jog on!' she exclaimed. 'I know your kind' she continued, slurring her words, and trying to maintain her balance. 'You're robbing us blind and pocketing the money to pay for your cocaine at the end of the night!'

On hearing this the man on the door straightened his back and puffed out his chest in front of her, instantly becoming larger and more intimidating.

'Just leave it! It's not worth it. Come on. Come on!' said her friend, tugging at her handbag and looking nervously at the bouncer. 'We'll go somewhere else instead.'

'Unbelievable!' exclaimed Robert as they watched the two girls stagger off down the road.

Girard smiled as the group passed the entrance to the club.

'There's something in the air tonight boys!' he exclaimed as they approached the venue.

'Tonight's gonna be one to remember.'

'Just shut up Girard and follow me!' said Robert, heading past the bouncer on the door and into the Seven club.

Girard glanced at the offers on the boards outside.

'Vodka Jelly!' he exclaimed as he entered. 'Stuff that!'

Patrick was just behind him, bringing up the rear. He was just about to follow his friend in when a bouncer stepped out in front of him.

'ID please?' he asked.

Girard stopped as he heard this and laughed at his friend.

'It's always you, isn't it Pat?' he chuckled.

'Yup,' said Patrick, fishing in his wallet for his provisional driver's licence. 'And I'm older than you!' Patrick handed the green card to the bouncer, who looked at it and looked at Patrick before giving him back the card and moving aside.

'Go on,' he said, motioning them into the club.

'Thanks,' Patrick replied, putting his license back into his wallet.

'Bad luck mate', said Girard as they walked through the entrance and into the club. 'We're not gonna see much of Rob tonight I don't think, but that doesn't mean we can't have a good night. To the Bar!'

\*\*\*

Claire and Joe were sat opposite ends of their sofa watching evening television. A child was currently yelling at their parent on the screen.

'Why not just lock in me my room then?' they screamed. 'Just because you're a complete loser with no friends doesn't mean I am!'

'Mind your attitude please,' came the reply after a moment's hesitation. The parent was clearly trying to control their emotions that were in danger of becoming irrational. 'You have run up a three-hundred-pound phone bill due to you constantly texting and calling your friends. Do you not bother to speak to each other in school? How do you expect me to pay that?'

'Should have got them a pay as you go, not a pay monthly plan,' said Claire. 'Have you caught any of your students playing snake in lectures?' she asked Joe. 'I have. Not so much during the practical, but the theory lessons are a different story.'

Joe just looked at Claire with a glazed expression. She could have told him the world was about to end and she probably would have been met with the same look on his face, his mind and spirit so far removed from his wife.

'Either way it doesn't excuse the way they are talking to them,' Claire continued. 'I can't begin to imagine what would have happened if I had spoken to my mother like that!'

She leaned forward and picked up her wine glass that was placed on the coffee table in front of her, before settling back down and tucking her feet into the chair beside her.

She glanced over at Joe.

'Do you ever regret our decision not to have children of our own?' she asked.

'No,' Joe said without hesitation. 'I'm close enough to them at work thank you.'

Claire sighed.

'Figures,' she replied. 'I just wonder if you'd be more open if we had...'

Saying nothing, Joe stood up and picked up his mug from the table.

'I'll be in the office,' he said as he exited the room, leaving Claire alone on the sofa.

'Whatever,' she called after him. 'I'm starting to think there's someone else Joseph!'

\*\*\*

With the tables located on and around the dance floor now cleared, the bars hours operating as a nightclub were in full swing. There were cues three people deep for the bar, with those at the front having to lean over and shout their order into one of the four bartenders' ears who were serving tonight to be heard over the noise. Some were avoiding trying to speak altogether. Instead, they were pointing at what they wanted before holding up the number of their fingers to say how many they would like.

On the dance floor, people were moving to the beat of the music. Some dancing with their drinks in the air, some dancing in a group, others dancing on their own. Couples occupying the floor were also dancing like they were the only two people in the venue.

Onlookers perched around the area, debating whether to join in or remain where they were.

Two girls had gone into the DJ booth. One was having a word in the DJ's ear, no doubt trying to get a request supplanted into tonight's pre-programmed playlist. Robert was shouting into the ear of the guy stood next to him.

Patrick had made his way upstairs and was stood at a urinal in the men's toilets.

He had just begun to silently read the framed notice on the wall in front of him when he heard a familiar voice coming from the person now stood beside him.

'That poor, poor girl!'

"You!" exclaimed Patrick.

Next to him was Kevin Ross, a student on the same history course.

'How you doing Kev?' he asked.

'All good bud,' Kevin replied.

The two of them walked in tandem towards the sinks.

'Who did you come here with?' Kevin asked.

'Girard and Robert. He's desperate to get in with what's his name? I forget!'

Kevin laughed.

'Fair enough. I'm here with Jess and Dom.'

'What do think of the armed patrols outside then?' Patrick asked.

'Whilst I'm horrified of them, I'm grateful they are there. They could've just shut everything down and locked us in our dorms,' Kevin replied, walking over to one of the basins opposite the urinals and turning the tap on.

'You're literal hell on earth!' said Patrick, stood over one of the other sinks washing his hands.

'Don't get me started Pat!' said Kevin, shaking his hands and pulling paper towels from the dispenser. 'If anything, it's gotten worse.'

'I best come say Hi to the others,' said Patrick. He walked over and stepped on the pedal of the metal bin in the corner of the room, allowing Kevin to drop his used towels in after him before removing his foot.

'Go for it,' replied Kevin. 'But for Christ's sake keep an eye on Girard! Jess is still embarrassed about that particular evening.'

Patrick put his right thumb up as he held the toilet door open for Kevin.

\*\*\*

Girard had been badgered into getting the next round of drinks. Despite offering to buy someone else's drink for them if they did it instead, he had eventually given in. It was all in good fun and in fairness his friends had coughed up their share of the money.

The queue at the bar was only two deep now, which would mean his wait would be significantly shorter than it was for his first drink earlier. He was stood bobbing his head and humming the melody of the music when somebody pinched his left buttock.

*I've been goosed! The very cheek of it,* he thought.

He spun around, fully expecting to see Kevin laughing himself stupid along with Patrick, but instead he was met with a blinding light that filled the room. Before his eyes had chance to adjust, his ears started screaming at him. Something warm and wet was running down his face. He put his hand to his forehead and held it up in front of his eyes.

Blood.

## 9.

'We must stop meeting like this,' said Rhys as Mills and Dee approached him from outside the Seven Nightclub.

'All clear?' asked Mills.

'Yes,' replied Rhys.

'If the powers that be continue to insist that public amenities stay open, then we're going to have to start sweeping the buildings,' said Mills. 'That'll be a massive headache.'

'It must have been planted earlier in the day during a gap in the patrols,' said Dee.

'I think assumptions were made that armed patrols would be enough of a deterrent,' said Mills, looking at the glass that littered the pavement in front of the building. 'It's extremely concerning that they are not.'

'Only one device again, this time concealed in a backpack that was hidden in the DJ booth,' Rhys continued as the three of them entered the building.

'The eight people nearest the explosion, including the DJ died instantly.'

Stood just inside the doorway was William waiting to greet them. To the right Buckland and his forensics team were swarmed around the square frame of what was left of the DJ booth.

There was glass everywhere. The windows had blown out on both floors, and every glass in the venue had shattered. The bar had been obliterated, with everything from soft drinks to hard liquor now on the floor between the debris. Unlike the relatively contained blood radius they had found in the aftermath of the previous bombs it was everywhere this time as most people were holding a glass object at the time of the explosion.

'My God,' said Dee, trying to come to terms with the site that was in front of her.

'I think he was absent tonight, Kate,' replied Mills behind her.

He started to rub his head, trying to work out where on earth to start going through this mess.

Buckland had left his team and wondered over to the waiting officers.

'As horrific as this looks, there may be some light in the darkness,' he said.

Mills just looked at him blankly.

'Please share,' replied Dee, her eyes fixated on the dance floor. It was impossible to tell what it had looked like prior to the explosion.

'We have recovered evidence in the upper part of the DJ booth over there,' said Buckland. 'I can't tell you anything concrete at this stage, but it looks like part of the backpack that was used to conceal the bomb. Once we've finished everything here, you'll find me wherever it is,' he said.

'Any indication that this device contained any shrapnel?' asked Dee.

'No. There's absolutely no evidence of that, and in a place like this it would be easy to spot in amongst the glass,' said Buckland.

'It's the same person, isn't it?' said Mills. 'The same person who targeted the cinema, then the centre and now this! They've simply changed how they are leaving them in these venues. Thank Christ they haven't done the same with making of the things!'

'We can't say that definitively at this stage I'm afraid Colin,' said Buckland.

'Do we know if there were any eyewitnesses?' asked Dee.

'Several. They were all outside when we arrived awaiting the first responders,' Buckland replied.

'Well, I'm sure our officers have used their initiative and started the process,' said Mills. 'Can we be of any use to you in here?'

'Not unless you feel like combing through the blood, wood and broken glass,' Buckland replied.

'Ok. In that case we'll head outside. See you back at the station.'

Buckland nodded and headed back in the direction of the dance floor.

'Run that evidence as soon as you can. I'll pay your overtime myself if needs be!' Mills called after his colleague.

Before they reached the exit, Dee's phone went.

'Say again? What? Are you certain?' she asked the voice at the other end of the phone, Mills looked at her quizzically.

'Yes, William and Rhys have secured the area. We'll send them in your direction now.'

'What is it?' asked Mills as she hung up.

'Possibly another bomb,' said Dee, looking at her colleague with a growing concern.

'Where?' asked Mills. He glanced round and caught William gaze, motioning him to come over.

'The Catacombs nightclub,' Dee replied. 'Near the train station.'

'I'm afraid there may be another IED William,' said Mills as William reached them. 'Your presence has been requested. Have one of the armed officers on patrol outside escort you and take one of the cars if needs be.'

'I believe Zoe Lee is that area so co-ordinate with her,' added Dee.

'That's Officer Zoe Lee to give you her full official title,' said Mills.

'Ok,' said William. 'We'll let you know the situation once we know more.'

'Thanks,' said Mills. 'Appreciated.'

'I need some air,' said Dee to Mills as they watched William and Rhys exit the building.

'So do I, but it's going to be a while before we get any that hasn't been tainted by this nightmare,' Mills replied as they walked towards the exit.

As soon as they were outside, Mills started to look in all directions.

'What are you doing?' Dee asked.

'Looking for the press,' he replied.

Dee spotted the tip of a boom mic between two ambulances.

'There' she said, pointing ahead of them. 'Between the ambulances.'

'Yes. I see,' Mills replied. 'As long as they don't obstruct us, they can stay there. Right now, we need to organise these people. It's utter chaos out here!'

As most of the clubs in the street had now been evacuated, people were everywhere. They filled the pavements and road, surrounding the emergency vehicles and personnel already in attendance blocking any chance of them leaving.

'Radio our colleagues and have any who are free meet us here,' said Mills to Dee. 'I expect most of them have been relocated to the other area where the second device is expected so we'll have to make do. I'm going to commandeer some of these barriers.'

Mills made his way through the crowd and approached one of the doormen of the largest nightclub in the road.

'DCI Mills,' he said as the doormen both looked at him. 'I need you to bring these barriers and follow me please?'

'What for?' asked one of them.

'Because we need to clear this street,' replied Mills. Dee, Wood, and several other officers had congregated in the middle of the road. The armed police officer was stood with them, not sure where best to position himself.

'I'm pretty sure I know what you're thinking,' said Dee, observing his awkwardness. 'But you are not responsible for what has happened here.'

'Absolutely,' added Wood. 'The device was probably planted before patrols were established. It's not like it hasn't been all over the news that they were coming.'

'Unfortunately not,' replied Dee.

'So, what's the plan now?' asked Wood.

'My guess is that Mills wants us to cordon off a section of the street using the club queuing barriers and have all these people leave in the same direction,' said Dee. 'We will need officers positioned by the emergency services and on both sides of the pavement to help shepherd people away. The plan is for them to leave in the opposite direction to that of the emergency access route. Is everybody clear?'

'Yes,' responded several voices in unison from those gathered in front of her.

'Where's best for me to be?' asked the armed Officer.

'Stood by the emergency vehicles I think,' replied Dee. 'The injured people there are the most vulnerable out here.'

Mills had managed to recruit several of the nightclub's security team, and with their help had moved the nightclubs barriers onto the road. Several other officers had followed his lead having been briefed by Dee. On both sides of the pavement, they had created zed barriers so those who went through could not double back.

Officer Wood spotted a group of people deliberately ignoring the instructions given to them, with other members of the public having to walk around them to leave the area as they had been instructed. He wondered over to them.

'Excuse me. What do you think you're doing?' he asked. 'This area is unsafe, and you need to leave as instructed.'

'Not until we've finished our drinks,' said one of them, lifting his bottle and taking a swig. 'Cheers pig.'

The group he was with then laughed.

'Look. We have enough to deal with without you lot giving us grief so please, do as you've been instructed,' said Wood.

'What right do you have to spoil our night?' slurred another of the group. 'Lousy coppers. You should be over there, not over here harassing us.'

'Police harassment, police harassment!' yelled another, causing several people to turn and stare.

It was at this point several other officers joined Wood, including Jons.

'My colleague here has asked you nicely, and I'm going to do the same. Please do as you've been instructed and move along. Under the circumstances you can take your drinks with you this one time, but we need to get you clear of the area,' Jons said, hopeful that now they had been spoken to than more than one officer the group would cooperate.

But the men did not reply. Instead, one of them threw his beer bottle at Jons who managed to dodge it, before lunging at Wood and punching him. It was at this point that Jons stepped behind him, and with Woods help got him onto the floor.

'You are being arrested Under section 89 of the Police Act, assaulting a police officer,' said Jons, removing and placing the man in his handcuffs. 'You do not have to say anything, but it may harm your defence if you do not mention when questioned something which you later rely on in court. Anything you do say may be given in evidence. Stand up.'

'Does anyone else fancy joining your friend here?' asked Wood to the rest of the group, who had backed away since the scuffle putting distance between themselves and the officers.

'Then please, leave the area as directed,' he said, watching Jons chaperone the man in handcuffs through the barrier towards a police car.

'Are you alright Wood?' asked Dee as he returned to where they had previously gathered.

Everyone watched as Jons shut the door of the police car having.

'Yes. There's always one isn't there?' he replied. 'And he didn't hit that hard. Before some lunatic started his personal vendetta a large amount of my job was dealing with the city's drunks of an evening.'

'Well, just as long as you're Ok,' said Dee.

Mills was looking up and down the street in both directions, watching as the lights from the emergency vehicles bounced off the buildings illuminating the nights sky. Most people had now cleared the area, with the last few making their way through the barriers away from the area.

'Fait accompli. Any word from Officer Lee?' he asked.

'No, nothing yet,' Dee replied.

'Fingers crossed it stays that way,' said Mills, as the group watched another ambulance move off slowly from its parked position.

\*\*\*

Wes Price was sat at the far end of the bar directly opposite the stairs that led down into the Catacombs nightclub. He was currently trying to mime the smallest amount of mixer possible to the barmaid in front of him. So far it seemed to be working, and he was beginning to feel the effects of the spirit. Tonight was both a necessity and a tactical change of scene.

Usually, Wes could be found in the halls of residence bar, but one evening not too long ago he had single handily finished off the contents of a whiskey bottle. Reasoning that he didn't need any further aggravation from those employed by the university, he'd headed off into the city. Several of his peers kept telling him he was well on the way to becoming a functional alcoholic, but now was certainly not the time to try and stop.

'Re-sits,' he said out loud to himself as he began lifting his glass. 'Why bother? Just let me fail and leave me alone like all the other faces who disappeared after the first year.'

Outside, William and Rhys were approaching Officer Lee and two others who had congregated outside.

'Evening all,' said Rhys as they approached the group. 'Does anyone have any idea how we can empty this club without causing mass panic? Usually, we deal with deserted or partially destroyed buildings, not full ones.'

'We've just been discussing that,' replied Lee. 'The most obvious thing would be to kill the power in the place and have their own security shepherd everyone out. What do you think?'

'Sounds like as good a plan as any I've heard recently,' replied William.

'Brilliant, please wait here a moment,' Lee replied as she started to make her way towards the club entrance and into the building. There was a ticketing booth just inside the doorway to the left of a flight of stairs that led patrons down into the main bar area where a security guard stood.

'Good evening,' said Lee to the girl in the booth and the man stood opposite. 'I am Officer Zoe Lee. Stood just outside are several of my colleagues. We have received an anonymous tip that there may be an explosive device hidden somewhere on these premises and need to move quickly.'

She paused and watched the expressions on both their faces change.

'Rather than risk a mad dash as people rush toward the exit in panic, I need someone to cut the venues power quietly and calmly. Once people start to leave, our team can begin their search. What's your maximum capacity please?'

'Three hundred and fifty,' replied the girl inside the booth. 'Although currently we have two hundred and ninety-seven in.'

Lee turned to face the security guard. 'I will need your help,' she said.

'Certainly,' the man replied.

'Can you access the venues control panel from here?' Lee asked.

'No, it's downstairs,' replied the girl. 'I'm not sure of its precise location but I know that Oscar behind the bar does.'

'Perfect. If you could accompany my colleagues down into the venue then please Sir, I'll help disperse folks once they emerge back out onto the street,' said Lee to the security guard. She walked over towards the entrance and motioned for William and Rhys to come forward and join them. 'I must apologise to you both,' she said suddenly. 'I haven't even asked you your names.'

'I'm Laura. Laura Kelly,' came the voice from behind the glass.

'And I'm Michael Long,' the security guard replied.

'If I could please ask you to remain where you are for the moment Laura,' said Lee. 'We need to count people as they exit to make sure that everyone is accounted for.'

'I can do that,' Laura replied.

'Thank you,' said Lee smiling at her.

'Are we on?' asked Rhys as he and William entered the venue.

'Yes,' replied Zoe. 'Michael here will accompany you downstairs. He will then speak to the barman Oscar who can shut off the club's power.'

'If you can guys, try and position yourselves in the far-right corner of the club before people start to leave,' said Michael. 'Both the DJ booth and toilets are in that area, and you'll be able to start your search more or less straight away. No one will have to walk past you on their way out.'

'Aren't people going to notice us in all this protective equipment?' Rhys asked.

'You'd be surprised how little people notice,' said Officer Lee. 'Unless you're in a uniform people recognise. I'd barely get downstairs before people would start to react.'

'If you move quietly and swiftly toward the back area, no-one will register your presence,' said Michael. 'It's not exactly bright down there.'

'In that case, we are ready when you are,' said William to Michael. Rhys nodded in agreement.

They descended the wide staircase down into the club, the volume of the music increasing as they approached the bottom. Florescent strips ran along the front edges of the steps. As they stepped into the main area of the venue, all their senses were assaulted at once. The sound of the music and the heat and the smell of alcohol engulfed them as they casually walked over to the bar area.

Oscar was stood behind the bar, handing change to a customer when he noticed Michael motioning him over. Both men walked over to the left end of the bar. William and Rhys could see Michael talking into the barman's ear. Oscar looked over at both men, before turning and approaching a solitary door on his right with a keypad and staff only sign upon it. He typed in the four-digit access code before disappearing behind the door.

Michael turned and nodded at William and Rhys. It was time for them to make their way over to the far-right corner of the club as the bouncer had suggested. However, it would not be straightforward. Most of the people in the club were either stood or dancing between their current position and where they were trying to get too. They split up, Rhys weaving his way through those on the edge of the dance floor, and William adopting to wriggle his way behind those currently stood up by the bar. He seemed to be making better headway than his colleague until he reached the toilet doors. Just as he was about to walk past the door to the ladies opened. Three girls walked out jumping and screaming, completely oblivious to where he was stood.

After they had passed him, he carried on past the doors and over to the far-right wall where Rhys was stood waiting for him. Both men were now in position to commence their search as soon as the lights and sound abruptly stopped.

\*\*\*

Oscar was stood with a flashlight in his mouth. He lifted the front panel to the electric unit, granting him access to the switches that controlled the power supply to the club. Finding the mains switch, he lifted it and plunged the venue into darkness. Screaming could be heard coming from the main club behind the wall, followed by Michael's voice trying to direct people to exit the club as quickly as possible.

'DJ booth first?' Rhys asked William. Both men were stood watching people leave with their own flashlights in their hands.

'Definitely,' William replied as they simultaneously turned on their torches. 'I'll give it another thirty seconds, then I'll go and check both the ladies and gent's toilets. We should then check the length of the bar.'

Rhys nodded at his colleague.

Ed Prior and Lucas Soons were making their way up the stairs amongst the crowd.

'Buzzkill,' said Lucas as they were reaching the top of the stairs. He felt each of his pockets in turn, checking their contents. 'Wallet, keys and mobile all still here thank God!' he exclaimed as they walked past the ticket booth and back outside.

Officer Lee was directing people who had begun to congregate outside of the venue.

'Keep moving please,' she said.

Ed and Lucas looked at her quizzically as they passed.

'This isn't just a power cut is it Luc?' said Ed to his companion, who was looking down at his mobile phone.

'I've had seventeen missed calls in less than ten minutes Ed,' Lucas replied, pressing redial on his phone and placing it to his ear.

'Jesus!' exclaimed Ed. 'I'd better check mine.'

Ed reached in and pulled his phone out of the inside pocket of his jacket pocket.

'You're not going to believe this Lucas…' he started.

'What?' replied Lucas interrupting him.

'I've had twenty-one calls,' replied Ed. 'Somethings not right.'

'Someone better answer!' said Lucas with growing impatience as he listened to the sound of an unanswered phone ringing in his ear. 'Now!'

Roberta Halliwell had taken it upon herself to approach the police officers to ask the question everybody seemed to want the answer to. Currently a journalism undergraduate, she had recently joined the team responsible for the weekly student newspaper that was distributed to accommodations across the city.

'Excuse me,' she said as she approached Lee. 'I've never known the police visit the scene of a power cut before. What's really going on here?'

Lee wasn't about mislead anyone, particularly regarding the potentially life-threatening situation.

'I initiated the power cut,' she said. 'We needed to clear the venue without provoking any panic.'

'Why?' Roberta asked, looking confused. Several others stood nearby were now looking over at them, waiting to hear the police officer's response.

'I can assure you that this was an extremely necessary action,' Lee said. 'There's been an incident involving an explosive device this evening in another venue and on our attendance in the aftermath we received word that there may be a similar device here.'

On hearing this, several people gasped.

'You don't happen to know where do you Officer?' asked a man as he stepped out from behind Roberta.

'Seven Sir,' replied Lee.

'Oh God!' exclaimed the man as he began to jog away.

'My advice would be for all of you to make your way home as quickly and as safely as you can,' said Lee to everyone around her. The last few people were now exiting the club doors, followed by Laura, Oscar, and Michael just behind them.

'Your colleagues are still downstairs,' said Michael to Lee as they group walked over to her.

'That's a positive sign,' said Lee reassuringly.

Oscar was staring at the club doors when William and Rhys appeared.

'Nothing down there!' exclaimed Rhys as everyone walked towards them. 'A god dammed hoax!'

'Who would have the audacity do to that at a time like this?' barked Oscar. 'It's sick.'

'At least we're all still in one piece boss,' said Michael.

Oscar scowled at him.

'Believe me, we want to find those responsible for this just as much as you do,' said Lee. 'But our force is already dealing with a serious incident this evening.'

She looked over at William and Rhys.

'Thank you for your swift arrival and assistance guys,' she said. 'I'll have our dispatch team try and trace the call.'

'I'm just relieved we didn't find anything,' said Rhys.

'Indeed,' added William. 'We've already attended the aftermath of three explosions as it is. To put that into perspective for you all, that's more than the average soldier encounters during a six-month deployment.

## 10.

Faye was sat in bed listening to the Radio, accompanied by the sound of running water coming from the ensuite as Mark was getting ready for bed. The couple liked to listen to the bedtime book series as a way of ending their day and, according to Mark, saving their eyesight.

'We interrupt our normal broadcasting schedule with breaking news,' said the presenter.

*Oh no...* thought Faye, as Mark emerged from their bathroom and turned off its light.

'It's now been confirmed that at least thirteen people have lost their lives after an explosion in an inner-city night club earlier today. This makes the third such incident in as many days. Despite the deployment of armed police...'

'Turn it off please Mark,' said Faye. 'I've heard enough'.

'Are you sure?' asked Mark. 'I'm sure the bedtime book will be on after this.'

'Yes. I'm in no mood for that now.' said Faye sadly.

Mark did as he was asked, before turning back the covers and getting into bed with his wife.

'I've been thinking,' Faye said after a pause, letting her husband rearrange his cushions beside her until he was comfortable. 'Did Joe seem a little off to you the other day?'

'Define off for me please?' replied Mark. 'He seemed pretty normal to me.'

'It's just what he said,' Faye replied. 'I don't know when I'll see you again.'

'Aren't you being a little melodramatic?' asked Mark.

'I don't know. Maybe,' said Faye.

'It's not like he's a regular guest these days like he used to be,' said Mark.

Faye turned to lie on her back.

'He told us he loved us,' replied Faye.

'He tells you that every time he leaves!' replied Mark, the sound of tired exasperation now creeping into his voice. 'If you're that concerned phone them. I'll go and get the phone.'

'No, don't!' said Faye, reaching out and touching his back. 'I don't want to disturb them.'

'Then please sweetheart, don't read too much into it,' said Mark, sliding down the mattress and pulling the quilt over himself.

'I'm trying not to,' replied Faye. 'But I just have this nagging feeling as the boy's mother that something isn't quite right.'

Mark leaned over and kissed his wife on the cheek. 'Your tired minds playing tricks on you. Get some sleep sweetheart,' he said. 'Goodnight.'

'Goodnight' replied Faye.

She reached up and pulled the light switch chord hanging down beside the bed, doubtful that sleep would come quickly.

\*\*\*

Lauren hit the save as tab on the document scroll bar and leant back in her chair.

*Thank God that's finished!* she thought to herself, switching off her computer monitor but leaving the tower on with its fan whirring.

She would re-read and edit her work in the morning. That was enough for tonight.

Besides which, she was itching to try out her new shower curtain with adjustable curtain rail. It would be a novelty not to have to use the toilet with her shoes on in a bathroom still wet for a change.

She stood up to open the wardrobe to retrieve her towels from the top shelf when she heard a loud cheer from outside.

*What the bloody hell is going on?!* she thought to herself.

She was used to the sound of people returning from their night in the city now; it was accepted as part of living in the university's hall of residence. But this was different. It sounded more like a mob than a group of happy drunk students or the now ever-present campus security.

She headed over to her windowsill and looked outside.

There were around thirty students, both male and female, gathered in the paved courtyard in between three residential buildings. They were all wearing superhero masks or bandannas around their faces and were clutching various items from within the flats; fire extinguishers, cricket bats, baseball bats, hockey sticks, frying pans and rolling pins. In front of this armed mob, stood on a wooden bench was Toby Gideon.

*I should've known*! thought Laura, rolling her eyes.

'Thank you, brothers and sisters, for answering our call to arms tonight,' said Toby, marching up and down the bench holding a baseball bat and wearing a Batman Mask. The crowd in-front of him cheered. 'As we all know, some sick persons have decided to blow their fellow humans up, and the police so far have done nothing to protect us!'

A chorus of Boo's echoed round the courtyard. 'Well no longer! For the Son of Sam (he pointed to himself) and his Superhero's (pointing to the students in front of him) shall rid our city of this evil by sunup. Who's with me?'

Another cheer went up from the congregation. 'Follow me!'

Lauren watched Toby jump from the bench and run off towards the city, with his mob following closely behind. She then saw two more people exit the building below her, one holding a belt and the other an Iron. They too ran off in the direction Toby and his mob had just run.

*Idiots!* thought Lauren, returning to her wardrobe to retrieve her towels.

\*\*\*

Stuart Riley was stood on the path waiting for his dog to finish her business up against the nearest tree. To the best of his knowledge, he was the only person in the park this evening. No matter what the city's human population were doing, his canine companion still needed her evening walk.

As a Veterinary nurse, Stuart had crossed paths with far too many dogs suffering from the effects caused by a lack of exercise. Owners had a lot to answer for, particularly the owners of a recent case whose poor dog required surgery after it ate a baby soother given to it by an unsupervised child.

He watched as his dog began to follow a trail of scent from the tree back in the opposite direction.

'Diana!' he called. 'This way silly.'

Diana looked up and began trotting back along the path towards her owner before stopping suddenly and pricking up her ears. A few seconds later, Stuart began to hear the shouting.

'Chalo! Revolution is our name!'

'Diana, come!' Stuart said quickly.

Dianna didn't move, so Stuart walked over to her. Bending down, he reattached Diana's lead to her collar. From this lower position, he watched though the trees as a group of students ran down the neighbouring pathway and out through the entrance of the park heading towards the city centre.

'We're going back this way now girl,' he said to Diana, standing and encouraging her to follow him back up the path towards the tree.

***

Toby and Matt, having exited the park, were waiting for the others who had begun to crowd around them again.

'First things first,' said Toby. He walked over the nearest bin and began pummelling the plastic casing. Matt laughed and did the same. The plastic shattered. Toby picked up what was left of the lid and threw it on the floor, before reaching in and removing the metal container inside it. He dragged it over to the group before reaching into his pocket and pulling out a box of matches. Flipping the box on its side, he lit a match and dropped it straight into the top of the bin. He then did the same with another, watching as the flames began to take hold of the upper items of rubbish.

'This marks the furthest point that anyone is reaching,' he said loudly to those stood around. 'They may have got past the coppers, but no one is getting past us!'

'We still haven't forgotten Hillsborough up where I'm from!' added Matt. 'Fourteen years and still spitting bullets.'

'I need a select few of you to stay here whilst the rest of us carry on further into the city,' continued Toby. 'Any volunteers?'

'I'm sure T was a general in a past life!' said Todd Barry, stood next to Matt.

'Maybe,' replied Matt laughing. 'We should have made him a helmet of justice to wear thinking about it.'

'Wouldn't work with the Batman cowl I fear,' giggled Todd. 'And if you're on about the same helmet of justice from Knightmare, then he wouldn't see a thing. But what a show that was!'

Before Matt could respond, a car screeched to a halt in front of them. Those stood at the front of the pavement could see a crude anarchy symbol graffitied on its bonnet in red spray paint.

'Moth!' exclaimed Toby, nearly falling off the curb onto the car.

'Get in Toby!' said Timothy Darrell, sat in the front passenger seat. Toby immediately opened the back door nearest to him. He threw his bat onto the seat next to him and shut the door.

'Go! Go!' he exclaimed as the car took off. 'Sleeper my man, nice of you to donate your vehicle to our cause,' said Toby to the driver as he looked out of the car's rear window. He could see the students behind him starting to separate themselves into smaller groups.

'Cometh the hour T,' replied the driver.

'We figured the psycho would be long gone from the bomb site by now and we'd need to get after him quick,' said Timothy. 'Where do you think they'd have gone?'

'Well, if it were me, I'd head toward the train station and I'm gone,' replied the driver. 'It's the closest and most anonymous way to travel.'

'To the station Sleeper!' exclaimed Toby.

'Just drive straight in the bus entrance Sleep,' said Timothy pointing ahead of them. 'No time to look for a space.'

'On it!' the driver replied, veering left suddenly into the area outside the station. He passed behind two busses before screeching to a halt. Two of the armed police officers stationed overlooking bus stop and station entrance immediately began walking towards them. 'Go!' he yelled.

Timothy and Toby quickly exited the car. They crouched down and made their way around the back of the vehicle, before standing and running as fast as they could towards the entrance of the train station. Once inside, they caught of sight of a man the other side of the turnstiles carrying a large bag flung over one arm.

'Over there!' exclaimed Toby, 'Get him!'

Both students ran straight at the electronic barriers, jumped, and clambered over them.

The stations lone security officer positioned along the wall of the ticketing booth stepped out and tried to grab them, but both Toby and Matt managed to dodge him as they made their way toward the staircases that led to the platforms. Toby bounded up the first set of stairs two at a time before scanning the platform.

'He's not up here,' he yelled as began making his way back down the stairs. 'Try the next one. Quick!' Just as Matt was about to race ahead, he saw Toby lose his footing and fall down the last four stairs before landing on the floor below.

'My ankle!' he exclaimed, sitting himself up quickly. He was now surrounded by the station guard and the two police officers he had seen outside. Matt was already being placed into handcuffs.

'Just so you know,' said Toby looking up at everyone surrounding him in turn. 'I will not be coming quietly!'

# 11.

Mills slammed his coffee cup on the desk, sending drips flying all over the various papers that had started to overrun his desk. 'Dammt!' he exclaimed.

'Morning Colin,' said Dee, sitting down at the desk opposite him. She could already sense the feeling of frustration from her colleague despite it still being early in the morning.

'Another day in paradise! I hear there was no second device last night. Someone though it would be amusing to call in a hoax.'

'Yes. They've traced the call to a pay phone. Forensics are dusting for prints, and we've released a statement appealing for witnesses,' replied Mills, flapping a document over the arm of his chair trying to salvage its text from the spilt coffee.

'Good,' Dee replied. 'Hang on. Released a statement? How long have you been here already?'

'Too long,' said Mills, checking another document. 'But I don't have the energy for another heated discussion at home right now.'

Not sure how to respond, Dee decided not to probe any further.

'I see a group of students decided to act last night too. What a night,' she said, taking a long swig from her morning coffee cup.

'Yes,' Mills replied. 'Not only do we now have to stop and detain a bomber and an idiot making hoax tip offs, but we also must waste precious manpower running round after a bunch of students in masks pretending to be Batman et al!'

'I know. I still can't quite believe that,' said Dee, shaking her head.

'They've all watched too many superhero movies if you ask me,' Mills continued. 'They forget that real people cannot stop bombs or bullets. And you'd think that supposed intellectuals would know better, wouldn't you? Not to mention that a criminal record would relegate even the best future qualification useless!'

'Wasn't Sam Gideon's son the ringleader?' asked Dee, checking her computer.

'Yes. Master Toby Gideon. That won't help his father's political career. And how on earth did they get off the campus and into the city in the first place with the extra security around?'

Before officer Dee had a chance to respond the phone rang.

'You better get downstairs,' said the familiar voice of Officer Buckland. 'We've found something in the upper fragments of what's left of the bombers backpack. It got torn off during the explosion as the bomb was hidden in the main compartment.'

'Have you been here all night?' Dee asked him. 'I can hear the fatigue in your voice.'

'Absolutely!' came the reply. 'I want to find the monster responsible just as much as you do. Sleep can wait.'

'It appears so,' replied Dee, looking over at Mills. 'We are on our way down to you now.'

***

The daily morning meeting and briefing was taking place at Hudson and James estate agents main offices in the city centre. The company was co- owned by brothers in law Abbas Hudson and Malcolm James, the latter being married to Abbas' sister.

Thankfully the city's redevelopment had not affected their ability to park on the road behind the building, saving them the hassle of having to apply for a parking permit since the introduction of on street parking meters. Had they been another road further east, their early morning commute would have been extended significantly.

The day started just like any other, with Abbas, Malcolm and three of their colleagues sat around Malcolm's desk ready to share information and roughly plan the day ahead.

'So, what would we consider to be our best achievement yesterday?' Malcolm asked those assembled around his desk.

'Well, I closed a deal on the five hundred-thousand-pound house in Bute Road yesterday,' said Tyler Perry smiling broadly. 'And all being well we should be near enough complete on the two-bed semi in Bont South later today.'

'Brilliant,' replied Malcolm.

'I must say, I am impressed,' added Abbas. 'Whatever issues your previous firm were having certainly wasn't down to you. You've been here less than a month and already have an impressive sales record with us.'

'Indeed, Hudson and James are lucky to have you,' said Malcolm.

'Thank you,' replied Tyler.

'I have two more valuations lined up this morning after the morning ring around,' said Abbas.

'Double check the surrounding area for a rough pricing guide will you please?' said Malcolm. 'The average house price around that area seems to be most inconsistent now.'

'Don't worry I will,' Abbas replied, taking the final sip from his disposable coffee cup. 'Although I think the properties unique selling point will assist me,' he said smiling.

Malcolm scribbled a note on the book in front of him before looking up to address his other colleagues seated next to Tyler.

'How are things looking on the lettings side? Ladies?'

'I am hoping to erect a sign in Torrent Close later, I just need to speak to landlord first,' said Natasha Adams.

'We had an email from a tenant late yesterday evening saying their shower tray is leaking water and entering the properly below,' added Ruth Chase. 'I hope to chase up the landlord and get our maintenance team to address that today as a priority. As far as we are aware there are no other issues in any of our other properties.'

'Great!' replied Malcolm. 'On a slightly less positive note, we have received some feedback on that four bedroom properly we lost yesterday.'

'These things happen,' added Abbas, a reassuring look on his face. 'What's important is we take this opportunity to learn and improve our service.'

'Absolutely,' said Malcolm. 'And it's not like we did anything fundamentally wrong. We were able to inform potential buyers about schools in the area, but not about all the local amenities.'

Everyone around the table looked at each other.

'And to be fair it was a very specific question that lost us the client,' added Abbas. 'A Father asking about the nearest swimming facilities in the area as their son has hyper joint mobility.'

'Indeed,' said Malcolm. 'It's just unfortunate we were unable to answer that particular question and one of our competitors was.'

'Which one?' asked Tyler.

'It doesn't matter,' said Abbas.

'No, it doesn't,' said Malcolm. 'The point is that all this extra knowledge all adds up in terms of potential sales. We have a database of local amenities on our computer system and should all refresh our knowledge before meeting a potential viewing.'

'It's not just you guys,' added Abbas. 'I was dealing with that particular properly in question.'

'Is there any other business, issues or just comments in general?' asked Malcolm.

Everyone assembled looked at each other but nobody spoke.

'Ok. Well, in that case we all have our phone calls to make. Have a good morning, everyone.'

\*\*\*

Joe was stood in front of the photocopier, printing resources for the students attending his next Seminar and trying not to yawn. More pressing tasks had meant that he was not as prepared as he had been earlier in the week, but no matter. So far so good. Hopefully the police would take the bait.

The photocopier was located on the back wall of the library between two bookshelves. Next to it was a table for people to rest the other books or papers they planned to make a copy of next. Having finished, he now had to walk past the front desk to get out through the alarmed doorway. There was a student stood in front of the desk handing money to the librarian.

*No doubt paying a fine for a late return*, Joe thought to himself. He continued to walk around the back of the student heading towards the door. Just as he thought he would be able to leave without being noticed he heard a voice.

'Have you heard about the latest bomb Joe?'

He stopped and turned. Carol Dixon the librarian was stood up behind the desk.

'Awful, isn't it?' she continued. 'One of the deceased used to come in all the time to complete his coursework. Said his halls of residence were way too loud and rowdy for him to concentrate.'

'Tragic,' Joe replied coldly as he continued towards the library's exit.

'These kids should be worrying about hangovers, not explosions!' Carol said as he walked out.

\*\*\*

Mills and Dee had descended the stairs to the forensic laboratory, located below the stations offices upstairs. Dee knocked on the door.

'Come in,' came a muffled voice behind it.

'Please tell me you've found something to go on,' said Mills as they opened the door and entered the room.

'Yes Sir,' said Buckland smiling, 'Take a look!'

Mills and Dee headed over to a table inside the station's laboratory with magnification equipment on one end. Suspended above it from the ceiling and stretching right along its length was a light. Buckland yawned as he approached the detectives, placing his hand over his mouth.

'Oh Dear, excuse me!' he said. 'Having now gathered enough evidence from the first three bombs, we've been able to reverse engineer and determine what explosive was used. Triacetone triperoxide, more commonly known as...'

'TATP,' Mills interjected.

'Correct,' said Buckland. 'TATP is an extremely sensitive crystalline powder that explodes when under heat, friction or using a mechanical shock as in this case. All three bombs were made of TATP, and all three were detonated using a timer. Therefore, we can say all three IED's were made by the same person based on forensic evidence.'

'That's a bonus,' said Dee, walking around the table.

'Aldehyde was turned into a carboxylic acid using aqueous acidified chlorite and acetone as the solvent,' continued Buckland.

Mills and Dee both looked back at him blankly.

'It sounds incredibly technical,' he continued. 'But they are all reasonably common chemicals. We also found this…'

Mills and Dee's eyes glanced down at the table as Buckland placed an evidence bag in front of them.

'This is part of a mosque community events leaflet,' said Buckland. 'As I said earlier, the force of the blast in the lower compartment caused the upper portion of the backpack to be torn off and thrown from the blast area.'

'Do we know which Mosque it came from?' asked Mills.

'Yes sir. It's in the middle of the city. Not hard to find. Located near to the fire station.'

'Any prints on the leaflet?' Dee asked.

'No, I'm afraid not. It's lucky we even recovered it,' Buckland replied.

'Ok Dee,' said Mills. 'When we get back upstairs, we'll have Wood and Jon's head over and get us a list of their regular attendees and staff to run background checks on. Thanks Buckland.'

'Pleasure Mills,' he replied.

'Now go and get some sleep! That's an order,' said Mills.

'I'm gone already,' Buckland replied as he picked up his jacket and yawned into his hand again.

'Try and get your team to ascertain where the chemicals may have come from in my absence.'

Mills nodded at him.

'We will,' he said. 'Thanks again.'

Mills held the laboratory door open for his colleagues. They watched Buckland as he headed towards the exit of the station, before ascending the stairs back to the offices above.

'At last!' said Dee. 'A tangible thread to follow.'

'It's certainly progress,' said Mills. 'But we are still a fair distance away from the edge of the woods just yet.'

# 12.

Officer Wood looked out of the window as they sat waiting for the traffic lights to change. 'Well, this is a first for me. I've never been to a mosque before,' he said.

'Neither have I,' replied Officer Jons, sat in the driver's seat. 'What time is it?'

'Eight thirty-two,' said Wood. 'Why do you ask?'

'Because we are not about to disrupt these people's morning prayers Wood. Half of society's problems can be distilled down to a lack of one thing. Respect.'

'That's a profound statement for this time in the morning Ryan,' said Wood. 'But I completely agree.'

'How's your head feeling this morning?' asked Jons.

'Thankfully that idiots punch didn't land fully,' replied Wood, looking out of the passenger window and watching the city as they drove. He had lost count of the sleeping bags, quilts, bags of clothes and people he had already seen huddled in the covered entrances to buildings that offered minimal shelter to the city's homeless.

*When are we gonna learn?* he thought to himself. *People keep ignoring a problem unless it becomes their problem, but this is our problem. All of ours. And it's getting worse and worse.*

He cast his mind back to that Christmas when he volunteered at the inner-city community hall. Every year it ran a special holiday soup kitchen for the city's homeless. Long rectangular tables were dressed in tablecloths, candles, and mini-Christmas trees. Volunteers from all occupations joined the halls usual staff, all dressed as elves.

'This definitely fits me better than my police uniform,' he had commented looking in the full-length mirror in the back-office room.

'Suits you better too!' a fellow volunteer had replied.

They had been preparing food for over two hours in the large kitchen next to the centre's main hall. The organisers were expecting at least fifty people to attend the event. Turkey and all the trimmings had been prepared, as well as some additional meat and a vegetarian alternative.

'No one can leave here hungry,' the head chef had said.

He smiled to himself as the police car passed a clothes and barber shop. Most people didn't realise that the food served at these centres was only part of their service. Visitors were also able to get their hair cut, and nails manicured if they wished. Clothes and toiletries that had been donated were also given to them wrapped in Christmas paper.

Wood was proud to be able to help provide the city's homeless some company and love during the holiday season, but one thing that grated on him was the fact that the events resources came mainly from charity donations and not the city council provisions budget.

'We're nearly there Keith,' said Jons. 'You can see the mosques Dome and Tower up ahead.'

Wood looked up. The dome and tower stood several feet above the rest of the nearby buildings, showing its position amongst the rest of the city's skyline. Due to the number of worshipers who visited the Mosque every day and its inner-city location, there was a car park on the opposite side of the road. Jons pulled in and parked in the nearest available space. They got out of the car, crossed the street, and walked up the stairs to the entrance of the Mosque. Jons held the door open for Wood.

On entering the mosque, they found themselves standing in a rectangular shaped lobby. To the right there was a room with shoe racks lining the walls, a sign on its back wall directing worshipers to the washroom just behind. Directly in front of them were three double door entrances that led into the carpeted main prayer hall. A mural of scripture from the Koran

ran around the ornate walls, with a golden chandelier hanging from the centre of the ceiling.

There were two rows of chairs positioned along the back wall for elder worshippers, a few of whom were sat saying prayers.

'Beautiful!' said Wood out loud.

Jons pointed to a transparent collection box located under a pillar labelled Zakat Fund which contained various coins and pound notes.

'Remember the report of those idiots who tried to break in and steal this last year?' he asked Wood, as they watched a man walking across the lobby towards them.

'Good morning, gentlemen' he said. 'My name is Saddiq Fazif, how may I be of assistance?'

'Good morning, Mr Fazif. I am Officer Keith Wood, and this is Officer Ryan Jons.

We are investigating the recent bombings in the city and need information regarding your mosque's recent attendees. Do you keep such records?'

'I must stress that this is simply a routine enquiry,' added Jons.

'You will need to see Adil Maulama officers. He should be in the office this morning. If you would please follow me.'

He led Wood and Jons to the left of the lobby past the entrances to the prayer hall. There was a set of stairs located beside the far prayer room entrance, with signs pointing upwards to the library and women's prayer area. Directly in front of them was the mosque office.

Fazif knocked on the door and opened it.

'Adil. There are some policemen here who require some information to help with their inquiries.'

'Show them in Saddiq,' said a voice from behind the door.

The police officers followed Saddiq into the office. It looked not dissimilar to the offices at the station apart from the ornate oak decoration that framed the room.

'Officers Wood and Jons, this is Adil, our operations manager here at the mosque.'

Adil stood up and shook both men by the hand.

'Thank you, Saddiq,' he said.

Saddiq left the room and closed the door behind him.

'Now. How may I be of assistance? What information do you seek?' Adil asked, sitting back down in his chair.

'We would like a list of your regular attendees, participants and employees to help us conduct our investigations into the recent bombings in the city,' said Officer Jons.

'Please understand,' added Wood. 'Some new evidence has come to light that deems this necessary.'

'I appreciate your position officers,' said Adil, opening the top drawer of his filing cabinet and removing a folder. 'My most recent list of those affiliated with our mosque,' he said, handing the folder to Wood. 'I am afraid it's quite extensive as we have a lot of social and community-based gatherings besides daily worship here,' he said.

'That is quite alright,' said Wood. 'Thank you for your co-operation and assistance.'

'It is a pleasure officers,' Adil replied. 'Anything I can do to assist you and help end our cities current tyranny. Please allow me to show you out.'

Adil escorted the officers out of the office, through the lobby and back outside. He then shook both Wood and Jons by the hand.

'I'm sure we shall speak again,' he said, before returning inside.

After crossing the street, Officer Jons unlocked the police vehicle and both men entered. Wood was skimming through the documents that Adil had just given the two Officers.

'That went incredibly well. If only everyone we encountered was as pleasant and willing to help us as that,' he said, knowing fully well that it wasn't and probably would never be the case.

'You best let Mills and Dee know we're on our way back,' said Jons. 'Then we can start going through that list properly together.'

\*\*\*

Stephen Gough was sat with his back to the train's toilet surrounded by business commuters dressed in their suits. He had closed his eyes, trying desperately to lose himself in his headphones. It was certainly a better option than staring at the plastic interior of the carriage having been unable to get a window seat. He understood where his parents were coming from, but he resented the fact that he was the only one of his friends on his way home. Taking the train was a thousand times better than having his parents threaten to drive and collect him if he didn't make his own way back.

'It's an unnecessary risk Stephen!' He could still hear his mother's voice ringing in his head.

He wasn't worried about missing lectures, as all but one of the notes could be accessed online. No, he was more worried about fitting back into the box that was life at home with his parents.

For the biggest part of a year, he had been experimenting with gender fluidity with his best friend Marie Robinson. He would go out for the night dressed as a girl, and she a boy. The sense of liberation was intoxicating. There was no one else who understood him, or he trusted more than her.

He had met Marie in a lecture and their friendship had grown from there. She shared his love of the comedian Eddie Izzard and classic horror movies, even going so far as giving him the nickname Dr Caligari after the classic nineteen twenties film. Most people assumed that Stephen and Marie were a couple, something they had both repeatedly laughed off initially. However, as he sat there feeling the rocking of the train as it crossed the points on its way from the station, he could no longer ignore the fact that he had fallen for her massively. What was he to do? Take the calculated risk and tell her how he felt?

*No. Stop it. You're just being selfish. Love is selfless,* he told himself. *If you love her let her go.*

He thought for a moment. *Only for her to meet someone you must smile at every day, whilst at the same time dying inside. Love resides in the deepest parts of us. In our hearts and stomachs as well as our heads. It's what creates the sense of wanting the person to feel complete.*

'Oh, shut up!' he said out loud, before sitting up and opening his eyes suddenly.

The man sat next to him turned and stared at him.

'Sorry' he said, forcing a smile. 'Talking to myself.' The man next to him scoffed and turned his attention back to the copy of the Financial Times he was reading.

Just then Stephen felt his phone buzz in his pocket.

*Oh Christ. Here we go*, he thought to himself. That's her.

Sure enough it was Marie, although he was not expecting what he was about to read.

*Hey You! Do you remember those first years we met in the SU? Robert and Patrick? Both were killed in last night's explosion :( xx*

Stephen looked up and stared at the carriages ceiling, trying to remember that evening.

The student reps had put on a Pirate themed night in the Students Union. If he remembered correctly, a friendly debate with Robert and Patrick happened. They were adamant that if it weren't for Captain Jack from that pirate's film, no one would care about pirates. However, Stephen and Marie countered that Edward Teach had been responsible for pirate themed novels and children's birthday parties for the last three hundred years. He gathered his thoughts before replying.

*The pirates? That's awful! I hope to God they catch whoever's responsible soon. Please stay safe. I'll let you know when my train gets in the other end xx*

He hit send before turning his gaze upwards again.

***

Joe had paid a rare visit to the staff room. Purple chairs were placed around a large, circular table. Along the back wall was a kitchen sink and worktop surface, along with a fridge, microwave, and the much-coveted coffee machine he desperately needed. He had just placed the cup under the nozzle when his phone buzzed. He sighed as he removed his cup from underneath the machine and placed it back onto the worktop and took his phone from his pocket. Claire had messaged him. Change of plan.

The warmth of the midday sun mixed with the fragrance of cigarettes greeted Joe as he descended the steps of the social sciences building and headed left towards the university's chemistry building. All the various faculties were situated along one road with buildings either side of it, punctuated by a staff car park. Claire's building was at the far end of the road on the corner.

Joe entered as he had done several hundred times before and headed straight down the corridor. He knew he would find Claire still in the laboratory, eating her salad whilst preparing her first lesson of the afternoon.

'You'll have to fend for yourself tonight,' she said as he walked into the room. 'Holly is coming over later.'

'You could have told me that in your message,' grumbled Joe.

'It's not as simple as that,' Claire replied. 'I'm finishing late today. We have a department meeting about the upcoming assessments that I completely forgot about, and I need you to take this box of papers home for me before I forget about them too.'

Joe went over and picked up the archive box next to her.

'I didn't mean you had to take them now!' Claire said.

'Might as well,' Joe replied. 'How are you getting home later?'

'Don't worry yourself, Sue is giving me a lift back,' Claire replied. 'If I had remembered the meeting was today, I would have bought my own car.'

Joe shrugged as he headed silently towards the door.

'Thank you, love you!' said Claire to no reply.

## 13.

DCI Mills put his sandwich wrapper and empty coffee cup into the station's canteen bin.

Running the hot tap, he squeezed out some soap from the dispenser and lathered his hands.

*I wonder if they're any closer to a name yet*, he thought. *I've never known Keith Wood to voluntarily skip a lunch break.*

He dried his hands on some paper towels and headed back towards the main room of the station.

'Have you found them Keith?' asked Mills as he approached his colleague.

'Do you mean the prank caller, or our friend who lost his backpack?' Wood replied.

'Either. Both preferably,' said Mills.

'Still nothing on the hoax so far, and we're still in the processes of elimination with the other. This is a big one!' replied Wood. 'Might take a few more...'

'I think I've found them!' exclaimed Jons, looking up from above his PC monitor on his desk.

'Dee?' shouted Mills into the station. 'Can someone get Dee for us please.'

'I'm right here, no need to shout!' came a voice from beside the canteen door. She walked over hastily to the others crowded round Jons desk.

'His name is Malcolm James, of Pakistani descent. Lists his occupation as an estate agent. Co-owns a company will his brother-in-Law,' said Jons.

'What the hell has that got to do with anything?' asked Wood.

'Let me finish Keith!' Jons snapped back. 'Three weeks ago, he returned from a visit to Pakistan's tribal region.'

'That's right on the Durand line into Afghanistan, isn't it?' said Officer Dee. 'There's known terrorist training camps located on that border.'

'That's correct,' replied Jons. 'Not only that, but that specific area of Pakistan has been used as a haven for newly radicalised terrorists.'

'How long was he there for?' said Mills.

'Ten days, and he travelled alone,' replied Jons. 'He could easily have crossed the border, spent a few days in one of the camps, recrossed the border into Pakistan and then home.'

'Can we confirm he travelled?' said Mills.

'Yes. I took the initiative of asking the airline for his check in confirmation and they confirmed it for both his departing and returning flights.'

'Good,' said Mills.

'I also spoke to the airport surveillance team and asked if there was anything they had given the severity of what we're dealing with. They've just sent us CCTV footage from the terminal,' Jons said. 'Justin's already worked his magic. Have a look at this.'

He moved the mouse over to a mpeg on his desktop and double clicked. Everyone crowded round tightly to his computer screen.

'As you can see here, he's clearly holding a copy of the Koran as he's boarding the plane,' said Jons.

'Well, I'll be damned!' exclaimed Mills. 'Does the timeline fit with the first bombing? I want to be doubly sure before we make a move on this.'

'Absolutely sir!' Jons responded. 'Like I said he returned three weeks ago; plenty of time to gather the resources he would need, especially if he had help from others.'

'Right,' said Mills.

Everyone turned to look at the detective inspector, ready to receive their instructions.

'Wood. Get back in contact with Adil Maulama. We need everything he has on Malcolm James and those closest to him at the mosque.' said Mills.

'Yes Sir' replied Wood. 'He did say if we needed anything he'd be more than happy to help. He wants to protect everyone just as much as we do.'

'Good.' replied Mills. 'What's Mr James's address? It's time we paid him a visit.'

'It's listed here as Eleven New Moon Road,' said Jons.

'Dee with me,' said Mills, heading towards his office to retrieve his jacket. 'We'll need some other officers as back up.'

He glanced round the room. 'Hughes?' he called.

'Yes sir,' replied Hughes, sitting at another desk just across the room.

'You're coming with us. Bring two more officers and the van,' said Mills. 'We shall meet you there.'

\*\*\*

The police van and cars pulled up on the pavement outside the house in New Moon Road.

Before they had even exited the vehicles, they could see neighbours in the nearby houses all looking through the windows or standing in their open doorways. A few people had also started to congregate on the street at either side of the vehicles; curious as to see what or who might appear.

Mills and Dee opened the garden gate and approached the blue front door with its silver door knocker, post-box, and house number. Hughes, Donovan and the two other officers waited outside. Mills knocked on the door. A middle-aged woman answered.

'Mrs James?' asked Mills.

'Yes? I am Mrs Nadia James,' she responded, glancing up to see the police van, vehicles, waiting policemen and the various onlookers outside. 'Have you come to the right address?' she asked, the shock and panic building in her voice. 'What's this all about?'

'I am DCI Mills, and this is DI Kate Dee' he replied. 'We're investigating the series of recent bombings in the city. Is your husband home?'

'Yes,' Nadia replied. 'He's playing video games with our son Samuel in the lounge.'

'May we come in?' asked Dee.

Mrs James held the door open, and the officers entered the hallway.

Polished wooden floorboards ran the length of the hallway into the kitchen at the back of the house. Middle Eastern vases with flowers flanked the framed photographs on a dark oak sideboard. Looking back from the middle of various sized frames were pictures of relatives, friends, Samuels school portraits and the three of them together. Mounted on the wall were four passages written in Arabic.

'First door on your right,' said Naida having closed the front door.

Malcolm James was sat next to his son Samuel, both holding a gaming controller and completely oblivious to the fact that two police detectives were now standing directly behind them.

'You cheated Dad!' exclaimed Samuel.

'Did not!' replied his father laughing. 'I beat you fair and square.'

'Oh yeah?' said Samuel. 'Let's see you do it again then.'

'Alright son, you are on!' exclaimed Malcolm.

'Excuse me,' came a voice from behind them.

Malcolm turned round and stood up.

'Malcolm James?' asked Mills.

DI Dee walked over and sat down where Malcolm had been next to Samuel.

'Hi,' she said in a soft voice.

'What are you doing here?' Malcolm asked.

'Malcolm James,' continued DCI Mills. 'You are being detained under section 41 of, and schedule 8 to, the terrorism act 2000. You do not have to say anything but, it may harm your defence if you do not mention when questioned something which you later rely on in court. Anything you do say may be given in evidence. Turn around please.'

Malcom turned and caught the look of horror on his sons face as Mills secured him in handcuffs.

'What?' he asked. 'I'm confused? What on Earth is this all about?'

Mrs James was now crying. Samuel had run over to his mother and was also crying.

'Samuel. Sam. Sam,' said Malcolm in a deep and reassuring voice. 'It's Ok son. This is just a simple misunderstanding. I'll be home before you know it.'

He turned to look at Mills and Dee.

'Before I come with you, I need assurances that my wife and son will be safe. Can you give me that please?' he asked.

'Do not worry Sir, officers will be posted outside of your house until further notice,' replied Dee.

'Thank you,' Malcom replied softly.

Mills led Malcolm out toward the front door and paused for a second whilst Dee caught up behind them and opened it. All of them could here mother and son crying in the living room.

From the moment they set foot outside the house they were met with a barrage of camera flashes and shouting.

'Mills. Is this the man responsible for these bombings?'

'Why has it taken this long to make an arrest?'

'He's innocent you racist!'

Ignoring the onlookers, Mills led Malcolm to the back on the police van. Looking back at his house, Malcolm could see his wife and son stood on the doorstep.

Suddenly and without warning, Samuel broke free of his mother's grip and came running out of the garden. Small and nimble, he weaved past several police officers stationed between himself and the van.

'Samuel!' screamed his mother, frozen in panic. Having reached the back of the police van,

Samuel stood and watched as they were opening the doors, tears running down his face.

'Dad,' he whimpered. 'Please don't take my Daddy away,' he pleaded, looking round at Mills, Dee, and Hughes in turn.

Dee crouched down so that her face was level with his.

'Don't worry. We'll make sure he's safe,' she said.

They both watched as Malcolm was assisted into the back of the van. Dee then led Samuel back to the house where his mother was waiting at the bottom of the garden and the two embraced.

'Who told the press?' Mills asked angrily as he watched his colleagues shut the doors of the police van.

'Could've been anyone Sir,' replied Hughes. 'Just look around you.'

Mills said nothing as he walked over and got back into the police car. Dee then joined him, and the pair fastened their seatbelts in unison.

'There's no containing it anymore I'm afraid,' said Mills, wiggling the gearstick before placing his hand on the key to start the engine. 'His face will be everywhere in a matter of hours.'

'As will his poor son and wife's,' said Dee solemnly. 'They clearly have no part in this.'

'Let's just hope we've got the right person,' Mills replied, releasing the cars handbrake.

With photographers' flashes going off surrounding the police van, they slowly drove out of the road on their way back to the police station.

***

This afternoon it was Joe's turn to listen to his students. The head of social sciences had introduced idea of an assessment based on a presentation as an alternative to modular coursework. The idea was to try and keep students better engaged through different methods of learning. Focusing on the course's previous topic of youth and drugs, the students had to present the knowledge they had learnt in groups of three. Despite the collective groan that Joe had received when he had announced that every student had to present something to everyone, it seemed that the majority had managed to accept their fates and focus on the task despite everything.

Several students had chosen to concentrate on the rehabilitation of addicts and the ongoing debate on the legalisation of certain substances that had caused quite a difference of opinion in previous seminars. Nearly half the inmate population of the United Kingdom and significantly more young offenders had been incarcerated due to drug related crime, and Joe was surprised to see the looks on his students faces when they had received the information during his lecture.

Joe was sat in the front pew of the lecture theatre with paper and pen, roughly grading each pupil based on their contribution to their group. He knew fewer names of his students this year than any of those previously, so a lot of time was spent with him asking for names after each group had finished. He was about to get up and turn on the overhead projector himself for the final group as an excuse to stretch his legs when one of them approached him.

'Do you have a spare plug sir?' Jake Collins asked.

'No, I'm afraid not,' replied Joe. 'Unless you don't need the projector?' he asked dismissively.

'No, we don't. I'll unplug that then. Thanks.'

Joe watched as Jake walked up to the front of the lecture theatre holding nothing in the way of notes in his hands. He was carrying a large tape recorder.

*Interesting*, he thought to himself. *I wonder where this is going.*

\*\*\*

Malcolm's uncomfortable journey in the back of the police van seemed to go on forever, until finally it stopped and reversed slowly. He could hear shouts from the crowd outside long before an officer opened the door and he stepped out of the vehicle. The light from dozens of camera flashes cast their shadows on the wall behind them as he was led into the police custody suite.

'Well, these are extraordinary scenes here just outside the police station. Just moments ago, we saw officers lead a suspect thought responsible for this week's horrific events into the building in handcuffs' said Gavin Jordan, looking right into the lens of the news camera in front of him. 'Whilst details remain scarce, we can however reveal that the name of the suspect is said to be a Malcolm James of New Moon Road, who has links to one of the mosques within the city.'

Gavin paused and lifted his hand to his right ear in an attempt to hear the instructions from his producer being fed to him via earpiece more clearly over the noise in the background.

'And we can now cross over live to the assembly building where the first minister is about to make a statement.'

Inside people's homes, university halls and bars over the city, everyone watching the breaking news were greeted with a camera shot from inside the government assemblies press conference room.

'I'd like to thank the police for their continued and tireless efforts at a time that has been unlike any other,' said the First Minister into a pencil thin microphone atop of a wooden podium. 'Hopefully this arrest will allow us to sleep a little easier tonight.'

The camera then panned out slightly, revealing standing flags at either side of the podium.

'As a result of this arrest, we will be able to reduce the armed patrols currently around the city. Hopefully visitors will also have the confidence to return here. Tourism has always been a vital source of income for our economy, and I am pleased to announce that tonight's big event at the arena is now able to go ahead as planned. Thank you.'

Viewers then returned to outside the police station. A slight delay from the programs control room meant a few seconds of Gavin standing I silence awaiting his cue.

'Well, as we've just heard from the First Minister patrols are to be relaxed. This comes after reports of growing concerns coming from the assembly over the cost of the extra security that has been used this week. We will of course keep you up to do date with this story as it continues to unfold, but for now back to the studio. This is Gavin Jordan, City News.'

# 14.

'Drunk students are nothing new,' said Lin. 'The odd hangover during a lecture used to be enough to discourage people, but since technology has allowed our students greater access to resources from home they've just stopped turning up. They'd rather miss the lecture than the party.'

'That's why I don't put my lecture notes online,' replied Joe. 'It means they need to attend to pass the course, and hopefully curbs such behaviour.'

'I don't think he meant to break his neck Joe,' replied Lin, sat at the table opening her sandwich.

'It's beyond ridiculous!' exclaimed Joe, pouring the milk into his cup. 'At what state of intoxication must you need to be to break your neck?'

'It was a tragic accident,' Lin replied as Joe sat down opposite her.

'Maybe,' Joe grumbled. 'But I would've assumed that a student predicted the result such as Chris Macintyre did would have the sense to not take the risk. I guess I presumed wrong. These kids are no different to anyone else. Drunks. Wasted Youth!'

The thought had continued to go round and around in Joe's head for the rest of the day. He became increasingly restless, feeling the anger and frustration growing in his mind. We have a problem.

He had driven the car up on the pavement outside the chemistry department and was impatiently revving the engine when Claire exited the building.

'Why are you so aggravated?' she asked as they sat at the red light at the end of the road.

'Chris Macintyre broke his neck!' Joe said, almost barking at her. 'The idiot got drunk.'

'Oh, how awful!' replied Claire.

'I can't stand it,' said Joe. 'And this is just the tip of the iceberg. I've lost count of the number of students I've seen sitting in my lectures looking ill due to self-inflicted behaviours.'

The traffic light changed, and he stamped on the accelerator, propelling the car forward.

'Calm down!' exclaimed Claire. 'I'd like to get home safely.'

After a quicker journey than usual, they came to an abrupt stop on the driveway outside their new house, narrowly missing the back of Claire's car.

'I don't care what you need to do, but you need to go and calm down,' said Claire. 'It's a miracle we weren't killed with you driving like that!'

She got out and slammed the passenger side door before marching up to the front door. Joe remained in the driving seat. Reaching over, he opened the cars glove box and took out some sheets of paper, before rummaging around the pocket of his door for a pen. Since his car accident he always carried such things just in case he needed to exchange details with another motorist. At the top of the page he wrote Wasted Youth, and then proceeded to write for twenty minutes about students abuse of alcohol, the future of higher education and his prediction of its impacts on wider society.

His right hand began to cramp as he came to the end of his second page. He put the pen down on the dashboard, pulled down his sun visor and lifted the little flap before staring at himself in the mirror.

*It's up to me*, he thought to himself. *And it can't wait.*

Would him releasing a paper be enough to make people take notice? Doubtful. Such a statement would require action. He cast his mind back to the incident at college. The very possibility that someone had a knife stopped everything, but that would be far too brazen and not sufficient for the scale of the issue he was faced with. *What to do?*

After moments pause, Joe turned the key and fired up the car's engine.

*The cities library will have the answer*, he thought to himself, reversing back out of the driveway.

\*\*\*

Malcolm found himself sat in a holding cell, replaying the events that had happened since leaving home. Having been greeted by custody officers after the ordeal outside, he then had to go through a series of biometrics. First, he was searched, an officer patting him all over to check he had nothing hidden on his person. Then his fingerprints were taken before he was photographed.

The officers also took a DNA swab from Malcolm, placing it in his mouth and rubbing it against his cheek. He had felt uncomfortable enough during his search, but the mouth swab made him even more uncomfortable.

'Do you suffer from any mental health conditions that require additional support?' the Sargent behind the desk had asked him.

Malcolm shook his head in response.

'Do you wish to have a solicitor present before being questioned?'

'Yes Sargent. Please contact Taz Abdullah,' Malcolm had replied.

Taz was a friend of Malcolm and a fellow member of his Mosque. Once the door of the holding cell in the custody suite had been secured behind him and he was alone, Malcolm silently wept.

Taz couldn't arrive soon enough.

\*\*\*

With his new prime suspect now being held in a custody cell just down the Hall, DCI Mills was preparing an interview room. Four chairs were tucked in either side of a rectangular table. At the far end by the wall was the recording equipment. Mills was so deep into his own thoughts that he didn't hear Dee knock before entering the room.

'You do realise your pacing don't you Colin?' she asked. 'I thought you'd have joined us upstairs by now checking we had all the necessary resources before his interview.'

'Am I?' he replied. 'Sorry. I hadn't even noticed!'

Dee could hear the element of surprise in his voice.

'I know you are under a lot of pressure,' she responded. 'But please try to remember you are not on your own.'

'I'll try' Mills responded, forcing himself to smile at her. 'Do you know if the press mentioned James and his links to the mosque?'

'I don't know,' Dee replied. 'I expect so.'

'Brilliant!' exclaimed Mills. 'Just what we don't need, added racial tension, particularly after recent global events.'

'At least we had the foresight to leave officers with Mrs James and their son,' replied Dee.

'Yes, and we had better ensure we have at least one car present at James's Mosque. Have Donovan dispatch one will you please,' said Mills, glancing at his watch. 'Hopefully James's brief will arrive sooner rather than later.'

'I'll do that now,' replied Dee. 'See you shortly.'

\*\*\*

Joe had stopped his vehicle in a loading bay near the cities arena, opposite a three-storey car park. He activated the cars hazard warning lights and assessed the area. This would be his first and only driving experience whilst wearing vinyl gloves. Thankfully despite its age, the cars power steering was still effective.

With a false disabled badge displayed in the dashboard and a bumper sticker on the back of the car, he was confident nobody would come and knock on the window and ask him to move. Indicating and pulling out into the traffic, he paused in the middle of the road before turning into the car park. He glanced in his mirror. All the security seemed to be staying on the opposite side of the road. *Good.*

He parked the car in the top far east corner of the car park. Just to the right of the space was a pay-meter and door leading out down the stairs to the lower level and exit. He opened the cars glove box and took out a timer and a screwdriver. Reaching around the back of the driver's seat with his left hand, he found the loose wires. After bringing them round the middle of seats, he carefully unscrewed the back of the timer. Placing the screws in the upper pocket of his driver side door, he attached the wires to the timer before replacing and tightening the screws. He then removed the battery from his pocket, placing it in the back of the timer as he had done previously and looked at the clock in the middle of the dashboard. What would be the optimum time for detonation? *Eleven. Two hundred and forty minutes.* He held the button down for what felt like an eternity before arriving at two four zero and pressed start. *Primed.*

Joe climbed out of the car and removed the protective plastic chair cover which he had used to cover the driver's seat. He then screwed it up and placed it in a pocket along with the screwdriver, before manually locking the car despite it being central locking. He carefully removed his gloves and placed them in the same pocket before looking around.

The car park was nearly full due to the fact it was across the street from the cities arena and a band were playing tonight. Thankfully the level he was on was only occupied by empty vehicles, their owners having already left. Rather than using the stairs, Joe walked behind a row of parked cars and made his way down the up ramp. A car narrowly missed him, the driver accelerating up the ramp not expecting to find someone walking down towards them. To the sound of several blasts on the cars horn and jeering from the passengers inside, Joe continued down the ramps towards the bottom level. On reaching the ground floor, he headed towards the exit.

For this evening's alibi, Joe had taken advantage of the fact that Claire was entertaining her friend and deliberately arranged to meet some of his colleagues from the university. He wouldn't call them his friends; these were just people who happened to be around him at this time in his life thanks to his current occupation. Now walking along the pavement, he headed away from the area and further into the city.

# 15.

Claire rolled down the blind in the kitchen. She walked over to a top cupboard and fished out two large wine glasses. Taking a few paces to her left, she reached down and grabbed the bottle of rose perched at the top of the wine rack. Clutching the wine and the glasses, she turned round to face her guest.

Holly was sat opposite her picking at a bowl of cheese nibbles.

'You know, I really shouldn't eat these, they're far too Moorish,' she said smiling.

Claire said nothing as she sat down next to Holly, uncorked the bottle, and started to pour.

'What's up with you?' Holly asked. 'You're not your usual smiley, chatty, optimistic self that I've known forever.'

'Sorry,' Claire remarked. 'I'm just knackered! Everything seems like such hard work these days compared to how it used to be.'

'What's he done now?' Holly asked.

Both ladies knew Holly was talking about Joe. She had been thrilled for her best friend when she was first introduced to him but didn't think for a moment that they'd end up getting married. After a long discussion between the two friends, Claire had proposed to him on the twenty ninth of February, taking advantage of the leap years tradition. Having initially done things as a three or occasionally a group of four depending on who Holly was seeing, times had certainly changed. Rare was it these days that both were in the same place at the same time. It felt almost as if they were time sharing Claire between one another.

'So, what's he done?' Holly repeated, trying to press her friend into opening up.

'Oh, nothing really.' Claire replied. 'I mean we're Ok, it's never been candles, flowers, restaurants, and romantic gestures between us even from the beginning. But…'

She paused and turned to her friend. 'He hasn't come anywhere near me in over 18 months.'

'18 months!' Holly exclaimed. 'Do you think there's someone else?'

'I don't see how there could be,' Claire replied. 'He seems to spend all his time either lecturing, holding seminars, playing with his car in the garage, or in the office marking whilst listening to The Cure. I took him to see them for his birthday once, and that's all he talked about for three months. Now we barely talk at all.'

'So, it's not just me he's become distant with then?' Holly said as she leaned back before taking a swig of wine.

'No, I'm afraid not,' said Claire, looking a little sombre. 'And he's been completely aloof about these bombings, despite both of us having known some of the kids who have died. I just don't get it.'

'Well, there is one positive. I know what to get you for Christmas now,' said Holly smiling.

'And what would that be?' asked Claire.

'A Vibrator,' replied Holly, beaming at her.

Nearly spitting out her wine, Claire doubled over as both ladies started to laugh uncontrollably.

***

Alicia Lane and Stephanie Myers had just left their flat, making their way down to the student car park which was situated just below them in the area at the south entrance to the halls of residence.

'Don't forget keep your ticket from tonight,' said Alicia to her friend. 'I want to try and keep enough of them to start a collage for our house next year which we can keeping adding too. I very much doubt this will be our last show we go to.'

'How many have you already got?' Stephanie asked her.

'Everyone since the very first theme night at the student's union,' Alicia replied.

'Bloody hell!' exclaimed Stephanie.

'Well people do have a habit of throwing them on the kitchen table when they get in, before trying to navigate the room for a glass of water to take to bed with them.'

'Whereabouts in the city do you want to live and when do you want us to start looking?' asked Stephanie. 'It obviously needs a parking space. I'm not going to park miles away from the place. I thought more people would have had cars, but I guess I was wrong. Seems to be more of a hindrance than help.'

'You're one of the lucky few that can afford one Hun. I'm sure if more people had the money, they would have one too,' said Alecia.

'It would be so much easier if we were allowed to park outside the halls like we did when we arrived,' said Stephanie.

They heard the muffled rumble of the tumble driers inside one of the halls on site laundrettes as they walked past.

'You know, if I'd have had more for-thought I would have asked my parents to buy me a condenser tumble drier,' said Stephanie.

'Why?' said Alicia quizzically.

'Because, if I had it set up in the flat, I could have made a fortune charging others to use it. It would also save us ladies the risking of losing our underwear or having some pervert stare at it.'

'That's genius!' replied Alicia, 'But a bit late in the day now.'

'Well rest assured, we'll have one when we move into the new house,' said Stephanie.

The pair had now reached the gradual sloping steps that led down into the car park, the grass verges next to them rising as the path gradually began to slope. They could see people playing tennis in the courts just beyond it. The site also housed a leisure centre and sports facilities for students to use. They had just started walking across the car park when they spotted one of their flat mates coming back from shopping at the nearby superstore. She was holding a shopping bag in either hand and had a packet of toilet rolls tucked under her right arm.

'Hiya,' she said. 'Where are you two off to?'

'The show at the arena,' replied Alicia.

'Fab!' came the reply, as she walked past. 'And very brave of you.'

'I love that girl,' said Stephanie to Alicia. 'Short and to the point.'

'What did she mean by brave?' asked Alicia. 'This is a good idea, isn't it?'

'You saw the news. The man responsible for those bombings is behind bars,' replied Stephanie. 'Don't let other people's scepticism stop you having a good time.'

'I won't,' Alecia replied.

'Good. Now where the bloody hell are those boys?'

'Not a clue, but here comes the campus security!' said Alecia as two figures approached them in uniform.

'Where are you ladies headed?' one asked.

'To the show at the arena, although we're waiting on two more,' Stephanie replied.

'Ok,' came the reply. 'Go careful.'

The pair then turned and walked away, heading in the direction of another group of students about to leave the campus site.

'Well, I feel so much safer now. How about you?' said Stephanie sarcastically before getting into the driving seat. Alecia sat down next to her and closed the passenger door. 'If we don't leave soon, we may as well just go back home.'

'They've still got five minutes,' Alecia replied. 'Besides, Chris has our tickets.'

'For the first and last time!' Stephanie replied. Just then there was a tap on the passenger window.

Both girls jumped. Chris Turvey was stood grinning at them, with his friend Will Poole close behind him trying to control his laughter.

'We're here!' exclaimed Chris.

'Git!' replied Alecia, climbing out of the passenger seat.

She smacked Chris on the arm.

'Ouch!' he exclaimed. 'What was that for?'

'You know what that was for!' Alecia replied.

'Just hurry up and get yourselves in the back!' Stephanie replied, growing impatient.

Chris bent down and lifted the level on the passenger seat and slid it forward.

He then climbed in the back and slid over to behind Stephanie allowing Will the room to get in.

Alecia pushed the passenger seat back into place before getting in herself and closing the door.

'Here we go!' exclaimed Chris excitedly as they pulled out of the car park on their way to the venue.

\*\*\*

Stephen was sat sprawled on the sofa in his parents living room, impatiently waiting for a reply from Marie having just text messaged her. Two minutes had turned to three, then five then ten. The longer it took, the more extreme his thoughts became.

*She's decided she hates me*, he thought to himself. *Some idiot has gotten his hands on her and changed her mind about me.*

He started banging his feet together angry as he looked back up at the clock. Fourteen minutes.

He sat up and grabbed the cushion from behind him before throwing it across the room towards an empty armchair, but the cushion missed the chair completely. Instead, it hit the uplighter floor lamp in the corner of the room causing, causing the lampshade to hit the wall behind it with a crack.

Luckily, it appeared that neither the shade nor the bulb had broken from the force of the impact.

'What in the hell was that?' came a shout from inside the kitchen.

'Sorry Mum,' said Stephen, standing up and heading over the retrieve the cushion.

'Missed the chair.'

'Haven't you got studying to do?' his mother barked back.

'I'm done for the day,' he replied dismissively, bending down to pick up the projectile.

Just then his phone went off, its vibration amplified by the sofa where he had been sitting.

He breathed a sigh of relief.

'Finally!' he said out loud, before heading back to the sofa to pick it up.

He highlighted the letter shaped icon and clicked.

*Hi. I'm Ok. Someone offered me a spare ticket for tonight's show at the arena, but I politely declined. It's not really me. How's home? x*

Stephen thought for a moment. By the sound of her message, not a lot was going on in his absence. Sensing the feeling of relief inside himself, he composed his reply before hitting send.

*Its ok, I guess. They keep showing bits and pieces on the news which Dad uses to remind me while I'm here. Missing you x*

\*\*\*

Stephanie and her car full of friends were now stuck at the temporary traffic lights. A sea of yellow cones stretched along the road and out of sight out. Alecia tapped on her passenger door impatiently.

'If we don't make it in time and they don't let us in, I am disowning both of you,' said Stephanie, glancing at the boys in her rear-view mirror.

Will looked around. A large, illuminated sign suspended over a building where they had stopped simply said Casino.

'Ever been there?' Will asked.

'Nope,' said Chris. 'I've never walked this far away from the university buildings before.'

'That's because he's too drunk to make it past the park!' Alecia replied.

'How dare you!' exclaimed Chris. 'I'll have you know there's plenty of places I frequent besides the bars, clubs and students' union.'

'Like the music shop for example,' said Will.

'Thank you, William,' Chris replied. 'Like the music shop! It's far better to invest your student loan there than to waste it gambling.'

'You bought a five-hundred-pound guitar, but never play it. How is that not wasting money?' said Stephanie, looking at Chris through her rear-view mirror and grinning.

'I'll get around to it sometime,' Chris replied. 'No doubt I'll be inspired by tonight.'

'Yes, he'll be playing one string making siren noises through a fancy pedal,' replied Alecia.

Both girls laughed.

The cars in front of them began to move. Stephanie followed them through the set of traffic lights and up the long city street.

'That's where all their student loan goes,' said Will as they passed an entrance to the shopping mall. 'Those bloody clothes shops. You're far better off doing what you did Chris. It's far more entertaining!'

Alecia looked at Stephanie.

'Boys!' she exclaimed.

'You love us really,' said Chris, leaning around the seat and looking out of the windscreen.

They were now approaching the end of the road.

Bars and restaurants were getting busy.

People were standing outside in small groups with smiles and muted laughter, the complete opposite to that of the stern looking security staff posted outside at the venue's doors.

'I hope that's a metal detector he's waving at her!' joked Chris.

'Why would anyone risk going to a bar after yesterday?' said Stephanie.

'The creeps behind bars!' exclaimed Chris. 'Let the party recommence.'

Stephanie took the right turn at the end of the road, and the area came into view. Lots of people were stood outside, with ticket touts walking between them shouting and waving tickets in their hands with arms aloft. Stephanie indicated right and they joined a small queue waiting to enter the car park.

'To be fair to the band, it's a miracle they didn't pull out anyway based on everything else that's going on,' she said, winding down her window ready to take the parking ticket when they reached the barrier.

'I expect once they had the reassurance that extra measures were in place, they were Ok. They need the money for God knows what, and we need them to help us escape from this nightmare,' replied Alecia.

'Not only that, but Gigs also bring in outside revenue to the city,' said Will.

'Check our Mr economics in here!' exclaimed Chris slapping him on the shoulder as they passed through the barrier and into the car park.

'Busier than I thought it would be,' said Alecia to Stephanie, both looking around in search of a parking space.

'Doesn't help that we're later than we planned to get here,' replied Stephanie, glancing in her rear-view mirror at Chris.

'Just head up the ramp,' said Chris. 'We'll yell if we spot an empty space.'

# 16.

Joe liked these pubs. No matter where you were, you knew what to expect. Same menu. Same wine list. Same atmosphere. Familiar layout. That was the beauty of pub chains.

The security on the door barely looked at him as he entered. He ordered a pint of coke from the bar and found a table by the window opposite the toilets. Putting his drink down, he took off his jacket which he hung on the back of his chair. Next, he fished into his pocket and removed his phone before placing it on the table. He then looked at his watch.

*They're always late*, he thought to himself. *It never fails to amaze me how people who appear so prompt in their working life are totally useless when it comes to time keeping in their personal lives. What doesn't help either is the two in question always carpool together. Still, needs must.*

He was staring out of the window about to take a sip of his drink when he heard a familiar voice.

'I've found him Dan!'

Peter Rowan, socio-economics teacher, and head of the social sciences department at the university pulled out the chair opposite Joe and sat down.

'To what do we owe this unexpected, rare pleasure this evening?' he asked.

'Give him a break Pete,' a voice from behind him said. "He's not a total recluse.'

Dan Silver, the departments lecturer in philosophy took his jacket out from under his arm and offered Joe his hand which he shook. 'It's nice to see you outside of work mate,' he said.

'Thanks,' Joe replied.

Dan threw his coat on the back of the seat next to Joe and put his wine glass on the table.

'Claire not with you this evening?' he asked.

'No, she's got a friend over,' Joe replied.

'Well, I'm grateful for the invite. I'm in need of a drink,' said Peter. 'We've never been this far behind at this point in the academic year before. The heads of the university are starting to get sweaty!'

He looked at his colleagues, both waiting for his plan.

'We're going to have to double the length of the upcoming seminars I think to make sure we cover all the necessary material.'

'Right o,' said Dan. 'Although I don't think I'm as far behind as Mr Darby here.'

'Not a problem Peter,' said Joe.

'Also, to give you boys a heads up,' Peter continued. 'I had a meeting earlier with the university executive board, representatives of our twenty academic schools, some local police officers, and the University security team.'

'Bloody hell!' exclaimed Dan. 'Rather you than me Pete. It was about the bombings, right?'

'Correct,' Peter replied.

'Well don't worry,' Dan continued. 'If you get the chop for whatever reason, Joe's here to step in. He was only complaining just the other day how he's become a vocal prospectus.'

Pete looked at Joe quizzically. 'Vocal prospectus?' he asked.

'Only to third year students during their final tutor meetings with me. You'd be amazed how few of them are aware of the options we can offer them once they graduate,' Joe replied.

'The quality of the lectures may also improve,' added Dan grinning. 'That Lecture he gives on voodoo and its influence on popular culture blows my mind! The origins of Zombies and his argument that dance music is essentially a stripped back version of shamanism. They kept the pulsing rhythms and drugs but stripped it of its spiritual qualities and purpose.'

'Cheers Dan' said Peter, lifting his glass as if toasting before taking a mouthful. 'To go back to what I was saying, there has obviously been some concern over student safety, but as none of the incidents have occurred on any grounds owned by the university the options are extremely limited.'

'What are they then?' asked Joe, leaning forwards in his chair.

'Well, the idea of introducing a curfew to students was passed around,' said Pete.

'I bet that went down like a lead balloon,' said Dan.

'Well, that would work for those living in the Halls of Residences yes, but not for those living in the city' Peter replied.

'Unless your Surnames Gideon!' exclaimed Dan.

'Did you know that over two thirds of our students live off campus, and that's without counting our mature students who commute from home?' Peter asked.

Joe shook his head.

'No, me neither' replied Dan.

'Therefore, it was concluded that we could only advise the students on how to stay safe when out and about. Not that we have any clue where the next problem might be. Seems it could be anywhere.'

'Yes, intuitions not what it used to be,' replied Dan.

'What do you mean?' replied Peter.

'We humans have neglected our powers of psychic perception for centuries,' said Dan.

'I think a lot of people find the idea uncomfortable,' said Peter.

'Stop please. That's far enough,' said Dan. 'We're here to unwind from work, not start a debate.'

'You started it, Daniel!' said Peter.

'Well, whether you believe in the religious idea of creation or the scientific theory of evolution, they both have one thing in common.' Dan replied.

'And what would that be?' asked Peter sceptically.

'The idea that humanity is all inbred,' said Dan.

'That would explain you then wouldn't it!' said Pete with a broad grin.

Even Joe couldn't help but smile at this.

'So why are we here?' Dan asked, pulling out a pouch of tobacco from his pocket.

'We're not exactly setting a good example to our students.'

'We are here because Joe asked, and the main suspect is behind bars. Mind you, I'm really impressed that despite the extra security and patrols that man managed to blow up that bar last night,' said Peter. 'Do you think he really did it?'

'I guess he's done something, otherwise why did they arrest him?' asked Dan, sprinkling a pinch of tobacco into his cigarette paper.

'Well, the details have been vague at best,' replied Peter. 'And isn't it a bit coincidental, especially after recent events in the United States? Makes me sceptical.'

Dan stood up.

'Just nipping out for this fag before we get stuck in. Either of you chaps coming?'

'Absolutely' said Peter, standing up and grabbing his jacket. 'I bought some specially for this evening. Are you coming Joe?'

'No, I'm good thanks,' replied Joe. 'It's been twenty-four months of hell that I'd rather not relive by starting again.'

'Fair play mate,' said Dan, taking a quick swig of wine from his glass. 'We'll be back in a bit.'

\*\*\*

'Well, we're too late to make the barrier, so we may as well check out the merchandise before we go in.' said Chris as they were stood in the foyer about to go through security.

'It's a miracle you remembered the tickets as it is!' said Alecia as the party edged forward. 'But I want to have a look at what they have too.'

'I'm going to check out the support band,' said Stephanie, as she stepped through the full body scanner and placed her mini backpack on the table to the right for searching.

'What about you Will?' asked Chris as the security guard checked the contents of the bag.

'I just need a beer and a good view,' replied Will. 'We will meet you in there then,' said Stephanie putting her backpack back on and heading towards the double door entrance to the main part of the arena. Will followed her as Alecia and Chris headed straight towards the merchandise stands that were already surrounded by people.

'How many more of these kids are there?' asked Dom, one of the security guards stood on the door to his colleague stood next to him.

'Can't be many more left,' replied David. 'Is everything in place?'

'I've been told the bomb squad checked the arena and its surrounding area earlier before the gig could be confirmed it was going ahead, and we've still got armed security out front as a precaution,' replied Dom.

'Yes, I heard that too,' said David.

'Not taking any chances then, are they?' said Dom.

'Can you blame them?' came the reply. 'And I appreciate the caution.'

'Hopefully they've got the right guy,' said Dom. 'I can't imagine what it's been like for our police this week.'

# 17.

Mills was stood in front of the growing case board, sipping coffee from his cup.

'So, despite everything that's already occurred, a concert is going ahead tonight,' said Dee, walking up behind him.

'Yes,' grumbled Mills. 'I've been staring at this board for so long my minds gone blank.'

'You need to stop Colin,' said Dee. 'Take five minutes and clear your head before we focus on interviewing James.'

Mills turned and faced his colleague.

'Thank you,' he said, placing his hand on Dee's shoulder before leaving the room.

She watched him slowly walk into his office and close the door.

*That's the biggest display of affection I've ever seen from Mills*, she thought to herself.

*The mounting pressure of this week must be catching up to him.*

***

Nadia James was talking to her brother Abbas on the telephone, pacing around the living room. Suddenly, she trod on one of the controllers left abandoned on the floor from earlier. Flinching, she threw herself backwards onto the sofa as tears stared to well in her eyes again.

'You alright?' her brother asked her.

'I have just stood on one of those stupid controllers the boys were using to play that game before Malcom was arrested,' she said. 'That really hurt.'

'Ouch!' Abbas replied.

'If I were you, I'd expect an early morning visit from the police to your offices Abbas,' said Nadia to her brother whilst rubbing her left foot.

'I will,' said Abbas sighing. 'What a day you've had! Is Samuel asleep now?'

'Yes. Finally. Although he's in my bed,' replied Nadia.

'Will you be sending him to school like normal tomorrow?' asked her brother.

'I haven't even thought about that,' said Nadia. 'It'll be an early start if I do. You need to be there almost forty minutes early to guarantee a parking space anywhere near that school these days.'

'Look. If you're telling me I need to prepare for a police visit, then you most certainly need to do the same,' said Abbas. 'Don't worry about sending Samuel to school, we will have him for the day. He can play and help entertain his younger cousin. It might help distract his mind for a while.'

'If you're sure?' asked Nadia. 'I won't want to burden you or Aleena.'

'Nonsense,' Abbas replied. 'The Holy Book. Two. Two eight six. Allah does not burden a soul beyond that it can bear. I'll pick him up before I head into the office.'

'Thank you so much,' replied Nadia. 'I'm going to ask Taz Abdullah if he will be here with me in the house whilst the police carry out their search. No doubt Malcolm will request him at his interview if he hasn't already.'

'A very wise idea,' Abbas replied. 'But I'm afraid I must go little sis. I shall leave you with passage from the Holy book to draw from. Three. One three nine. Do not lose hope, nor be sad. You will surely be victorious if you are true believers.'

'Thank you, brother. I love you,' replied Nadia.

'Speak to you later,' said Abbas before hanging up.

\*\*\*

'You, Holly Wilde are a bad influence!' giggled Claire. 'Thank god I'm not teaching until tomorrow afternoon.'

'Yeah, go on blame me! At least you've snapped out of your mood,' Holly replied.

Claire help but smile at this. If anyone could turn her frowning into laughter it was Holly.

'So, what do you think he's got stashed in that office of his then?' Holly asked.

'Nothing I expect,' said Claire. 'There's a tour t-shirt and ticket stub from The Cure show mounted on the wall above his desk. His PC and mini hi-fi. Shelves full of sociology books and box files. The obligatory archive boxes for taking paperwork to and from university, and an in and out tray. That's about it!'

'Seriously? When's the last time you went in there?' Holly asked.

'Last Thursday evening, I think. I find I usually need to coax Joe out for dinner these days,' Claire replied.

Holly stood up and took another sip from her glass.

'He's definitely hiding something,' she said walking towards the hallway. 'Let's go find out what! My moneys on pornography stashed in the desk drawer!'

Claire laughed dismissively.

'You coming with?' Holly shouted, already halfway up the stairs now.

'Yes. Ok. Ok,' Claire called back, placing her glass on the table as she stood up. 'But you're wasting your time.'

***

They were stood in Joe's office, laid out exactly as Claire had described.

'Ok. First things first. What's in the desk drawer Joseph?' Holly giggled.

She opened the drawer. Inside she found three red pens, three black pens, tip-ex, hole reinforcers, plastic wallets and several hundred treasury tags.

'Well. That was disappointing!' Holly exclaimed. 'Now there really is no excuse to neglect my best friend forever.'

'See!' Claire smiled. 'I told you.'

'Well, since were in here we might as well have some fun!' smiled Holly.

She pressed the on button on the mini hi-if. Switching its function from Cd to radio, she found her favourite dance station and turned it all the way up.

'Let's dance honey!'

She extended her hand which Claire took. With both ladies smiling and laughing happily together, they began to dance around the little office in abandonment.

## 18.

Having been given all the relevant Information with regards to the reason for his arrest on his arrival, Taz had spent the last twenty minutes chatting to Malcolm. They now found themselves sat in the police interview room.

Mills entered the room first, followed by Dee. They both sat down facing Malcolm and Taz on the opposite side of the table. Mills removed the plastic wrapper from a new disc and inserted it into the recorder before pressing record.

'This interview is being audibly recorded should it be tended in evidence before court,' he began. 'Interview Room 2. I am DCI Colin Mills, also present is DI Kate Dee. At the end of the interview, you will be given a notice with information about what will happen to the disc and how you may have access to it. Do you understand?' he asked.

'Yes,' replied Malcolm solemnly.

'Please state your full name and date of birth,' Mills said.

'Malcolm James. Twenty third of the fifth, nineteen seventy-two.'

'Also present?' Mills looked over at Taz.

'Taz Abdullah, Mr James Solicitor,' Taz responded.

'You are not just here to watch Mr Abdullah, but rather to advise, observe and assist Mr James,' said Mills.

Taz nodded at the detective inspector. Mills then readdressed Malcolm.

'You do not have to say anything, but it may harm your defence if you do not mention when questioned something which you later rely on in court. Anything you do say may be given in evidence.'

He opened the folder in front of him and took a breath.

'Mr James. You were arrested on suspicion of planting Improvised Explosive Devices at a cinema, the site of a science fiction exhibition, and bar in this city,' said Mills. 'We believe that you recently returned from a trip to an Afghanistan training camp where you were radicalised in the weeks leading up these attacks.'

Malcolm shook his head. He could not believe what he was hearing.

'What evidence do you have that links my client to these events may I ask?' said Taz.

'We have recovered a document fragment from the bar that we can link to him, as well as details of your time travelling and footage from the airport,' responded Dee.

'Circumstantial evidence then,' Taz replied.

'Can you account for your movements up to and during the times of the bombings Mr James?' continued Mills.

'Yes,' Malcolm responded. He took a deep breath, fully aware of the importance of what he was about to say should he get it wrong.

'I travelled to Pakistan after the death of my grandmother. I travelled alone as me and my wife believe that our son Samuel is still too young to attend such an event.'

Sensing the emotion rising within him, Malcolm paused for a moment before continuing.

'I arrived a day prior of the three days mourning period that is custom in our religion.

I was not only present at service but after the funeral, when the casket was taken to the burial site by myself and three other men from my immediate family.'

Mills and Dee looked at each other. 'Can anyone confirm this?' Mills asked.

'How many people would you like to confirm it Sir?' responded Malcolm. 'My Father met me at the airport when I arrived in Pakistan. My mother and brothers were with me during the initial mourning period, and several hundred people attended her funeral. I then spent the remaining three days at my aunt's house with my mother and father prior to us all flying back to England.'

'And what about your movements once you returned home Mr James?' continued Mills.

He was clearly not expecting the answers he had just been given. 'As stated previously we found a document at the scene of the bar explosion that can be tied to you.'

'Well, I have attended all five daily prayers and other social gatherings at the mosque since my return. If you contact our administrator Adil Maulama he will be able to clarify this.'

'What if contacting Adil Maulama is a way for you to obtain an alibi?' asked Mills. 'Maybe you had accomplices. Friends and acquaintances from the mosque.'

'I can assure you Sir that this is not the case,' replied Malcolm.

'What about when you haven't been at the mosque?' asked Dee. 'Who can vouch for your whereabouts then?'

'Contact my brother-in-Law, Abbas Hudson. He can give you my work itinerary and list of clients I have seen around the times in question,' Malcolm responded. 'We co-own an estate agency together here in the city. Other than that, I was at home with my wife and son.'

'If I may add something please?' said Taz. 'After a brief discussion Mr James has agreed to grant you full access to his financial records to verify his movements. This includes all business transactions as well as personal details.'

'Despite how it may seem, we do thank you for your full cooperation, Mr James,' said Dee. 'I'm sure a judge would take that into account during your sentencing.'

'I believe that the law will find me to be as I am, not guilty of these crimes,' replied Malcolm. For the first time since the beginning of the interview he sounded confident.

'I will need that list of names now please,' said Mills.

'Certainly,' replied Malcolm. He glanced over at Taz who nodded at him. 'I am happy to proceed when you officers are ready.'

***

Claire could not stop smiling. Holly was jumping up and down, waving her arms in the air. It was as if the small and plain office had miraculously been transformed into a club dance floor. The only things missing were an impressive lighting rig and pyrotechnics.

Suddenly, Holly lost her footing and toppled backwards.

'Shit!' she exclaimed as she fell backwards onto the desk, knocking off the archive box that had been left there. It fell open and emptied half of its contents over the floor.

'Oops!' said Holly with a giggle. 'Joe won't like that!'

Claire sighed at being torn away from a rare moment of fun as she bent down to pick up the box. All she had expected to find were students completed essays with red pen comments and a circled grade, but as she turned the box the right way up to re-fill it, she caught sight of things she had not expected to see. Electric wire, wire cutters, and half a dozen small black timers were also on the floor. One page also stood out amongst the others as it had been laminated.

'What is that?' asked Holly, turning down the music and squatting next to her friend.

Claire picked up the laminated paper and turned it over. They both looked down upon a pipe bomb diagram. Around the outside were notes written in Joes handwriting, including a list of chemicals and the method to weaponize them.

'Oh God!' Claire shouted, the pitch of her voice rising with panic. 'Oh god, oh god, oh my god, oh my god!'

She got up quickly and without warning ran out of the office, heading towards the bathroom.

'Claire!' Holly yelled after her, but Claire did not reply.

Holly stood up, stepped over the items on the office floor and headed towards the door.

She shouted again from just inside the office, hoping this time her friend would hear her.

'Claire!'

She walked out of the office into the hallway. It was only then she realised that Claire was unable to reply. Holly could now hear her best friend being violently sick in the bathroom.

\*\*\*

The Pub was getting busier now, with staff walking in between the tables carrying plates of food.

'Man, that smells good,' said Dan, watching as a waiter walked past with a freshly made pizza. He turned back to face Pete and Joe.

'Better make this the last one I suppose,' said Peter. Joe could hear the disappointment in his voice. 'Back to it all too quickly come the morning, and I could do without being pulled over on top of everything else.'

Joe said nothing and looked at his phone only to be greeted by its locked screen and time.

*Nothing. Good. No news is good news*, he thought to himself.

'Are you ready Dan?' Pete asked.

'Yeah, I guess so,' he replied, downing the last of his drink.

'I best get going too,' said Joe.

He stood up and started to put on his jacket.

'Do you want a lift back with us Joe?' asked Peter.

'No, I'm good thanks.' he replied. 'I got a taxi in, but I'll walk back.'

'Walk!' exclaimed Dan as they walked back towards the pub entrance. 'You are aware we live in the age of the motorcar, aren't you?'

Joe nodded silently as the trio stepped outside.

'It's a bit nippy out here, but the cars not far thankfully,' said Peter. 'Are you sure you don't want a lift Joe?'

'No, I'm good thanks Pete,' he replied. 'I'll see you both on campus tomorrow.'

As Pete and Dan turned and walked in the direction of Pete's car, Joe headed off through the city in the opposite direction. There were no patrol officers around.

\*\*\*

There was a long snake of people stretching from the bottom of the stairs all the way up to the pay station on the upper floor of the car park. On the opposite side of the road, people were still exiting the arena and being chaperoned away by its security.

'Man, what a show!' exclaimed Chris. 'I'm still buzzing!'

'I'm glad someone is,' replied Alecia, stood on the step behind him with Stephanie. 'I'm bloody freezing!'

'Well once we get to the pay station we can pay and get out of here,' said Stephanie. 'Besides which, this was your idea!'

'Correction, this was our idea!' said Chris, putting his arm round Will with a beaming grin on his face. 'And they didn't disappoint!'

'You say that...' said Will. 'But they left out one of their biggest songs! I feel kinda cheated.'

'Says the man who's sang along with every word for the last ninety minutes!' exclaimed Chris.

'I must admit, I'm glad I didn't miss it,' said Alecia.

They had made their way to the top of the stairs and were stood on the upper floor of the car park by the meter with only a few people in front of them.

'Right. I have the parking ticket. Cough up your change everyone!' said Stephanie.

Will fished in his jeans pocket before planting a handful of coins into her hand.

Chris laughed.

'What the hell!' Stephanie exclaimed.

'Here. Take this,' said Alicia.

She guided Stephanie's hand full of change back to Will with a ten-pound note between her fingers.

'I'll shake those two down for their share tomorrow. I just want to get back now,' she said.

Just as Stephanie placed the ticket into the machine, the car parked in the disabled space directly next to them exploded.

# 19.

Mills had just finished writing down all the names of the various witnesses put forward by Malcolm when there was a knock at the door. Dee left her seat quietly to deal with the interruption.

'For the record, DI Kate Dee has just stepped out of the room,' said Mills.

He had barely finished speaking when the door reopened, and Dee re-entered the room.

She walked straight over to Mills and whispered into his ear. He looked up at her, trying his hardest to control the look of shock that had begun to creep across his face.

'Well Gentlemen. If we're all happy I suggest we leave it here tonight,' he said.

Malcolm and Taz look at each other, then turned and nodded at him.

'Please state your agreement for the recorder,' Mills prompted.

'Yes,' replied Malcolm.

'Mr James, you will remain in custody here overnight. Our interview is now suspended and will continue tomorrow morning once we've had chance to search your house and any other properties on your portfolios. It's 11 pm. I am switching off the tape recorder.'

\*\*\*

'What do we know?' asked Mills as he entered the room where he had left the rest of his team to conduct Malcom's interview. His face was like thunder.

'Car bomb on the upper tier of the car park opposite the arena Sir,' said Jons solemnly.

'How many dead?' asked Mills.

'Too early to say Sir, but from what I understand the concrete pillar that the vehicle was parked near cracked and gave way. The explosion also took out most of the wall by the stairway which caused the ceiling to collapse.'

'This is a living nightmare…' said Dee, trying to control her emotions.

'Do you think James did all this?' asked Wood.

'After what he's just said in interview, it's looking extremely unlikely,' said Mills. 'Do you think this could be in protest at me arresting him?'

'Whatever it is, the area will need to be cleared and secured before we're allowed to enter the scene,' said Jons.

'I had William and Rhys go over that arena with a fine-tooth comb!' said Mills angrily. 'And for what!'

'No-one could have predicted this Colin,' said Dee, trying to reassure him. 'We did what we could under the circumstances. People have been the target, not cars, and we can't possibly check every building in this city. The best thing that we can do now is to join our colleagues and secure the area so the other emergency services can do their jobs before questioning any survivors and eyewitnesses.'

'Forgive me, but that still doesn't make me feel any better,' said Mills, heading towards his office. He opened the door and slammed it shut behind him.

'Wow,' said Wood, looking around at his fellow officers. 'Just wow.'

\*\*\*

Karl Wass was sat at a bus stop with a woman, her two shopping bags placed on the floor between her legs. Another man was stood at the far side of the shelter talking incoherently into his mobile phone.

'These bus stops are naff!' Karl grumbled. 'The seats are always cold, and I can guarantee that if it starts to rain it'll be coming in from the only direction where there's no side to the thing!'

Beth Day, Karl's girlfriend was stood up next to him looking at the bus timetable behind its Perspex frame.

'Will you stop complaining!' she exclaimed. 'You did offer to take me home, remember?'

'Yes, and I reserve the right to complain.' Karl replied. 'Not to mention the added risk of being blown up!'

Beth laughed sat down next to him. She leaned over and kissed him on the cheek playfully.

'My Hero,' she said with a grin.

Karl didn't respond. He was watching a figure strolling on the opposite side of the road.

'Isn't that Mr Darby?' he asked Beth.

'What? Walking around at this time of night. It can't be,' she replied.

'No. I'm pretty sure it is,' said Karl. 'Mr Darby!' he yelled.

Joe stopped walking and turned towards them, before crossing the road after the passing traffic towards the bus stop.

'To what do I owe this unexpected pleasure?' he asked as he reached the bus stop.

'I was going to ask you the same thing,' said Karl.

'My wife is entertaining this evening,' replied Joe. 'Where are you two headed?'

'Oh, I'm just taking the lovely Beth home,' said Karl.

Beth leaned round him and smiled. 'Hi Sir,' she said.

'She lives in a different dorm to me,' continued Karl. 'I'm just making sure she gets home safe.'

'How very gentlemanly of you,' said Joe. Both students laughed.

'I'll see you two tomorrow,' said Joe.

*Good,* he thought to himself as he walked away from the students. *I've now been seen out here.*

\*\*\*

'When did you guys get back?' Jons asked William and Rhys as they made their way through the lower corridor of the police station.

'A while ago, our job was to secure the area and then re-check it once the gig had started which we did,' replied Rhys.

'I just wished we've had the foresight to check the car park opposite,' added William.

'None of us would be standing here if we had foresight,' said Buckland from behind them.

'Where did you manifest from?' Jons asked.

'My office is right there Jons,' replied Buckland, pointing to the labelled door on his right. 'I've been on standby in case the boys found anything suspicious,' he said, nodding at William and Rhys. 'I was hoping to share some new information.'

Dee approached the group.

'Mills not with you Kate?' Buckland asked. 'He's taking a moment,' she replied.

'Not anymore,' came a familiar voice from behind the group.

Everyone watched as the detective chief inspector approached them.

'Informal staff meeting?' Mills asked.

'No,' said Wood defensively. 'We're just…'

'Relax Keith,' said Mills interrupting him. 'I'm just trying to diffuse some of my own tension.'

'I think you owe your door an apology,' said Wood.

'Oh dear, said Buckland. 'Should I refrain from what I was about to share?'

'No, go on,' said Mills.

'Our teams have managed to identify some possible chemical sources used to make the explosives,' said Buckland.

'Which are?' asked Wood.

'You could get them via industrial or laboratory sources,' he said. 'But if we talk simply in terms of accessibility, the easiest place in this city they could be found is in the chemistry department at the university. All these chemicals are included on a list the university are obliged to keep. They are regularly used and stored on site,' said Buckland.

'So, if I were a chemistry student or lecturer, then I would have regular access to these chemicals?' asked Dee.

'I believe so,' Buckland replied. 'Otherwise, there would be no need for them to keep them on campus.'

'It fits Colin,' said Dee. 'Now I think of it, did you notice the student signs on the way into the bar? We may have unknowingly discovered our bombers main targets. Bars. The cinema, a science fiction exhibition, and now a concert. There's no way any of these places wouldn't have had students there. They make up such a considerable percentage of the city's population.'

'Thanks to our valiant head of forensics, I believe we now have our next steps,' said Mills. 'And your timing couldn't be more key to this case. As a starting point, we need a list of all current and former chemistry students and teachers going back five years, paying particular attention to individuals with expulsions or dismissal in their records. Cross reference those names with the names we have from the Mosque, along with any students that happen to be in rented houses that are on James company portfolio.'

Everyone looked and nodded at him in agreement. 'Sargent Donovan can get to work on that whilst we're dealing with this latest mess.'

'Whether this is the same culprit as the previous bombings, or a different person responsible, please prepare yourselves,' said Rhys clearing his throat.

'How do you mean?' asked Mills.

'This time a vehicle- borne improvised explosive device was used,' replied Rhys. 'What you are about to encounter will be nothing like what we have already seen with the last three bombs. I encountered such a device whilst on my last tour with the army. I'll never forget the sight of the blood from the unfortunate civilians caught in the blast staining the street, or the giant dust cloud suspended above the area.'

Dee shuddered. For a moment no-one said anything. William placed a reassuring hand on Rhys shoulder.

'I'd like to thank you two for your persistent work on this case,' said Mills, turning so he could address the two men directly. 'You have more than earned the right not to be exposed to anymore such horrors, although I must admit I am selfishly grateful that I have had access to your expertise.'

'Thank you Mills,' said Rhys. 'If only it was that simple.'

'Indeed,' continued William. 'Just because you've spent time in the army on active duty doesn't mean you earn the right to an early retirement. I've got bills to pay and a family to feed just like everyone else.'

'Hmmm,' said Mills, turning a thought over in his mind.

'Why are you real heroes always sickeningly modest?' said Dee.

\*\*\*

Holly was sat on the floor of the landing. She'd had to use the wall as a walking aid to get there as she too was now in shock at what they had discovered. Claire was still being sick in the bathroom but had managed to let Holly know she was Ok by faintly yelling in between urges. Holly picked up her phone and dialled 999.

'Emergency service operator. Which service to you require?' said the voice at the other end.

'Police please,' said Holly. Her voice had begun to shake.

'I'll connect you now,' replied the service operator.

'Police. What's your emergency?' asked a different voice.

'I'm at my best friend's house. We know who the real bomber is.'

'Where are you calling from, please?'

'My friend Claire's House. Number five, East Gardens.'

'Is anyone injured?' the operator asked.

'No,' said Holly. 'But Claire is still being sick after discovering her husband is the bomber.'

'What's your name?' asked the police dispatcher.

'I'm Holly. Holly Wilde.'

'Where is your friend's husband now Holly?' asked the voice.

'Out with colleagues from the university. He's a lecturer there like my friend is.'

'Ok. stay on the line please.'

Claire emerged from the bathroom. Her eyes were red raw, and she was as white as a sheet.

'Who are you talking too?' she asked Holly.

'The police,' she replied. 'I have to protect you.'

Claire sat next to Holly and put her head on her shoulder.

'Thank you,' she said through her tears.

'Are you still there?' asked the operator.

'Yes.' replied Holly. 'And my friend is here with me now.'

'May I speak with her too please?'

'Er. Sure.'

Holly moved the phone away from her ear and activated its speaker mode. She then looked at Claire and nodded, prompting her to speak.

'Hello?' said Claire faintly.

'Is that Claire I'm speaking too?' asked the operator.

'Yes. This is Claire,' came the reply.

'Your friend says you have discovered Bomb manufacturing equipment in your home. Is that correct?'

'Yes,' replied Claire, trying to fight back the tears and stop her lips from trembling. 'We found it in my husband's office.'

'What's your husband's name please?'

'Joe. Joseph Darby.'

'Do you know where he is right now?'

'He said he was going to a bar with some of his colleagues, but I'm sure he'll be home soon.'

'Can you confirm you address for me please Claire,' the operator asked.

'Five East Gardens,' replied Claire, before folding up her legs and bowing her head.

'Ok. I need you two to stay together and stay on the line please. We'll get someone out to you now.'

# 20.

Mills was about to climb into his car along with Dee when they heard yelling.

'Mills. Mills. Wait!' yelled Donovan, running up to the car.

'Apologies,' he said trying to catch his breath. 'I'm not used to running like that anymore.'

'It's OK. Take a breath,' said Mills. 'What's up?'

'The call handler is currently on the line with two women who have discovered bomb components hidden in one of their husband's study,' replied Donovan, taking another deep breath.

'Excuse me?' said Mills, taken aback.

'Where are they?' Dee asked.

'Five East Gardens,' replied Donovan. 'The husband is out, but his wife reckons he'll be home very soon.'

Mills stood silently for a moment thinking as he watched a cloud roll across the night sky.

'How do you wish us to proceed Colin?' asked Dee.

'Wood, Jons and Hughes, I want you to head down to the car park as planned with Buckland and his team,' said Mills, still looking skyward. 'Dee and I will go to straight to Five East Gardens now, but we're changing our tactics slightly this time.'

'How do you mean?' Wood asked Mills.

'When we arrested Malcom James, we went in hot. Sirens and the van and the whole force,' replied Mills looking at him. 'This time we shall make the arrest quietly and discreetly so as not to alert the public and press.'

'Makes sense,' replied Wood. 'Plus, if this turns out to be what I know we all collectively hope it is we don't want the husband running.'

'Correct. Keep in contact please Keith,' said Mills.

'And find Zoe Lee!' Dee added, holding up a cupped hand to her lips to make sure he heard her.

'Will do,' Wood called back, giving her a thumbs up.

'Once we know what's what in East Gardens, we will head towards you,' said Mills.

Wood climbed into the police car with Jons, who rolled out of the car park and onto the main road with sirens blazing. Buckland and his team followed on, with Officer Hughes in another vehicle. The two detectives watched their colleagues leave before pulling out into traffic with only their indicator light on.

'This changes everything doesn't it?' said Dee once they had left the station, heading silently in the opposite direction to the other cars.

'If we can't link the two men then yes it does,' replied Mills. 'Significantly.'

\*\*\*

'When you hear your door, I need you to answer it. It'll be the police officers,' said the dispatch operator.

'Ok. Thank you,' said Claire, her brain pounding against her skull.

'Should be with you any moment now,' came the reply.

Holly was still sat beside her friend. For the first time in forever she had absolutely no idea what to say to her. She stood up, stretched, and looked at Claire feeling guilty.

The detective's car entered the road passing the East Gardens Road sign. It was several hundred yards long, with detached and semi-detached houses running its entire length.

'So do you think these are the same components used in the previous explosions?' Dee asked Mills.

'I hope so,' he responded. 'Do we know what the husband's occupation is?'

'He's a lecturer,' responded Dee.

'At the university?' Mills asked.

'Not certain of that Colin,' she replied. 'I guess we'll find out soon enough.'

'Quite,' said Mills, as their car crawled slowly up the road.

Dee was looking up the road in both directions, looking for the house number.

'There on the right,' she said, pointing to the house.

Mills brought the car to a stop in front of the driveway.

'Do you have a plan?' she asked Mills as they exited the vehicle and headed towards the door.

'That will depend on what we find,' he said.

'Understood,' Dee replied.

Mills knocked on the front door.

'That'll be the police,' said Holly on hearing the door.

'They're here,' said Claire to the dispatcher. 'Let them in please Hun,' she asked Holly.

Holly headed down the stairs slowly to the front door and opened it.

'Claire Darby?' asked Mills.

'No, I'm Holly Wilde,' she replied. 'Claire is still in the hallway upstairs. Please come in.'

She opened the door. Mills and Dee stepped in. She led them up the stairs to Claire, who was still sat with her back leaning on the wall.

'Good evening, Mrs Darby,' said Mills. 'I am Detective Chief Inspector Colin Mills, and this is Detective Inspector Kate Dee.'

Claire gave both officers a faint smile.

'Our top priority is your safety,' Mills stated. 'But first we need you to confirm some details you relayed to our colleague during your 999 call.'

'Ideally, I'd like to talk somewhere that would be more comfortable for you. Do you think you can stand?' Dee asked.

'I'll try,' said Claire. 'The living room is not far away from the stairs.'

'I'll help you,' said Holly. She approached Claire and helped her to her feet.

With Holly stood in front of Claire, they slowly descended the stairs with Mills and Dee behind them. Holly waited for Claire at the bottom of the stairs before holding her hand and escorting her round the bottom of the staircase and into the living room. Claire and Holly sat next to each other in the middle of the four-seater sofa that rang along the back wall of the room. On the walls opposite each other hung two large canvas pictures of a lion and an elephant. A large mirror was hung over the fireplace opposite the sofa. Mills and Dee entered after them. Dee positioned herself on the end of the sofa next to Claire with Mills stood just in front of them.

'Do you mind if I perch on this?' he asked, pointing to the coffee table just behind him.

'No. Please do,' said Claire.

'Can I ask you what you and your husband do for a living please?' Mills said after sitting down cautiously on the tables top.

'Yes. We're both lecturers at the university. I work in the chemistry department, and he is a social sciences lecturer,' replied Claire.

Mills and Dee both looked at each other.

'Does your husband ever visit the chemistry department?' Mills continued.

'All the time,' said Claire. 'He meets me most days there to drive us home. If I'm running late, he'll often kill time in the department.'

*Buckland maybe spot on,* Mills thought to himself.

'Do you know if your husband has any connection to Malcom James?' Mills asked.

'No,' Claire replied. She bowed her head and started to sob. 'We'd never even heard that name before his public arrest. He's innocent. It's my husband you want. I can't believe this is happening…' Her voice trailed off.

'It's ok. You're doing really well,' said Dee reassuringly.

'Would your husband have access to the chemicals in your department?' Mills asked.

'Yes,' Claire said. 'He knows the very last thing I do is secure the storage facility before we leave for my own piece of mind. He's watched me do it hundreds of times.'

'So, it's open when he's in the building?' asked Mills.

'Yes,' replied Claire. 'But only for a few minutes at most.'

'Would you mind if I had a quick look in the office, please?' said Mills.

Claire nodded in agreement.

'Thank you,' he said.

'It's all my fault,' said Claire as Mills exited room, making his way back up the stairs.

'You're doing really well Claire,' repeated Dee.

Throughout her career, Dee had seen many wives and partners trying to cover for their spouses, but there was not a trace of Claire trying to deny Joe had any involvement. Quite the opposite in fact. She certainly wasn't quiet, or desperately thinking out loud for a rational excuse.

***

Mills was stood in the office. He could not get over how superficial it looked as he slipped on a pair of gloves.

*This room is the literal meaning of hiding in plain* sight, he thought to himself. *It's disturbingly plain.*

He then caught site of the framed T-shirt on the wall behind the desk.

'No!' he exclaimed out loud. 'You can't taint them. I love The Cure.'

He crouched down in front of the box that Claire had turned the right way up. Right next to it was the Electric wire, wire cutters, and the timers. He then picked up the laminated piece of paper with the pipe bomb diagram. His eyes scanned the list of chemical notes Joe had made. The names aldehyde and acetone he had heard were there. He then picked up another document and turned it over. It was a student's essay that had been graded at the top. Mills held the bomb paper and the essay side by side and compared the handwriting on each. A match. It would still have to be verified before it could be submitted as evidence, but it was good enough for now. If the writing had been different, then a case that someone might be trying to frame the lecturer would need to be added into their ever-growing lines of enquiry.

He placed the papers carefully back where they were. Standing up slowly so as not to disturb anything he exited the room, removing his gloves and pocketing them as he went.

He walked back down the stairs and into the living room to join Dee, Claire, and Holly.

'Well. That is pretty self-conclusive,' Mills said as he approached the sofa.

'Now back to my priority, keeping you two ladies safe.'

Claire and Holly looked at each other in apprehension.

'Safe?' asked Claire quizzically.

'Safe from what?' Holly added.

'What I don't want is for your husband to return home and realise what's happened. It could cause him to panic or even retaliate,' Mills replied. 'Therefore, I must ask you ladies to stay together somewhere else tonight. Is there a safe place you can go?'

'My house,' said Holly. 'It's not far, and I don't think Joe even has the first clue where it is these days.'

Claire looked at her best friend and squeezed her hand.

'Thank you,' she said.

'Rest assured Mrs Darby, I plan to arrest your husband tonight based on what I have already seen as soon as he returns home,' Mills continued.

'You will be able to return home tomorrow,' said Dee reassuringly.

'We will need to fully search the property in the morning for further evidence just to pre warn you,' said Mills. 'But your husband will be in custody and therefore no threat to either of you being here.'

'Let alone anyone else…' added Holly, staring straight ahead, her eyes widening with anger now.

'Can you remain with Claire until tomorrow, Holly?' asked Dee. 'You don't have any prior commitments that you cannot miss?'

'Nothing that cannot be changed,' said Holly. See smiled at Claire who returned her look. 'I'm not about to leave her on her own now after all this time.'

'I'll call for a car to have them dropped off and then station at Hollys residence Mills,' said Dee.

'Good,' said Mills as Dee stood up, walking towards the living room window. 'Usually, we would ask you both to come and make a formal witness statement. However, under these circumstances I think we will have them bring the necessary paperwork to you when they pick you up,' she said.

'We appreciate that,' replied Holly.

'Once our colleagues arrive and take you to Holly's residence, we shall move our vehicle around the corner so that your husband doesn't spot it,' said Mills as he sat back down in front of Holly and Claire.

'Car and paperwork are on the way Colin,' said Dee, wondering back to the group near the sofa.

'Great,' Mills replied. 'Where would you ladies usually be when your husband returns home Mrs Darby?' he asked.

'In the Kitchen most likely,' said Claire. 'It's far enough away from the office and our bedroom so as not to disturb him. We just keep the back door open so we can nip outside and smoke.'

'Then leaving the kitchen light on for him to see as normal when he approaches the house is a good idea,' said Mills.

'I'll do that now,' said Dee, leaving the living room and heading for the kitchen at the back of the house.

'I'd use these last few moments to throw some things in a bag if I were you,' Mills said to Claire.

'I'll do it,' said Holly standing up. 'I know where everything is.'

\*\*\*

Joe was whistling as he rounded the corner, watching his warm breath curl in the cold night air. For the first time in as long as he could remember he was in a good mood.

The streetlights were casting uninterrupted beams of light out over the pavement and road. A cat ran past him along the bottom of the wall that provided the boundary between the private gardens and public street. He watched it jump up and over into what he assumed was its home garden. He put his hands into his pockets to fish out his keys before rounding the hedge and into the driveway. He could see the glow of the kitchen light still on through the windows as he approached.

*Still entertaining then,* he thought to himself as he stepped up onto the welcome mat outside his front door. He was just about to place the key into the front doors lock when we heard a voice from behind him.

'Joe Darby?'

'Yes,' he replied without even turning around. 'This is a very desperate visit before the deadline tomorrow,' he said as he began to turn the key in the lock. 'Most students don't know where I live.'

'We are not students Mr Darby,' replied another voice.

Before Joe had chance to open his front door any further, he glanced over his left shoulder as he felt his left hand being directed towards the centre of his back.

'Joe Darby,' said Mills. 'You are being detained under section forty-one of, and schedule eight to, the terrorism act two thousand.' He moved Joes right hand away from the door, placing it behind his back with his left. 'You do not have to say anything, but it may harm your defence if you do not mention when questioned something which you later rely on in court. Anything you do say may be given in evidence.'

Joe said nothing. He was now stood on his front doorstep in handcuffs.

Mills led him in the direction of their car, whilst Dee shut the houses front door and removed the key. She walked back down the drive and after a brief jog along the road caught up to Mills and their suspect. Dee then opened one of the vehicles passenger doors as Mills bundled Joe into the back of the police car before shutting it. Both detectives then climbed into the front seats and fastened their seatbelts.

With the cars police lights and sirens still disengaged, they drove their suspect out of East Gardens, heading back towards the police station.

## 21.

Joe had been photographed, fingerprinted, and processed since his arrival in custody.

To everyone's surprise he had not requested anyone be contacted or notified of his arrest.

The officer had just finished taking his DNA swab, and they were waiting for someone to escort him to his holding cell which was being prepared.

Joe was then led from the desk through another locked door and into the stations other holding cell opposite Malcolm James. Mills had insisted on overseeing the process.

'Keep an eye on him please,' he had said to the officers before leaving the custody suite.

'He is unnervingly quiet.'

'You're not going to interview him straight away?' asked a bemused Officer Grant after Mills had watched him lock the door of the holding cell.

'No. I plan on letting him stew for a while.'

Having exited the building and re-joined Dee who had remained outside, they were now on their way to join their colleagues already at the scene of the car park Bomb.

Mills had his phone to his ear listening to a dial tone that seemed to be lasting forever.

He hit the car door with his other fist and hung up.

'No answer from Keith Wood,' he said. 'Although why I was expecting one is beyond me.'

'You do know we could leave this one to the team and go home and rest don't you Colin?' Dee asked.

'No, we can't, we both know we're far too entrenched for that,' replied Mills. 'Besides, I need to see this with my own eyes to believe it.'

Dee paused for a moment.

'So do I,' she said, slowing the car down before indicating left.

'I thought the first thing Darby would do is lawyer up,' said Mills to Dee as they drove down the wide city centre street on their way to the arena. 'But to our surprise he didn't request we contact anyone.'

'Maybe he thinks we don't have anything we can use to charge him,' said Dee.

'He should know better!' replied Mills. 'I've asked the officers to keep an eye on him. We know that these events have taken meticulous planning. It wouldn't surprise me if he has an endgame.'

'I'm not sure,' said Dee hesitantly. 'He doesn't fit the profile of someone who would take his own life.'

'He doesn't fit the profile of someone who would blow up half of his own city…' countered Mills, as both detectives spotted the brown signs directing drivers in the direction of the arena.

'So, I take it we're going to search East Gardens tomorrow morning before we interview Darby then?' asked Dee.

'Correct.' said Mills. 'I want some proper evidence in our possession before we sit down, especially after our interview with James.'

Dee followed the road and they caught site of the arena for the first time. It was swamped by dozens of emergency vehicles, including the city's air ambulance helicopter that was currently touched down in the centre of the road, having been closed off to all traffic in both directions. Tire tracks and footprints were clearly visible on a road that was covered with dust and debris. Mills and Dee both glanced up and to the right. What was left of the car park now came into view.

'My God,' said Dee. 'I know Rhys said we should be prepared but…'

'Nothing could prepare us for this!' interrupted Mills. 'The press better give us some room!'

\*\*\*

'It won't be possible for us to enter for some time yet I'm afraid,' said Buckland, as Mills and Dee approached him. They were all stood in a line on the edge of the curb looking up at what was left of the car park opposite.

'Where are Rhys and William?' asked Mills. 'Checking again that there are no secondary devices hidden in the area,' Buckland replied.

'If only we had thought of the car park earlier,' grumbled Mills.

'We can't police the whole city, Colin!' exclaimed Buckland. 'It was the first minister's decision to relax security, even if we all disagreed with it.'

'That's what I said to him earlier,' replied Dee.

They could see Wood, Hughes and Jons by the various emergency vehicles talking to people who had already received first aid and were able to stand unaided. Three were talking to Hughes. One had their arm in a sling and an eye patch over one eye. The two others had bandages wrapped around their heads. It was then that they caught sight of a team of people negotiating the car parks ramp with a body bag on top of a trolley. The sullen expression on everyone's face indicating that there were still yet more bodies to retrieve from the building.

Buckland sighed deeply.

'So, as you can see the vehicle was deliberately parked in that corner of the building causing the most amount of damage,' he said pointing upwards.

'I wouldn't be surprised if tamping was used to ensure the direction of the blast.'

'Tamping?' said Dee.

'Yes. You place objects around the bomb to direct the force of the blast in a specific direction,' replied Buckland. 'Rhys explained the process to me.'

Both Mills and Dee remained silent.

'The glass shattered in all the cars on two levels and people who had already started to exit were trapped in their cars from the falling debris,' said Buckland. 'Apparently the tremors from the explosion were felt half a mile away. Several other people were killed outright, either directly from the blast or from the wall next to it blowing out and the roof structure coming down on top of them.'

Dee shook her head in disbelief.

'And I've been informed that the coroner's office has now been forced to use a cold storage facility in the bay as a temporary morgue after the events of the last few days. The club incident yesterday pushed them to their absolute limit, but this is too much,' said Buckland.

'The bomb was deliberately detonated at the time it was I presume?' asked Mills.

'No doubt about that,' Buckland replied. 'The entire car park, including the stairwell was full of people who had just exited the arena after tonight's performance and were heading home.'

'Son of a..!' exclaimed Mills. 'If only we had found him sooner.'

'The fact that a vehicle was used this time to create a VBIED armed with at least twenty times the amount of explosive we've already seen means we are very unlikely to uncover much solid evidence,' said Buckland. 'Not very helpful when it comes to comparative analysis from the previous devices.'

'VBIED?' said Dee questioningly.

'Sorry,' replied Buckland. 'Stands for a vehicle born improvised explosive device.'

'Hopefully we'll be able to trace the vehicle they used,' said Mills.

Just then a figure appeared directly opposite them below the car park. It jogged across the road in their direction.

'Rhys,' said Mills as he recognised him. 'All clear?'

'Yes,' Rhys replied. 'Although it's going to be some time yet before anyone can head up to the site of the explosion. Not only are they still having to remove bodies, but they need to deal with a significant amount of the debris and rubble before they are able to secure the roof.'

'Where would you like us to start?' Dee asked Mills.

'We need to be pre-emptive here,' Mills replied as he scanned the area. 'Due to what has happened, I'd put money on a swarm of parents arriving soon if they aren't already here. Desperate parents looking for their children or any news of them. We need to respect how their feeling, but we must also stress the vital importance of keeping the area clear so we can finish doing our jobs.'

'So, we need a stationed area for them then?' asked Dee, scanning the area looking for a suitable location.

'Yes,' Mills replied.

'The most obvious place would be at the entrance to the arena,' said Dee. 'We can take all the relevant names and contact information and have a paramedic and few police officers there to answer any questions. It's also where they knew their children were tonight.'

'Let's head over now,' said Mills. 'We can pick up Hughes enroute.'

\*\*\*

Mick was accompanying two of his colleges from the ambulance service out of the car park with a casualty on a stretcher and their companion. Just moments ago, they had been cut out of their car by the fire brigade. The small party crossed the road and headed in the direction of the air ambulance where Carenza was stood, coordinating her team in her role as senior paramedic team leader.

'This is Greg, and his friend Jack. Greg has a suspected broken back; his breathing has become increasingly irrational and as you can see, he has begun posturing,' said Mick as he approached his colleague.

'The last thing I said to him was if we get separated for any reason, meet me at the car,' said a voice from an ashen white face stood next to him.

'He's going to be ok,' said Mick, placing a reassuring hand on Jacks shoulder.

'In that case we best get him into the helicopter and off to hospital,' said Carenza.

With the pilot climbing into the air ambulance to begin his pre-flight checks, Carenza assisted Mills and their colleagues as they manoeuvred the stretcher alongside a horizontal board from the back of the helicopter.

'One, two, three lift,' directed Carenza as the stretcher left the trolley and was placed into the back of the helicopter.

'Come aboard,' motioned Mick, as Jack climbed aboard and sat in a chair behind the stretcher where Greg was. Mick handed him a headset that he put on, before taking up his own seat beside the casualty once he had double checked everything was in place.

'Won't be long and we'll be on our way,' he said reassuringly. 'Did you travel far this evening?'

'About two hours give or take,' Jack replied. 'We just love the band and were willing to take the risk despite everything that's happened, especially after the first minister's announcement.'

Mick fastened his own belt buckle.

'This was the nearest place to us that the band was playing,' Jack continued. 'We have no arena or anything other venue of this size. It's either smaller or a football stadium, although your stadium is newer and more attractive anyway!'

Mick smiled at him.

'Your very good at your job Mick,' said Carenza, who had been standing on the tarmac outside watching her colleague. She took a step backwards. 'Have a good flight.'

The sound of a mechanical whirl then began, growing louder and louder as the helicopters rotary blades began to turn. Those from the emergency services who were not currently treating casualties paused to watch with everyone else in the area. The sound grew even louder as it reached a sufficient speed. The pilot then lifted the helicopters nose off the ground slightly followed by the body of the aircraft before rising into the air. Having safely left the ground hovering higher than the surrounding vehicles, the aircraft's nose titled forward before it flew over the heads of the crowd below. With increasing altitude, it disappeared over the top of the arena and out of sight.

\*\*\*

Mills was stood talking to a group of eyewitnesses, all of them having just witnessed the air ambulance leaving the area.

'Please, please, one at a time!' he said after everyone had tried to relay what they had seen to him all at once.

'Ok. I'll go,' said Damien Brown, looking at Mills right in the eyes. 'So, we're out of the area and about to make our way across the road. Suddenly Bam! The heat hit us first, then this rumbling. Like a tremor.'

'People in front were blown backwards by the blast,' added Austin Farr, stood right next to Damien.

'I looked up and told D to go back,' added Pamela Stan, positioning herself between the boys.

'But I couldn't, because there's like, a thousand people still behind us,' said Damien. 'So many of them all just stood staring up.'

Mills nodded, trying to focus whilst fighting his growing fatigue.

'Then a rain of debris from the dust cloud,' said Pamela pointing skyward. 'One group walking on the pavement the other side got covered with dust from the blast. They looked like ghosts.'

'And then there's the people who were covered with blood,' said Austin solemnly.

'It went dead silent for a couple of seconds, then the screaming started,' said Damien. 'Happened so fast.'

'So, none of you were able to see anything or anyone acting suspiciously moments before then?' asked a dejected Mills.

'No Sir,' said Austin.

'Those people are probably in the body bags,' said Damien.

'Quite' said Mills. 'Well, thank you all for your time everyone.'

As he turned to leave the group, he caught sight of an open wound on Austin's arm.

'Hey. Your arm,' he said, pointing at it.

Austin rotated his left arm clockwise and anti-clockwise before lifting it towards him and looking at his wound.

'Oh That? It's nothing compared to others out here,' he replied. 'Doesn't even hurt.'

'Go get it looked at please,' said Mills. 'All this dust flying everywhere, it'll easy get infected.'

'I'll drag him over there if needs be Boss!' said Damien.

'Good,' replied Mills. 'Stay together, keep each other safe and follow all instructions given to you,' he said as he left them, making his way back towards his colleagues.

Dee had perched herself on the bonnet of their car, taking in deep breaths of the nights air. She was still trying to come to terms with her surroundings when Mills walked over to her.

'You know, I'm not naïve Colin. Far from it,' she said. 'When I became a detective, I expected to be dealing with more extreme crimes, but nothing like this!'

'I've been doing this job longer than I can remember,' Mills replied. 'I've never seen anything like this. It certainly wasn't in any part of our training.'

Officer Wood appeared from behind them.

'It's going to be several hours to process all this lot,' he said.

'Ahh, there you are Keith,' said Mills.

'Where's Officer Lee?' Dee asked. 'Did you co-ordinate with her on your arrival?'

'Haven't seen her Kate,' Wood replied. 'I'm told she was chaperoning people out of the arena at the time of the explosion.'

'Excuse me,' said Dee, before jogging back towards the entrance of the arena.

'Did you get anything out of your group Mills?' Wood asked.

'Nothing of any significance,' Mills replied. 'Everyone was too fixated on their evening to notice, and I guarantee the person who did this knew that and deliberately used it to his advantage.'

'Why's Dee so concerned about Officer Lee?' Wood asked Mills.

'She's her younger cousin,' Mills replied. 'Kate has told me about their summers in a fixed caravan eating jam sandwiches on the south coast of England, but she wants Zoe to succeed on her own merits so deliberately hasn't told anyone else.'

Mills phone went. He automatically put his hand into his right pocket to retrieve his phone, only to remove it empty handed.

'Damn!' he exclaimed, feeling the outside of his right pocket.

'I think it's in your jacket Colin,' said Wood.

Reaching up, Mills put his hand inside his jacket and retrieved the device.

'Mills,' he said, pausing to listen to the person at the other end of the line. 'Ok, thank you.' He hung up. 'We've just been given the green light to enter the car park,' he said to Wood. 'Buckland and Rhys are greeting us over there.'

'I'll see you when you come back down,' Wood replied.

Mills nodded as he crossed over the empty main road towards the car park opposite.

\*\*\*

'It's safer if we walk up the main exit ramp,' said Rhys as Mills approached him and Buckland who were stood waiting.

'Can we give Dee a moment to join us before we head up?' Mills asked the two men. He glanced round the area trying to locate his partner.

'Sure,' replied Buckland. 'I forgot to ask you earlier how the arrest went?'

'Without resistance,' replied Mills. 'And he was silent all the way back to the station. Only spoke to answer the questions Neil asked him during processing. I've got them keeping an eye on him.'

'Jesus!' exclaimed Rhys.

'Do you think he's going to try anything?' Buckland asked.

'I don't know,' replied Mills, shaking his head. 'But if he is responsible for all of this, then I'm not taking any chances by giving him the easy way out. He must be held accountable.'

He looked up and saw Dee approaching them.

'Sorry. Thanks for waiting for me,' she said. 'No problem,' said Mills.

'Watch your feet,' said Buckland as the group started to approach the car park.

Sure enough, no sooner had they started their ascent up the ramp they could see that Buckland wasn't over exaggerating. There were a few empty parking spaces on the first floor, but most of the now windowless vehicles were empty.

'How is Lee and her unit?' Mills asked Dee as they started their slow ascent.

'They're Ok,' said Dee. 'Shaken like everyone else who witnessed the explosion. The blast knocked her off her feet, and she landed on her radio.'

They turned right and walked along behind the parked vehicles before turning left to start their walk up to the upper floor. Blood was already visible.

'I should warn you now,' said Buckland. 'It gets worse from here on up.'

'We can only go as far as the top of the ramp,' added Rhys. 'There isn't enough room to get beyond that point until the rubble has been fully cleared, but that probably won't be completed until late tomorrow morning.'

'My God!' exclaimed Dee. 'Is this Bosnia?'

On reaching the top of the ramp the party stopped. In front of them was the rubble from the roof, which had crushed all but the car in the far corner opposite the exit ramp. To the left where the stairwell wall used to be was an empty hole, revealing another giant hole in what would have been the stairwells outside wall. The pay meters were mangled and black, with coins everywhere and a pool of blood radiating outwards from their location in every direction between the glass and debris. They could just make out the crushed and charred frame of what had been the car bomb.

'It was deliberately parked in that location, next to the stairs and pay meters,' said Buckland. 'It's a space for disabled badge holders that allows for a bigger car and easier access to the exit.'

'Are there any cameras that look over the area?' asked Dee hopefully.

'No,' continued Buckland. 'The CCTV only covers the pay meters in here.'

'Damn!' exclaimed Mills.

William had now joined the group at the top of the ramp.

'Looking at what remains of the car, I'm confident you will be able to retrieve the chassis number Buckland' he said.

Buckland nodded.

'Well, that's something at least,' said Mills. 'Do we have any idea of the current numbers?'

'At least thirty dead, a further forty seriously injured plus numerous other casualties.' replied Rhys solemnly.

'Is there anything else you need me and Dee to do at this stage?' Mills said after a moment.

'No, I don't think so,' said Buckland. 'I'll have a wait myself until I can get anywhere near that vehicle, and that's before all the DNA testing on the blood that we may sadly need to identify a few individuals.'

The group of officers fell silent for a moment. 'Me and my team will try and find anything and everything that we can,' said Buckland.

'And we will help,' said William.

Rhys nodded in agreement.

'Thank you for your offer gentlemen, but you need to be mobile in a second's notice,' said Mills. 'Wood, Jons and the others are outside.'

'Go and get some rest, both of you,' said Buckland. 'It'll be dawn in a few hours.'

'Just before we go, we will need teams to head out to the James residence and the other houses in the company portfolio for a routine sweep in the morning,' said Mills. 'But it is of utmost importance that the James house is checked whilst his son is at school.'

'Right,' said Buckland.

'Ideally, I want you to accompany Dee and myself to the James house. Do you think you'll be finished here and able?' asked Mills.

'If it means ending this madness, I'll gladly forgo sleep,' said Buckland seriously. 'I'll organise the second unit we need once were finished here.'

'Allow me to escort you back down,' said Rhys.

'That would be much appreciated. Thank you,' said Dee.

Mills was stood staring ahead, trying to retain as much visual information as he could.

'Come on Colin,' said Dee, touching his shoulder. 'Time to go.'

Leaving Buckland and William at the top of the ramp, Mills, Dee, and Rhys started heading back down the exit ramp. As they exited the car park and headed over in the direction of the police cars, Mills could make out the figures of Damien and his friends stood in front of a camera, with Austin holding up his newly bandaged arm to the lens.

*Appalling circumstances to receive your fifteen minutes,* he thought to himself as they neared their vehicle. *But no surprises.*

# 22.

Officer Grant undid the observation window at the front of Joes custody cell and looked inside.

He had been observing Joe every twenty minutes as Mills had instructed them to do so and had found him in the exact same position every time; sat on his bed staring at the wall opposite him.

'He's got nothing on him he shouldn't have,' said Officer Neil reassuringly and Grant shut the observation window again.

'I know, I was the one who searched him,' Grant replied. 'He's just sat in there staring at the wall. Usually, the people that come through here are either shouting, crying, screaming or being sick. This guy, nothing.'

'Best check our other guest whilst we are here,' said Neil.

He walked over to Malcolm's cell and undid the window in the door.

'Good evening, Officer,' said Malcolm. 'I wonder if I may be permitted to have some time in your custody exercise yard?'

'Are you sure? It's pretty cold out there,' Neil replied.

'I will weather any temperature for some fresh air and a glance at the night sky, if I may?' Malcolm said.

'One moment please,' said Neil.

He closed the observation window and walked back in the direction of the custody suite entrance. After unlocking the door between the cells and the entrance, he walked up towards the custody officer on the desk.

'James has just asked for some time in the exercise yard Shaun. What should I tell him?' asked Neil.

'Certainly, although you'll have to be handcuffed whilst being escorted,' came the reply.

'Right. Ok,' said Neil. 'Thanks.'

Feeling somewhat embarrassed that he'd forgotten a significant part of his job, Neil re-joined Grant in the main area of the custody suite. Grant watched him as he took out his handcuffs and headed in the direction of Malcolm's cell. Neil undid the observation window again.

'If you could please place your hands through this window Mr James, it will allow me to put these handcuffs on safely before escorting you to the exercise yard.'

Malcolm silently headed over to the door and did as he was instructed.

'Step back please and I can unlock the cell door,' said Neil.

Once outside the cell, Neil escorted Malcolm through the custody suite. They passed the other holding cells and through another locked door that led them outside to the exercise yard.

Malcolm breathed in the cold night air deeply as Neil removed his handcuffs.

'Which way is east please?' he asked.

'That way,' Neil replied, pointing. 'I'll be stood just over here.'

Malcolm nodded as the officer took up his position by the door. After a moments silent prayer, he looked upwards.

'I see Sirius is glowing tonight,' he said. 'Although I fear my dog days are upon me now before the summer.'

'Did you say Sirius?' asked Officer Neil.

'Yes. In the Canis Major constellation. The brightest star in the sky. Look.'

He pointed out the star to Neil.

'How do you know this?' he asked Malcolm. Malcolm smiled at him.

'Oh, my son Samuel chose to do a project on stars and constellations for school,' he said.

'I was ignorant of the knowledge up until then, but after that it has remained with me. My wife even bought me a telescope later that year.'

Neil had started to rub his hands together. 'It's cold out here, isn't it?' he said.

'Well, I am ready to return inside now whenever you are Officer,' said Malcolm.

He walked towards Neil with his hands out ready to be cuffed again before being led back to his cell.

\*\*\*

'Can I Drop you home?' asked Mills as he drove. 'Your cars in the safest car park around.'

'The irony that would be,' replied Dee. 'If someone picked tonight to try and raid the stations car park.'

'Best of luck to them if they did,' said Mills. 'Donovan's like the guard dog of the place. A Bullmastiff no less!'

Dee smiled.

'Well, I'm not going to say no to remaining a passenger,' she said. 'I am extremely tired now, not that the cat will leave me alone when I get in! Are you a dog or a cat person?'

'Neither,' said Mills. 'It's my wife I'll get it from, and not in a purring and affectionate way I'm afraid. She'll no doubt have to say her piece before I'm allowed to sleep.'

Dee smiled.

'What about your partner?' Mills asked her.

'She understands,' said Dee. 'This just better not become a habit.'

'Quite,' said Mills.

He stopped the car in front of Dee's front door. 'You best go inside and get some rest,' he said. 'I'll see you at the Darby house in a few hours. Do you want me to drive you over there in the morning as your cars still at the station?'

'To be honest Colin, I'll probably need the walk to wake me up enough to function properly' Dee replied, getting out of the car and leaning on the open door. 'But please, please bring coffee!'

'Done!' replied Mills. 'I'll get several, I think. Buckland is bound to need some. Remind me if I haven't done it already to issue the statement relating to the car park would you please?'

'Sure,' replied Dee with a smile.

She shut the passenger door and walked up the half a dozen steps to her front door. Mills watched her enter the house safely before driving away.

Dee shut the front door as quietly as she could. With her back turned and her mind elsewhere she didn't notice their cat Sabrina run silently towards her and position herself between her feet. Dee nearly tripped over the cat as she made her way into the hallway.

'Jesus Sabrina!' she exclaimed. 'You scared me, you silly thing.'

The cat sat down and looked at her as Dee removed her shoes.

'Yes, Yes I'm coming,' she said.

Dee scooped up the cat in her arms and tickled its stomach.

With the sound of contented purring, she carried Sabrina to the far end of the flat and into the bedroom. She placed the cat quietly on the floor as she made her way over to the left side of the bed. Her partner Dawn was fast asleep, curled up tightly in the duvet. She had left the bedside lamp on for Kate, something they had always done since moving in together. Dee's hours were a lot more antisocial than her own.

Dee wondered over to the chest of drawers near her and opened it as quietly as she could. Having retrieved her clean underwear for tomorrow, she quietly walked back over to her side of the bed and sat down. She then methodically undressed and left a neat pile of clothes on the floor, before gently lowering herself into bed next to Dawn. She rolled onto her side and turned the light out before rolling back onto her back. She then felt four paws run up her legs and over her stomach before Sabrina sat down on her chest and began to purr again.

Dee stroked their cat in the darkness of the bedroom.

'OK, OK,' she whispered. 'But Mummy desperately needs some sleep.'

***

Having abandoned his vehicle on the road outside his house with none of his usual precision, Mills had then been blinded by their security light as he approached his house.

After his promotion to Chief Inspector, his wife had insisted they take extra security measures.

Mills had argued that he thought it drew more attention to the property, but like most debates with his wife he eventually conceded.

With next doors dog barking loudly outside having been disturbed, he shut the front door and typed in the security code on the house alarm panel. No matter what time or circumstance he returned home in, he would never forget those numbers. They were chosen deliberately as it was their sons date of birth. He wondered down the hallway and into the kitchen. He picked up the nearest glass that was upturned on the draining board and filled it with cold water. The effect of the dust and debris from the car park had made his mouth extremely dry.

He drank all the first glass before placing it back under the tap and filling it again. Heading out of the kitchen and back toward the front door carrying his drink, he walked around the lower banister and up the stairs.

'I wish you'd take those boots off when you come in,' came a voice when he reached the top of the stairs. 'Now I'm awake.'

Mills said nothing as he crossed the landing, past their son's bedroom door and into his own.

His wife, Joy, was sat up in bed staring at him as he entered the room.

'Your son's getting hard time at school. Did you know that?' she said.

Mills could tell instantly by the tone in her voice that she was tired and irritated.

'The other kids keep teasing him about his father being useless at his job, and that we're all going to be blown up!'

'It's just kids being kids,' said Mills. 'It'll stop when this is over.'

'He's not like you Colin,' Joy replied. 'He's a lot more sensitive to this stuff.'

'Look!' snapped Mills. 'I haven't got time to discuss this now. I've barely got four hours until I must be up again and back at work.'

'You haven't got time to discuss your family?' countered Joy, her voice rising in growing anger.

'Look. You know I can't discuss cases with you,' said Mills, pulling on his pyjama top and pulling back the duvet. 'But I can say I think we're closer to the end now.'

'I hope so,' Joy replied. 'Right now, there's absolutely no work life balance, and our son is suffering.'

Mills rolled over with his back to Joy and closed his eyes.

'If he's up in time tomorrow, I'll talk to him before I leave. Ok?' he said.

'You best Colin,' said Joy. 'Otherwise, you and I will need a lot more serious conversation. Did you hear me, Colin?'

It was at that point she heard her husband snoring. 'Is it all worth it?' she said out loud, looking over at him.

## 23.

The early morning fog hid the tops of the trees as Claire and Holly were waiting impatiently on the doorstep for the police to arrive. Holly was rubbing her gloved hands together and leaning from one leg to another.

'Cold?' asked Claire, who stood still staring at the front door.

'No,' replied Holly. 'I need the loo! Shouldn't have had that second cup of coffee.'

'You can go in if you want,' said Claire. 'I'm just procrastinating. I'll never look at this house in the same way again after today…'

She sighed as Holly tapped her on the shoulder.

'They're here.'

Mills and Dee came walking up the driveway in unison, holding disposable coffee cups.

'Did you know someone had the audacity to call my home asking for a statement?' said Mills as they headed towards the front door where the two ladies were waiting for them.

'How on earth did a member of the press get my home phone number?'

'God only knows,' said Dee.

'Anyway, that'll keep,' said Mills.

'Good morning,' smiled Dee as the two detectives reached the front door. 'Did you manage any sleep last night?'

'No,' replied Claire.

'I'd be surprised to hear if you did,' said Mills.

'Having to write it all down did not help any,' Claire replied, handing her key to Holly. 'Please,' she asked.

Holly silently took the key from her friend and opened the front door.

'The rest of our team shall be along imminently,' said Dee as the group entered the house.

'A lot of our resources are still tied up with last night's bombing and searching additional properties,' added Mills.

'We saw what was left of the car park on the news over breakfast,' said Holly. 'Truly horrifying.'

'Even more horrifying is we know who did it. I've been sharing a bed with him,' said Claire solemnly.

They made their way straight down through the hallway towards the kitchen.

'Please excuse me a second,' said Holly, quickly running up the stairs in the direction of the bathroom.

Mills allowed Claire time to remove her coat which she placed on the nearby worktop before he spoke.

'As you know Mrs Darby,' he said. 'We are here to search the premises for evidence in relation to what we believe is a series of crimes involving improvised explosive devices. I have the necessary paperwork here.'

He put his hand in his coat pocket and took out an envelope containing the court issued search warrant.

Claire looked at Dee.

'It's just the formal legal process we have to go through before we can carry out our search,' Dee said. 'Please open it and have a look.'

Claire sighed as she opened the sealed envelope and unfolded its paper contents.

The others watched as her eyes scanned the document.

'Are you happy for us to proceed?' asked Mills.

'Yes,' replied Claire.

'Thank you,' said Mills.

'What did I miss?' Holly asked as she entered the kitchen.

'Just us giving Mrs Darby her copy of our warrant granting us consent to search the house,' said Mills. 'Once our colleagues have arrived, we will begin. I don't wish to take up any more time than is necessary.'

Holly placed her bag on the table and rummaged inside briefly before removing what she wanted.

'That reminds me, here are our completed witness statements,' she said handing them to Dee who was stood nearest to her.

'You did fill these out independently as instructed, didn't you?' asked Dee. 'Otherwise, they will be invalid, and you'll have to do others under supervision at the station.'

'We did,' said Claire with a sigh.

'Cup of tea anyone?' asked Holly as she picked up the kettle, heading in the direction of the sink.

\*\*\*

Dan and Peter were talking to each other whilst walking up the steps outside the social sciences building.

'Have you heard anything from Joe this morning?' Dan asked Peter as they neared the entrance.

'Nothing since we parted company last night,' said Peter.

'I did try and get hold of him earlier, but his phone went straight to answerphone,' said Dan. 'He's not as proficient in the art of school nights out as the present company.'

'No,' replied Peter dismissively, his mind preoccupied.

They entered the building and headed to the right. They had to pass Joe's office to get to either of theirs or the staff room beyond.

'I'll give him a knock Pete,' said Dan, pausing in front of Joes office door whilst Peter continued walking.

'Ok,' Peter replied walking past 'I'll be in my office.'

Dan gave Peter a quick army salute, raising his right hand to his temple before knocking on Joe's office door.

'He's not there,' said Dan, entering Peters office a few moments later.

Peter was sat behind his desk checking his emails on the computer.

'Really?' he replied in a surprised tone. 'Let me check if Claire's in.'

He picked up the receiver of the phone on his desk and dialled the four-digit internal link number to the chemistry department.

'Morning Clara, it's Peter from social sciences. Is Claire in this morning?'

Dan looked on as Peter paused to hear Kelly's response to his question.

'Ok. Thanks.'

He then put the phone down.

'Claire's not in either, and she too hasn't contacted Clara or anyone in their department to tell them.'

'Strange,' said Dan. 'Do you think everything's alright?'

'I hope so,' Peter replied. 'But we haven't got time to muse on the Darby's. They've probably overslept or something stupid.' He paused for a moment. 'Better get everyone in here for a quick staff meeting please Dan. Hopefully between us we can cover him until he shows up. We can't afford to let these kids get any more behind.'

***

The forensics teams white Van pulled up and parked along the bottom of the driveway. Though their presence had yet to be noticed in the neighbourhood, that didn't mean that they hadn't been spotted at all. Plenty of commuters had already spotted them on their morning travels, no doubt wondering what had happened. Who had passed of unnatural causes or suspicious circumstances whilst they were at home asleep?

After the Van had pulled in and parked outside the Darby's house, three people exited the vehicle. They opened the doors at the back of the van and began to suit up in their protective cover all suits, masks, and gloves. Once they had done this one of them headed towards the entrance of the house to speak to Mills who was stood waiting at the front door.

Immediately Mills recognised the figure approaching him.

'Morning Buckland. I presume you have everything we need for a comparative investigation?' he asked.

'Sure do,' Buckland replied. 'I made sure we had some presumptive test kits for initial analysis as I know we need to move quickly on this and sent the same over with the second unit to James's house.'

'Perfect,' Mills replied. 'Have you had much sleep?'

'Barely three hours,' Buckland replied.

'I meant to grab you a coffee earlier, but it completely slipped my mind,' said Mills.

'No bother,' said Buckland. 'Luckily, we had some fresh faces I could call in to help be my eyes on this one this morning as were spread over a few properties.'

'Alright for some,' commented Mills. 'We want to concentrate on trace evidence and chemical residue that matches the manufacture and storage of TACP. Hopefully we will also find fibres belonging to the suspect at the same time.'

'That's great,' Buckland replied. 'Once we have finished, I am optimistic that we will have some swabs to take back to the lab for further analysis and confirmation.'

'I do hope so,' said Mills.

Behind them, the rest of the team had placed Hazard tape around the property. One was approaching the house with yellow evidence markers and a case full of equipment. Bringing up the rear was the forensic photographer, carrying a thirty-five-millimetre camera to capture overall, midrange and close up pictures of whatever they found. The group of scientists paused just outside the front door awaiting Mills and Buckland's instructions.

'I would like to begin our search in the office upstairs and proceed from there,' said Mills. 'You shall see why when we enter. Please follow me.'

Dee headed into the kitchen from her position in the hallway. Claire was sat on a breakfast stool, with Holly putting the dishes away.

'Just to let you ladies know, our team have now arrived and are in a position to formally start our search' she said.

Holly looked over at Claire, who smiled weakly at her.

'I know it's not an easy thing to hear. It's never easy to say it. I'll keep popping back to see you every now and again throughout,' said Dee.

'Thank-you,' replied Claire.

Just as Dee was leaving the kitchen to re-join her colleagues Claire called after her.

'Officer Dee!'

Dee reappeared in the kitchen doorway. 'Yes Claire?' she asked.

'Whilst I think of it, don't forget to check the garage. It's been Joe's dumping ground for years. The complete opposite of his office, I can assure you of that.'

Dee turned and smiled at her.

'When were you last in there Claire?' she asked.

'Oh, I couldn't tell you,' Claire replied. 'I got fed up arguing with him about the mess, so I just stopped going in.'

'I understand,' Dee replied. 'Thank you for your help.'

Dee left the kitchen and headed through the hallway and up the stairs. She found Mills and Buckland talking on the upstairs landing just outside the office.

"Did you manage to uncover anything of significance last night after we left you?' Mills asked.

'Not a lot as we feared,' said Buckland. 'However, we did manage to get the chassis number of the vehicle. Hughes and Donovan are looking into it this morning whilst we are here.'

'Good,' said Mills as stepped through the doorway into the office. 'That's something.'

'We need everything photographed, tagged and bagged please,' said Buckland to his team. 'Particularly the articles on the floor as they are.'

'We can have Justin look at the computer when we get back,' said Dee. 'Once it's been photographed just unplug it and take it with you when we leave, please.'

'Make sure you also go through the various books and box files on the shelf as well,' added Mills.

'Might it be worth us heading down to the garage to continue our search ahead of the team before they start the rest of the house?' Dee asked. 'Claire has just referred to it as her husband's dumping ground and has barely been in it.'

'Good idea,' said Mills.

'I'll oversea the team up here,' said Buckland. 'Once we've completed a search of all the upstairs rooms we will come down and join you.'

'I'd start with the spare room,' suggested Mills. 'I think based on what we've already found, there's more likely to be something hidden in there than in the master bedroom.'

'I agree,' said Dee.

She took a few steps across the landing and walked over to the entrance of the room.

Glancing in she saw a double bed with storage drawers' underneath with oak beside tables either side. Two lamps, one on each table matched the light shade attached to the ceiling that carried a floral theme. Running along the far back wall was a fixed wardrobe. It was the height and width of the room. Two sets of double doors were separated by a single door in its middle.

'Maybe start with that wardrobe?' she said to Buckland. 'Hopefully that's where he's hidden the clothing.'

'We shall look shortly,' Buckland replied.

'If you need us, we'll be in the garage,' said Mills as they approached the top of the stairs.

'I'd wait a second if I were you,' came a voice from inside the office.

Buckland dipped his head inside the room before motioning for Mills and Rhys to accompany him.

'Mills. Dee. You both need to see this.'

The two detectives accompanied Buckland back inside the office. Rested on the desk in the space Joe's computer had previously occupied was an open box folder. One of the forensic team was stood beside it.

'And we've only just begun.'

He sidestepped to allow them to approach the desk.

Placed directly behind him on the tabletop was a printed document.

'Wasted Youth,' Mills read out loud. 'Extremists throughout history have grossly miscalculated. One sporadic explosion is not enough.'

He looked at Dee, a mixture of shock and horror appearing on her face.

'To help end the wasted youth and safeguard our country from the hands of so called higher educated delinquents, join our cause! Visit double-u, double-u, double-u, dot wasted youth dot blogspot dot com.'

'What do you think he means by wasted youth?' Dee asked. 'Students?'

'Could be. It also says here at the bottom there will be unavoidable collateral damage,' said Mills still reading the document.

Dee shuddered.

'The rest of the box file next to you also contains dozens of the same document,' said Buckland. 'This is definitely significant.'

Mills turned and scratched his head.

'Tear this room apart piece by piece,' he said. 'We shall head downstairs to the garage as planned. It's getting a little crowded in here, and it's crucial we gather this evidence correctly.'

## 24.

'Well, this takes practical training to a whole new level,' said Murray Boyd as he opened and held the gate open for his colleagues.

'It's not ideal is it, Murray?' said Daniel Robin. 'This is only the second time I've led a team in the field. But put it this way, if we do this properly and professionally it'll help our careers no end.'

'Whoosh,' said Murray, miming an aeroplane gaining altitude with his right hand.

'Enough now,' said Daniel reaching up and pressing the doorbell. Both men saw movement in the hallway through the glass in the front door, before the sound of the front door being unbolted from the inside.

'Good morning, Mrs James,' said Daniel as Nadia greeted them at the door. 'I am Daniel Robin, acting head of forensics. May we come in please?'

Nadia silently opened the door to reveal the figure of Taz stood next to her.

'This is Taz Abdullah, our family solicitor,' she said as the two officers entered the property.

'I am here to check the necessary paperwork is in order before accompanying you Gentlemen throughout your search of the property, presuming that's ok?' said Taz.

'Certainly,' replied Daniel, handing Nadia a sealed envelope. 'This contains all the relevant paperwork.'

Nadia handed it straight to Taz.

'One moment Gentlemen please,' he said as he stepped into the living room followed by Nadia.

Daniel and Murray stood silently surveying their surroundings as they waited for their return. Both men were stood looking up at the four Arabic passages on the wall when Taz and Nadia re-entered the hallways.

'Those are known as the four quls,' said Taz. 'Protecting Surahs.'

Daniel and Murray both smiled at him.

'I assume that you have now both fully read and understood the paperwork I presented to Mrs James?' asked Daniel. 'We shall soon commence searching your properly looking for materials relating to the manufacture and storage of TACP. Are you happy for us to proceed?'

'Yes. I am,' replied Nadia. 'Please excuse me.' She disappeared back into the living room.

'Our colleagues shall be entering the property shortly,' said Murray. 'If you have any questions about what we are doing during our search, please do not hesitate to ask us.'

'Thank you,' replied Taz.

Daniel had left the other two men in the hallway and was currently glancing around the kitchen at the back of the property.

'Are there any freestanding buildings in the garden?' he asked.

'None whatsoever,' Taz replied entering the kitchen behind him.

'In that case it won't take long for us to check the garden before starting at the rear of the property and work our way through,' replied Daniel.

'There is a side gate in which your colleagues could enter the house if that would assist you?' said Taz. 'It's a double gated entranceway.'

'If we could, that would help significantly,' Daniel replied.

'I'll have a tent erected directly outside the gates to shield the back garden from view,' said Murray.

'One minute please gentlemen,' said Taz. He left the kitchen and headed back down the hallway into the living room to speak to Nadia.

***

A concrete step led into the conservatory from the short, recently cut grass that filled most of the houses back garden. Satisfied that they had completed their search outside, the forensic team were just beginning to relocate their equipment inside. One white sofa and a telescope pointing towards the glass ceiling occupied the room, with most of its wooden floorboards obscured by a Persian rug. Taz had remained with the team from the moment they entered the property, watching the forensic photographer take multiple photographs of the room. No one had told him yet that he could not be present.

'After we are all finished in this area, then we can move into the room,' said Daniel to his team.

'The art decor in this house is wonderful,' commented Murray, pointing towards a painting depicting a man sat in a mosque reading the Koran illuminated by sunlight. A White sofa ran the length of one wall beside the door. Opposite from it in one alcove sat a wooden toy box. Fixed inside another alcove were three bookshelves, all filled with leather bound books.

'Once we've completed our search of this room, we'll head into the kitchen behind that wall,' said Daniel, entering the room with the rest of his team following closely behind.

Taz stood in the doorway watching the scientists methodically working. One opened the toy box lid and brought out a yellow digger.

'Some toys just hold too many memories to be parted with,' he said. 'That used to be Samuels.'

'Yes,' said Nadia appearing from behind him. 'It's moved dirt, sand, leaves and gravel to name but a few things. Do any of you require any refreshments?'

'No thank you,' said Daniel, walking towards her. 'We're about to enter your kitchen shortly.'

'Very well,' she replied before exiting the room.

On their way out of the room, the team noticed a door to a room located under the stairs.

'Downstairs toilet,' said Taz. 'Not a lot of room, particularly for taller persons such as yourselves.'

'I'll look around and we'll photograph it,' said Murray.

'Thank you, Murray,' said Daniel. 'We shall make a start in the kitchen. After you Mr Abdullah.'

Taz led the rest of the scientists into the kitchen. Large clean pans were currently occupying a large area of one of its worktops. Steel utensils hung from a metal rack within reaching distance of a large electric cooking hob.

'That's the most incredible spice rack I think I've ever seen,' said Daniel as he surveyed the room.

'Thank you,' said Nadia, filling a cut glass with water from the sink and taking a sip. 'Makes no difference to Samuel. Fish and chips are his all-time favourite meal.'

Everyone in the room tittered at her remark.

'Do you Gentlemen have any idea how long it will take you to search the rest of the house?' Taz asked, glancing at his watch.

'Presuming that all the rooms are as the two previous rooms we have been, we could be done around midday,' replied Daniel.

'The reason I ask is that I'm conscious Nadia and myself don't miss Dhuhr,' said Taz. 'Particularly under these circumstances.'

'Forgive my ignorance sir,' said Murray. 'But what is Dhuhr?'

'Dhuhr is the name given to our midday prayers Officer,' replied Taz.

'Even if we have to temporarily pause our search, I can assure both of you that you will be able to pray at this time,' said Daniel, looking at Taz reassuringly.

'Thank you,' he replied.

'I too am most appreciative,' added Nadia.

\*\*\*

Mills and Dee opened the inside door that led to the garage and surveyed the space in front of them. On the back wall was a metal shelving rack filled with various items. Next to that was a metal cabinet. Leaning on the opposite wall near to the cabinet was a fold up chair. Below the shelving units were old car hub caps, car mats, the empty packaging from a wind deflector box and some discarded car headrests.

'Likes his cars then,' remarked Dee.

'Well with no kids and his salary he can afford to,' said Mills, heading towards the metal cabinet. 'I always wanted a Porsche nine eleven myself'.'

Dee smiled as she turned to look at the items on the shelves.

'Engine Oil. Antifreeze. WD40. Gloss paint. Nothing out of the ordinary.'

Mills opened the cabinet in front of him.

'I think I've found the home chemistry lab Kate,' he said. 'Come and look.'

Dee wondered over to join her colleague.

There was only one shelf in the unit, deliberately placed at desk height. Upon it was various distilling equipment, vials full of chemicals, and a Bunsen burner. A tube ran from its base down the back on the shelf and into the gas canister sat in the bottom of the cabinet. A pile of the small steel plumbing tubes, sealed at one end and complete with a fuse in the other was also on the floor.

'So, what are the odds of these being innocent home experiments with completely different chemicals?' she asked Mills.

'Extremely slim,' he replied, taking a step back and glancing up at the top of the cabinet.

'What is it?' Dee asked.

'See those ten litre emulsion tubs?' he asked. 'There used to be at least two others up there, maybe more. You can see the dust marks around where they were if you look closely.'

Dee stepped further forward and leant up onto her tip toes.

'So, you can,' she replied. 'There were probably other tubs on top and underneath the shelving unit by the looks of things, and there's similar dust markings to the left if you look.'

'Nobody needs to store this amount of emulsion paint,' said Mill. 'Not even professional decorators.'

Buckland entered the garage.

'The team haven't found anything in the other rooms upstairs yet,' he said. 'We even took apart the miniature lighthouse and boat in the nautical themed bathroom. Have you found anything in here?'

'Yes,' said Mills. 'We need to check the shelf in that cabinet for traces of chemicals and check the contents of these tubs,' he said.

'How many are there?' asked Buckland.

'At least two, but we suspect there were more,' Mills replied.

'Good job we brought the mobile test kit with us,' said Buckland. 'I'm afraid I'm going to have to ask you two to step outside please.'

'Any particular reason as to why?' said Mills.

'If these are tubs full of TATP, they are extremely unstable,' said Buckland.

'Fabulous,' said Mills sarcastically. 'What's the biggest area you could cover with a forensic tent?'

'If we used a multi- tent system we could obscure the front of the property from view, including the driveway,' Buckland replied.

'If we could, please,' said Mills.

Dee led Mills and Buckland back out of the garage.

'Oh no,' said Mills, glancing left out of the front door as they re-entered the hallway. 'The press scouts and wannabes have arrived.'

A group of reporters had gathered and were currently grilling a younger police officer who had been stationed outside the house for information whilst their photographers were taking pictures of the house.

'I'll get the team to assemble the tents as quick as possible,' said Buckland.

'Time to make your statement,' Dee said, turning and heading in the direction of the kitchen. 'I'll go and update Mrs Darby.'

She left Mills standing with Buckland rubbing his head.

'I was naïve to think that we could pull this off without being disturbed,' he said.

'It could be worse Colin,' said Buckland opening the front door. 'At least the television vans are yet to descend upon us!'

# 25.

Hughes had been assigned by Mills to visit the office of Hudson and James prior to searching the properties on their portfolio.

'It's a lot of work, isn't it?' said policeman Brian Davis as they walked towards the door.

'Hopefully not,' replied Hughes. 'Friends of ours recently moved into a new rental property using Hudson and James. Apparently, they mostly deal with long term tenancy agreements as well as sales which should help us.'

They entered the estate agent's office. Abbas was sat at his desk replying to an email.

'Good morning officers, please give me one second to send this,' he said, clicking the right-hand button on his computers mouse.

'Done. I am all yours,' he said, looking up.

'As I am sure you are aware, we are conducting a series of searches in connection with the arrest of your business partner Malcom James,' said Hughes as he placed a hand in his inside jacket pocket to retrieve an envelope.

'This contains written authorisation to search both the office premises, and that of those that appear on your company's portfolio.'

He handed the sealed envelope to Abbas, who placed it on the computer keyboard directly in front of him.

'Please check the paperwork, and then with your consent I can contact our forensic team and we can start our search,' said Hughes.

Abbas reluctantly picked up the sealed envelope in front of him and began to open it with his thumb.

'I'm presuming the search of Nadia and Malcolm's house left you empty handed then?' he asked as he unfolded the paper and began to skim read.

'I'm afraid I cannot discuss our findings with you sir,' replied Hughes.

'I understand,' said Abbas. 'May I suggest whilst your forensic officers are carrying out their search that we start phoning people listed on our books. I'm afraid it's quite a comprehensive list, but myself and my colleagues are more than willing to assist you.'

'I appreciate that,' said Hughes. 'It cannot be easy for you folks.'

'Tyler?' called Abbas. 'Where are you?'

Tyler appeared at the back of the office. 'Yes Abbas?' he asked.

'Is there any possibility you can assist myself and these gentlemen making phone calls?' Abbas replied. 'Do you happen to know if Natasha and Ruth are still on the premises?'

'I believe Ruth had an early viewing appointment at one of the vacant properties,' Tyler replied.

'And Natasha?' asked Abbas.

'Just nipped out to get us some fresh milk,' said Tyler. 'She'll be back any moment.'

'Great,' replied Abbas. 'It appears we can offer you even more assistance officers.'

\*\*\*

Donovan was in the police station conference room with the previous owner of the car whilst a sketch artist was busy setting up their equipment. He had managed to track him down via the DVLA records, and it just so happened he was able to come down to the station almost immediately.

'Thank you so much for coming in so quickly Mr Lewis,' he said. 'As you know, we've invited you in today to help us make a facial composite of the man who bought your vehicle, but would you mind answering some quick additional questions before that starts?'

'Certainly,' Mr Lewis replied. 'But there's not much to tell. He was just Mr average. No outstanding features or charisma. He was wearing a woollen hat if that helps.'

'Did he give you a name?' Donovan asked. 'Yes. Robert Smith.'

Donovan jotted down the name on a piece of paper.

'As I was telling my wife,' Lewis continued. 'Unlike the other folks who came and looked at the car before him, he didn't want to know half of the information that the others asked.'

'How do you mean?' asked Donovan.

'Well, you expect people to ask if I was the only owner, if I had the vehicles full-service history, that type of question.'

'And he didn't?' Donovan replied curiously.

'No. Quite the opposite actually. He just looked in the boot, asked if the back seats folded down and then offered me ninety five percent of the asking price in cash.'

'That's different,' remarked Donovan. The sketch artist nodded at him.

'Ok, I think you're ready to go, do you both need anything? Tea, Coffee?' Donovan asked.

'A glass of water please if it's not too much trouble?' said Mr Lewis.

'Certainly,' Donovan replied. 'Marcus?'

'No, I'm fine thanks Donovan,' the artist replied, taking a seat next to Mr Lewis at the conference table.

'Ok. Back in a moment,' said Donovan as he stepped out of the conference room and closed the door behind him. Both met sat at the table smiled at each other before one of them spoke.

'Hi Mr Lewis. How are you? I am Marcus Tim, a forensic sketch artist with the police force here. My plan is to work with you on a composite sketch of the man who bought your vehicle from you. To begin, can you please describe in your own words what the person looked like?'

'He had white skin. I couldn't tell you for certain what colour hair he had as he was wearing a woollen hat.

'That's ok,' Marcus replied. 'Go on.'

'He had blue eyes. I'd say he was in his mid-forties. I also noted that the man looked tired, with a few days' stubble on his face.'

'Great. Thank you,' said Marcus.

He picked up the book in front of him, opened it, and pushed it over the tables top towards Mr Lewis.

'This is a facial recognition comparison reference book,' he said. 'Please have a look through it until you find a similar face we can use as a start off point.'

Lewis scanned the various faces looking out at him in the book. He flipped the first page over and continued. He then went to flip over the next page but changed his mind when he spotted a face on the side he was lifting.

'He looked a bit like that,' he said, placing his hand under the picture he had spotted.

'Great,' said Marcus. 'Please give me a moment to use this and your initial description to work up a first sketch.'

Buckland knocked on the door and re-entered the room.

'Your water sir,' he said, placing the glass on the table beside Mr Lewis, who picked it up and took a sip.

'Thank you,' Lewis replied before picking up the glass and taking a sip.

'Have a look at this,' said Marcus, showing his sketch book to Lewis.

'Not bad at all,' he said. 'His hat was pulled down lower over his eyes though.'

'Ok. Any other changes you want me to make?' Marcus asked.

'Yes,' said Lewis. 'His skin was a lot darker around his eyes. Judging by that and his voice I would say he was sleep deprived.'

'One moment,' said Marcus, amending his sketch.

'It's not surprising he's in trouble really,' Lewis remarked. 'As I've always told my wife, fatigue is the demon's playground.'

Marcus's pencil stopped moving. 'Ok. I think we are finished.'

He showed the picture to Lewis again. 'Is that better?' he asked.

'That is very, very good,' Lewis replied. 'I can definitely say that's what the man who bought my car looked like.'

'Great,' said Marcus, taking the sketch back. 'I am now going to sign and date the sketch, and if you are happy, please sign and date the back.'

He added the details to his picture before turning it over and passing it back to Lewis, along with the pencil.

'May I ask what the reason for my signing this is?' said Lewis.

'It can be entered into evidence if you do,' replied Marcus.

'I see,' Lewis replied before signing and dating the paper.

Marcus stood up.

'Thank you, Mr Lewis, we are done,' he said, offering the man his hand.

Lewis stood up and shook it.

'We're all finished then?' asked Donovan, who had been standing quietly in the corner of the room so as not to disturb the men. 'Please allow me to see you out.'

'Thank you,' said Mr Lewis. 'That's very kind.'

Donovan opened and held the door before following Lewis out of the conference room.

## 26.

Buckland and his team, having now obscured the house from view of the growing crowd outside, had set up their equipment and moved one of the tubs into the centre of the garage floor having opened the door from the inside. Mills was on the phone watching the team when Dee approached him.

'Ok. Keep me informed,' she heard him say before hanging up.

'Was that Donovan on progress on the car from last night?' she asked.

'Yes,' said Mills. 'They tracked down the registered owner of the vehicle via the DVLA only to be told he had sold it a week previously. The buyer paid in cash and never registered as the vehicle's new owner.'

'Interesting,' replied Dee.

'Smart,' commented Mills. 'Thankfully, the previous owner was able to go straight in. He sat down with a sketch artist at the station and having looked at the completed composite sketch. Donovan is almost certain it's Darby.'

'That's good,' replied Dee, watching the team of forensic scientists carefully extracting a sample from inside the second paint tub. 'Why would he not lock that cabinet do you think?'

'It automatically looks suspicious,' replied Mills. 'If it's not locked then people can't make assumptions that the other person wants the contents hidden. Being in the garage, Claire would simply have assumed that it's full of junk and not bothered to check.'

'It's so simple it's almost funny,' replied Dee.

'How's Claire?' Mills asked, watching the team of forensic officers repositioning a tent.

'Not good, as to be expected,' Dee replied. 'Thank heavens she's not going through this all alone.'

Buckland approached the two of them.

'Well as we all suspected we found traces of chemicals all over the shelf, but no fingerprints I'm afraid,' he said. 'But I'm confident that the first the second tub will contain TATP.'

'Do you think the spaces on the shelving units were from other similar tubs that contained the same thing?' asked Mills.

'Probably,' responded Buckland. 'There is also the matter of the car parts. One of my team couldn't help noticing the headrests at the back of the garage.'

'What about them?' asked Mills.

'Well, he's not certain, but he's pretty sure that they aren't from either of the cars parked out front on the drive,' said Buckland.

'Then we best check the cars,' said Mills. 'I will head back inside and retrieve the keys from Mrs Darby. You and your team have got your hands full as it is.'

'Thanks,' responded Buckland. 'I'm not moving now until all the TATP has been safely removed from the premises.'

\*\*\*

Having collected the car keys from Claire, Mills let his eyes survey the kitchen.

Nothing particularly stood out, quite the opposite in fact. Monochrome coloured appliances and a dishwasher disguised as another kitchen cupboard occupied most of the room.

It was then that his eyes noticed the two pieces of paper attached to the front of the fridge with magnets. On one magnet was written that the only thing other than a best friend was a best friend with chocolate. As the Darby's had no children, he could only predict that the child's picture in the other magnet was one of their nieces or goddaughters.

He took a further step forward. On the two pieces of paper were printed two university timetables, the top one was Claire's and the one underneath Joe's.

Mills took them both out from under their magnets and observed them one at a time in his hand.

'We'll need to take these,' he said.

'That's fine,' replied Claire. 'I can easily print another copy, and Joe won't be needing his anytime soon.'

\*\*\*

'Thank heavens we've been able to narrow it down to just two properties,' said Hughes to Brian as they drove across the city. 'Although I do find it slightly odd that no one seems to have gone on holiday though.'

'Maybe all the tenants don't like airports,' replied Brian. 'I hate them, particularly the ridiculously big international ones. I end up spending more killing time before the flight then I do whilst I'm on holiday.'

Hughes laughed out loud. 'Nervous flyer Bri?' he asked.

'Yes. I admit that I do need a few before I can get on a plane.'

'Did you read that article about the popularity of the staycation amongst the A listers?' Hughes asked. 'That's probably contributed too.'

'What's a staycation?' asked Davis.

'American term for a holiday at home,' Hughes replied.

'Ahh, I see,' Davis replied. 'Did Robin say if they have found anything at the James' house?'

'Nothing,' said Hughes. 'Not even a shred of evidence James had anything to do with this.'

'Oh dear,' Davis replied.

'I'd give Mills a wide birth if you can,' said Hughes. 'Unfortunately, I'll have no choice but to report back to him.'

'That Natasha was nice, wasn't she?' said Davis, glancing at Hughes.

'Can't say I'd noticed Brian,' Hughes replied.

'Oh, I know you did!' said Davis giggling. 'Unless I'm riding shotgun to a corpse!'

'Now now!' said Hughes. 'Maintain the professionalism, Bri. Didn't they say one property is completely unfurnished, or did I mishear that?'

'No, I am certain the estate agents said it was indeed unfurnished,' replied Davis. 'Shouldn't take the team long to go through.'

'Makes it more important to concentrate on both the garage and loft space in that case,' said Hughes, slowing the car as they approached a traffic light ascending from amber to red.

'I'm sure Robin and Boyd will be relieved,' said Davis.

'Can you remember what they said about the second property?' asked Hughes.

'Where were you?' Davis asked him. 'You were sat no further away from them that I was!'

'Don't forget I've been running this gauntlet with Mills as soon as the first call came into the station Bri,' replied Hughes.

'I'll shut up then, shall I?' said Davis, smiling at his colleague awkwardly. 'In answer to your question,

I think the other property is presently occupied. I'm amazed that Mr Hudson went as far as telling us they recently had contractual work done to replace the landing floorboards.'

'It's extremely rare,' said Hughes. 'But thank heavens! Makes our lives considerably easier.

## 27.

After a thorough search of Claire's car, Dee closed the boot and locked the vehicle.

'There's a logbook and a pack of tissues in the glove box. Oh, and a used coffee cup and a pair of sunglasses in the driver's side door,' she said, walking back towards Mills who was inspecting the outside of the other car.

'Nothing then. That doesn't surprise me,' he said. 'What about the headrests?'

'All in the car,' Dee replied.

'Best check in here then,' said Mills.

He unlocked the other vehicle and, having put on a pair of gloves, sat in the driver's seat of Joes car, and put the key in the ignition. He hit the button that turns on the car stereo and gradually increased the volume.

'The local city radio station,' he said to Dee, who had walked round and was stood next to him outside the car.

'He's probably been listening to the regular news updates to check our progress,' she replied.

'That would be my guess too,' Mills said. He opened the glove box. 'Nothing in there.'

'Is there a storage department underneath the passenger seat?' Dee asked him, walking round the bonnet of the car to the other side. 'We found a lot of different things stashed in them during my time with the roads policing unit. Drugs, needles, knives, even a taser once.'

'Be my guest,' said Mills as he watched his colleague open the department she had described.

'Nothing.'

'Where's the internal boot release switch?' asked Mills.

His eyes scanned the dashboard and round the various controls surrounding the steering wheels.

'Got it!' he exclaimed before pressing the switch.

'Nothing under the seat either,' said Dee as Mills watched the boot open in the car's rear-view mirror.

'And all the headrests are here too.'

'Then they definitely came from another vehicle then,' replied Mills.

He climbed out of the driver's seat and walked to the back of the car to look at the contents of the boot. 'Another archive box,' he said, removing the lid to look inside. 'This one actually contains only paperwork for a change by the looks of it.'

'I think this is how he's been transporting the bombs all along,' said Dee. 'Just like in his office, he's probably been hiding the explosives under the paperwork. If he was ever stopped and searched, you'd just assume it was a box full of university papers he was returning.'

Mills put the lid back on the box and lifted it out.

'What's that?' said Dee, leaning into the boot space and picking up a small rectangular piece of white paper as Mills placed the archive box on the driveway behind the car.

'It's a New Start charity shop receipt,' replied Mills. Several purchases were made, although they never list the actual items, only their classification area. Toys, clothes etcetera.'

Mills took out his phone, hit redial and held it up to his ear.

'Jons? It's Mills,' Dee heard him say. 'I need you to go to the New Start charity shop and request their CCTV footage. We are looking to identify Darby as a customer. Once you have that, take it back to Justin at the station for analysis. You can then compare it all with Darby's mug shot and the footage we have from the previous bombings.'

He paused to listen to Jons reply. 'Very good,' he continued.

He hung up and turned his attention back to the car.

'Considering all the other lengths he's gone too, why would he risk leaving that?' asked Dee, still searching the vehicle.

'Distraction,' replied Mills. 'Probably before his first offence at the cinema.'

'There's nothing under the boot lining apart from the spare tire and car jack,' said Dee.

Mills watched Dee as she placed the boot liner back into position in the vehicle and shut the boot.

'Do you reckon forensics could find any trace chemicals in here? I know the bombs were concealed, but it would be great to get confirmation that they were in here,' she asked.

'I'll ask them to run it now,' said Mills. 'We will seize the vehicle anyway regardless.'

\*\*\*

Claire and Holly were stood just outside the back door when Dee and Mills re-entered the kitchen. Claire exhaled a puff of smoke into the air and waved her hand through it, directing it away from the house.

'I know I shouldn't,' she exclaimed when she caught site of the officers. 'But...'

'No need to explain,' Dee said. 'It's understandable given the circumstances you find yourself in. Take your time.'

Claire dropped and stood on the end of her cigarette to put it out. She then put it in the nearest vacant plant pot and headed back inside, closely followed by Holly.

'Have our team been in here?' Mills asked them.

'Yes, earlier' replied Holly. 'We relocated upstairs briefly whilst they were in here.'

'We must have been searching the cars at the time Colin,' said Dee.

'In that case ladies I can now inform you that we have pretty much concluded our search,' said Mills. 'We have found a significant amount of evidence to link your husband to the bombings, including explosives he manufactured here on your property. Those gentlemen who were last to arrive are members of the bomb squad.'

'We will also be seizing his car and computer along with the various other items he used and stored. You will be given a full list of what we take,' added Dee.

Claire looked at Holly before putting her head in her hands.

'Is it wrong that I am no longer shocked?' she asked, looking back up. 'I should be distraught.'

'Only you can answer that,' Mills replied.

'We will keep you up to date as things proceed,' said Dee. 'And you can call us at any time if you have any questions.'

'Thank you for your cooperation at what I know is an extremely difficult time,' Mills said. 'One of our units shall remain here with you. I'd suggest keeping a low profile until the press outside dies down. That is unless you would prefer us to chaperone you somewhere else now?'

'No, it's ok,' said Claire. 'Once I leave here, I don't think I'll be coming back.'

She glanced over at Holly who walked over to her friend. She took hold of her right hand and squeezed.

'You two take care,' Dee. 'We will talk to you soon.'

They ran into Buckland as they made their way towards the front door.

'We haven't found any of the clothing he used I'm afraid,' he said to both detectives.

'I'm not worried at this stage,' said Mills. 'We have more than enough.'

'What happened to the explosives?'

Dee asked Buckland.

'William and Rhys are taking the lead with their disposal,' he replied.

'Did you find any trace of the chemicals in the back of the car?' asked Mills.

'Not at this stage,' said Buckland. 'However, with stronger laboratory equipment we may yet find something.'

'Can one of your team drive Darby's car back with you then please?' Mills asked Buckland.

'I shall do it personally,' said Buckland.

'Drive safe,' said Dee.

Having found their way out of the forensic tent, they caught sight of the public and press gathered outside. The congregation had grown significantly larger since earlier.

'Oh hell!' exclaimed Mills. 'We haven't had time to think, let alone prepare anything else for this lot.'

'So, it's no commenting it all the way to the vehicle then?' said Dee.

'Correct,' Mills replied.

To the shouts from of the various onlookers, both detectives put their heads down and quickly walked towards their vehicle.

'Please let Buckland know the piranhas are now circling outside,' said Mills once they were safely inside the car.

# 28.

Dee yawned as they crossed the station car park and re-entered the building.

'Please excuse me Colin,' she said.

'No need for apologies Kate. Have you seen the bags under my eyes?' he replied.

'First things first. We get the coffee on. Then we sit down and go over any potential evidence our second team found at the James properties.'

'Do you know how many properties they have in their portfolio by chance?' asked Dee.

'Not a clue,' replied Mills.

Once they were upstairs, Dee immediately walked over and started picking up and turning over several clean cups on the drainer before finding one of suitable cleanliness.

'Do you think they've found anything?' she asked.

'I haven't heard anything,' replied Mills, watching as she placed the first cup below the coffee machines nozzle. 'But we should know imminently.'

Several officers entered the upstairs area with Hughes.

'We are going to sit whilst we do this aren't we?' Hughes asked Mills, heading in the direction of the conference room, the other policemen following him automatically. 'Only standings proving more difficult this week than it has in a long while.'

'No need to ask that,' Mills replied. 'We are right behind you.'

Mills and Dee entered the conference room. Two chairs had been left unoccupied just inside the door. Furthest away towards the back of the room sat Hughes, with the other officers sat between him and the detectives.

'I would like to personally thank you all for assisting us again,' said Mills after taking his seat. 'I know that most of us were at the scene last night and have had very little sleep. I made the decision to place our main forensic resources elsewhere based on what was discovered by Claire Darby in her home. I feel confident that this decision was correct based on what we found, but we still had to make sure beyond a doubt that Malcolm James was not involved in these crimes before he can be released.'

'The shorter version of what Mills is saying being did you find any evidence that links James to the bombings?' said Dee.

There was a collective giggle from everyone in the room, including Mills.

'Sorry Colin, but we're all exhausted,' she said.

'Well thankfully we've had full co-operation from everyone,' said Hughes. 'James Brother in Law Abbas Hudson was more than happy to assist us. His sister as you can imagine is distraught worrying about her son and husband.'

'No doubt,' said Dee.

'So along with Mr Hudson we telephoned everyone on their companies list asking if they had been absent from the property for any length of time or had they seen Mr James. None were able too, so that just left us with two unoccupied buildings to search.'

'And did you find anything?' asked Mills.

'No Sir,' replied officer Brian Davis, who was sat next to Hughes. 'An unfurnished building doesn't give you many places to hide things. There was nothing in the garage or the loft space as well as the house.'

'It was the same with the other property,' added police officer Lloyd Jonas. 'We were even able to check under recently laid floorboards. Again nothing.'

'And what about his house?' asked Mills.

'Well Mrs James was there. As instructed, we waited for his son Samuel to be at school,' said Hughes. 'I personally didn't attend, but Robin over here did.'

He pointed to his colleague.

'Mrs James had their Solicitor present when we carried out our search,' replied officer Robin Gunn.

'We were able to consult with those at the Darby house as to what we were looking for.'

'And?' asked Mills.

'Well, like Lloyd said. We too did a thorough sweep and found nothing that warranted further investigation. It was a perfectly normal family home,' said Robin.

'I should also add that all the alibis he gave you checked out Colin,' added Hughes. 'Donovan received dozens of pictures of him with his family in Pakistan for the funeral.'

Mills lent back in his chair.

'And we're certain there's nothing that links James to Darby?' he asked the room.

'No. Nothing. They have never crossed paths. Darby is neither the copycat nor accomplice of James. He just set him up in the hopes to evade us,' said Hughes.

'I know our first investigation into the mosque after we were presented with the leaflet fragment didn't show up anything, but what about those with the closest links to James himself?' Mills asked.

'We found two parking fines, one of which was successfully contested, and one speeding ticket,' replied Hughes. 'Other than that, nothing. Every person interviewed cooperated fully and as far as I'm concerned proved to be dedicated members of both their religious and our wider city community.'

'Then we have no more reasons to hold Malcom James,' said Mills. 'He is about as far away from a radicalised terrorist as we are likely to encounter. Sadly, we pigeonholed him based on what was found at the bar, and the fact he was holding his Koran when he boarded that flight. It sounds horrendous in hindsight, but unfortunately that was all we had to go on at that time in the investigation. He can go home, but we must offer him assistance in getting home.'

'I'll arrange all that,' said Dee.

'And I'm also going to need to make a statement,' said Mills. 'I think we should contact the media this time Kate. Arrange a press conference in conjunction with James's release. We can also let them know that we already have someone else in custody. Hopefully that will reassure the public.'

'Good plan. I'll have the others get on that,' Dee replied.

'Hughes, if you could make sure Mr James custody documents are ready for me, please?' asked Mills.

'I can do that Mills,' Hughes replied.

'Thank you all again,' said Mills as he stood up. 'Dismissed'

\*\*\*

Taz had been allowed to see Malcolm in his cell before the conclusion of his police interview.

'How are you feeling my friend?' he asked as he entered the custody cell.

'More nervous than when I arrived,' Malcolm replied.

'Only natural, but don't worry,' said Taz, trying to reassure him as Officer Grant entered the cell.

'If you gentlemen are ready, I will accompany you to the interview room. Mills is waiting for you.'

Both men followed Grant out of the cell and across the hallway towards interview room one. They entered and sat down opposite Mills who had positioned himself next to the tape recorder.

'Interview Room One. Conclusion of Malcom James Interview. Present are Detective Chief Inspector Colin Mills, Malcolm James, and his legal representative Taz Abdullah.'

Mills took a deep breath.

'Having checked all alibis and financial records voluntarily put forward by Mr James, including his movements up to and including the bombings, I can state that we have found no evidence linking him to the crimes. Searches of his home and subsequent properties related to his occupation also failed to provide any evidence.'

Malcolm glanced at Taz, who smiled back at him. 'I have only one final question to put to you Mr James,' said Mills. Have you ever had any association with an individual named Joseph Darby?'

'I have never heard that name before, let alone had any association with that individual,' Malcom replied confidently.

'In that case you are hereby released from police custody,' replied Mills.

'May I request a copy of Mr James custody record should it be needed at any point in the future?' asked Taz.

'Certainly,' Mills replied.

'Thank you,' replied Taz and Malcolm in unison.

'Due to the circumstances surrounding your arrest, may I take this opportunity to apologise and offer you assistance getting home Mr James.'

Malcolm looked up from reading and looked at Taz, who exchanged his look.

'How does that work?' Taz asked.

'Well, my plan would be to drive Mr James home from the station in an unmarked police vehicle. The officers would then remain outside his home indefinitely for his and his family's safety.'

'Is that really necessary?' said Malcolm.

'I'd feel a lot happier if you'd accept it,' said Mills. 'Even though you are innocent, there may be a slim public majority who still believe you are responsible. We cannot rule out the possibly of you being a target once you leave.'

'In that case I accept,' said Malcolm. 'For my son's sake if nothing else. The only vigilante he should be aware of at his age is Batman.'

'Very good,' said Mills. 'This interview is now concluded. The time is fifteen forty-nine, I am switching off the tape recorder.'

***

DI Dee, along with Officers Wood and Jons were stood in the police station foyer.

Outside the front doors they could see a wall of press ready to greet whoever emerged from the building.

'Bloody hell!' exclaimed Wood. 'They can't all be local surely.'

'I doubt it,' replied Dee.

They watched as Mills appeared from the direction of the custody suite with Malcolm and Taz following close behind.

'Hopefully my statement will appease the press and they'll leave you and the family alone,' said Taz to Malcolm as they approached the congregation of officers. 'I would have preferred more time to prepare it, but I know you are anxious to get home.'

'That's my fault gentlemen,' said Mills. 'But not having this press conference will only prolong things for all of us.'

'Everything is in place Colin,' said Dee.

'Are you ready Mr James?' Mills asked. Malcolm took a deep breath.

'Yes,' he said. 'I think…'

'Let me do the talking,' Taz said to his friend. 'You just focus on getting home.'

Dee stepped forward and opened the door for them as Mills, Malcolm and Taz stepped out of the station. Instantly they were engulfed by the wall of cameras and shouts from the assembled press. Taz was deliberately stood next to Malcolm. He took a step forward towards the dozens of microphones and dictaphones he suddenly found pointing at him and proceeded to read aloud.

'My client is happy to be free and looks forward to returning to his family. Whilst he acknowledges that officers treated him with dignity and respect whilst in custody, questions need to be asked and lessons learnt around the stereotypes and assumptions that led to his false arrest. Thank you.'

He stepped back to Malcolm.

Before anyone in front of the men on the steps had time to respond to what Taz had read, Mills had already taken his place at the front.

'I have given Mr James an unreserved apology,' he said, pausing to take a breath. 'We recognise the significant impact this incident and our response has had, and we will seek to discuss these matters with him to identify learning opportunities. Our officers and staff work with commitment and professionalism to provide quality policing to the public, and I am happy to announce that we already have another individual in custody based on new evidence.

Thank you.'

With the help of Jons, Mills then ushered Malcolm and Taz to the waiting police vehicle below.

Several journalists were shouting after the men. 'What new evidence have you found that has led you to this conclusion?'

'Who is it that your now holding?'

'Are you linking them to all the incidents, or just the latest one?'

Mills opened the car door for Malcolm and Taz and then shut it behind them.

After watching the vehicle safely pull away along with most of the press, the two men turned to make their way back into the building.

Gavin Jordan had finished his latest piece to camera and was stood talking to his crew.

'So, do we stay put do you think? I'd much rather we use the police station for a background rather than a static shot of a tent outside a generic suburban house.'

## 29.

'You handled that incredibly well,' said Wood to Mills as he re-entered the building along with Jons. Mills nodded sheepishly at him as they walked past, making their way across the foyer. Wood and Dee followed them.

'So, what is it about the press Colin?' Dee asked. 'It's been one of your primary concerns over the last few days.'

'An old colleague of mine had a bad experience with the press,' replied Mills. 'It cost him his career, his marriage and his children.'

'How?' asked Wood, as the group approached the bottom of the stairwell.

Mills stopped walking and turned to face his colleagues.

'There had been a series of rapes in the area. Naturally the press wished to know more to help alert the public.'

'Of course,' said Wood.

'So, they approached the police asking for a description of the man. My former colleague told them that the attacker had worn a distinctive scarf around his head when carrying out the attacks. However, whoever was working for the press mistakenly thought he said a distinctive scar.'

'Oh god!' exclaimed Dee. 'I think I can see where this is going...'

'Nowhere good I'm guessing?' said Wood.

'No' said Mills, staring straight ahead. 'The press then issued the description with the wrong information, which in turn led to an innocent man with a distinctive scar ending up in intensive care and two further women being attacked.'

'Christ!' exclaimed Wood.

'But that was the presses mistake!' exclaimed Jons.

'Yes, it was, but naturally the big corporate company, rather than accept any responsibility, blamed it on the source of their information which so happened to be my colleague,' replied Mills.

'And he really lost everything?' asked Dee. Mills nodded at her.

'That's tragic,' added Jons.

'It's also a warning,' replied Mills.

He made his way up the stairs towards the offices with his colleagues following close behind him.

'Please round everyone up and have them head into the conference room with any and all information we now have on Joseph Darby,' he said.

***

Joe had spent most of his time pacing up and down his cell. It was now mid-afternoon of the day after his arrest. He had not touched either of the trays of food that had been given to him that morning. *What's taking them so long?* he thought to himself, pacing faster and faster.

Upstairs, all the officers had started to congregate around the tables in the conference room as Mills had instructed. He opened the conference room door and held it for Buckland to enter.

'After you,' he motioned.

Everyone already assembled in the room was casting their eyes over the case board that had been placed at the front. Stuck to it was the photographs of all four crime scenes, the remains of the car chassis, mosque leaflet and pieces of the recovered backpack. Next to that were pictures of the evidence they had collected during the mornings house search which included the receipt found in the boot of the car, the tubs of explosive themselves and the cabinet in the garage with its manufacturing equipment inside. Also pinned to the board were the other car components that were removed along with items discovered upstairs in the office, including a copy of the Wasted Youth. Next to Joe's mugshot on the other side of the board was the portrait the sketch artist had rendered based on the previous car owner's description of the buyer. Below that were screen captures of all the CCTV footage that had been obtained. Also present were the copies of Joe's and Claire's university teaching timetables.

Buckland wondered over to the evidence board and started adding other pictures to it.

Mills was stood just behind him.

'I'm a little late in the day I know Colin, but I had a hunch' he said.

'Go on,' said Mills inquisitively. 'What was it?'

'Well, after we had wrapped up our search of Darby's house and found none of the clothes he had worn that were captured on CCTV I thought to myself on the drive back, what the hell could he have done with them?'

'I do admit that thought had also crossed my mind,' said Mills.

'We found no evidence of burning at his house, and nothing in the bins,' Buckland continued. 'But it wasn't until we followed up on the charity shop receipt that it hit me; could he have re-donated them?'

'That...' Mills started then hesitated, 'should have been thought of sooner.'

'I wouldn't worry, we're all tired,' replied Buckland. 'So, I had Wood over there check with the charity shops in the city. Sure enough, after a few phone calls he visited one and found the cap in the window, along with the high vis vest and shirt he's seen wearing in the centre.'

'Seriously?' said Mills.

'Yes,' Buckland replied.

'Which one was it, Keith?' Mills asked, turning to address Wood.

'The Empower charity shop,' Wood replied from his position at the back of the room. 'It's a tiny little place at the end of a row of terrace houses. You could easily drive past it if you didn't know it's location. Sure enough the hat was in the window, and the high vis vest was on a rack.'

'Could they tell you who had donated them?' asked Mills.

'Unfortunately, not,' said Wood. 'And there's barely any CCTV inside the shop, let alone outside it. It was just another anonymous donation left outside in amongst several board games and crockery. They steam clean all the items of clothing they receive by donation before they resell them.'

'We ran them regardless but were unable to get a print or fibre from it,' said Buckland. 'All the items can now be found in evidence. I only wish I had such hunches more frequently!'

Mills smiled at his colleague and patted him on the shoulder.

'Take a seat,' he said.

Pouring himself a glass of water from the jug in the middle, he took a sip before looking up to address his colleagues in the room.

'Ok. As I'm sure we're now all aware, Malcolm James has been released without charge. No evidence was found at any properties associated with him, and we've had several people account for all his movements both here and in Pakistan. Our new prime suspect is Joseph Darby, and we have found nothing to indicate that he had any accomplices to carry out these crimes.' '

Any red flags from his past?' asked Wood questioningly.

'There was an incident of a suspected knife on site during his time during sixth form, but he was not directly involved,' said Dee.

'Incidentally that turned out to be a false alarm,' said Mills. 'But no doubt it made an impression.' He took another sip of water from his glass. 'I think we can surmise that he deliberately placed the mosque leaflet into that backpack in the hopes that it would be recovered and subsequently interfere with our lines of enquiry. Another part of a premeditated campaign.'

'It worked though, didn't it?' said Jons.

'Yes, Jons it did,' replied Mills solemnly. 'But now is not the time to dwell on past mistakes.'

'No offence Sir,' interrupted Wood. 'But despite all this other work we've been doing on Darby, some are still insisting that James had something to do with it.'

'I am aware of this Keith,' replied Mills. 'As I think are most of us seated around this table. Dee and I agreed before his release that we would assist him home and have officers remain in the vicinity for that very reason. Hopefully once people hear that we have charged someone else they will let it go.'

He turned round to face the board behind him. 'This is an overview of all the evidence we have collected against Mr Darby, and the first time I have seen it all in one place,' he said. 'I am extremely satisfied with what we have, but I would like to go over a few final points before we head downstairs and formally interview him.'

'So, we're not visiting the university first then?' asked Wood.

'No,' replied Mills. 'But I do plan to pay them a visit after Darby has been charged before I hand all the evidence we have collected over to the prosecution.'

'That process is not uncommon,' said Dee. 'It's just rarely heard about. Having been with Mills during our search of the Darby House, I think we will find a deliberate separation between home and work. He would have done this to not appear overly suspicious when cyphering chemicals from the chemistry department.'

'Hopefully my team can recover a fingerprint from the lab storage unit to confirm this,' added Buckland.

'That would tie in nicely with what we found at his home,' said Mills. 'As well as confirm the theory. We must also remember that everyone who currently has any association at or with people who are involved with the university have all suffered. The ripple effect from these atrocities will be felt for many, many years to come.'

'I thought there was no such thing as bad publicity?' blurted out Jons suddenly.

Everyone in the room turned and stared at him.

'It is when it involves death Jons,' Mills snapped back.

'No parent would risk losing a child Ryan,' said Dee 'You should know that being a parent yourself.'

Jons slunk back sheepishly in his chair.

'Your right,' he said after a moment. 'I can't think of anything more horrifying. Forgive my remark.'

'Not only that, more students and staff are likely to come forward after a conviction, safe in the knowledge that Darby's no longer a threat to them,' added Dee. 'It's the same in domestic violence cases. The fear of retaliation if the person found out.'

'Our recovery and study of both Darby and his wife's university teaching timetables explains how he could have done all this and have his wife and colleagues be completely unawares,' said Mills. 'Not only does it help Mrs Darby maintain her innocence, but it also helps us by being directly linked to our suspects opportunity.'

'Mills is of course referring to opportunity as part of the triad,' said Dee. 'Means, motive and opportunity.'

'Yes, I am,' replied Mills. 'Everyone keep that in mind as we progress, please.'

He wondered over to the case board and cast his eyes between Joe and Claire's university timetables.

'Darby clearly had more than enough free time in his week without his wife to manufacture his IED's and frequent the public places in which he planted them.'

'I'm still impressed how his wife didn't notice anything,' said Jons.

'Teaching chemistry involves a lot more classroom teaching hours than that of the social sciences,' said Dee. 'You can see the contrast in both their timetables by simply looking at them.'

'Not only that, but there was also the way he operated. Do you regularly open your paint cans and cabinets in the back of your garage to check their contents Jons?' Mills asked.

'Or ask your wife if her box files only contain paper?' added Dee.

'No!' Jons replied. 'It wouldn't even cross my mind too if I'm honest.'

'Precisely,' replied Mills. 'There's that mutual trust between spouses to not need to regularly check such things.'

'It's also part of the reason why Claire Darby feels so bad,' added Dee. 'That mutual trust she took for granted has been exploited and completely shattered.'

'All of which overlaps with the evidence we have to support Darby's means to carry out these attacks,' continued Mills. 'Having stolen the chemicals from the university and manufactured his bombs in the garage, we believe Darby was then transporting them in archive boxes along with his student papers to and from his house.'

'I'm presuming he then transferred the bombs from the archive boxes still hidden in his boot to the coat, box, and backpack as and when required?' asked Wood.

'That was our conclusion as well,' said Buckland. 'He would also have probably set them once he had reached his location to avoid them going off during transportation. He would have taken several timers with him each time should one have a fault, directly matching what we found in the study. These methods were probably used for the car park bombing, except on a much larger scale.'

'Escalation is a big part of this case. It is also one part that disturbs me the most,' said Mills. 'From concealed pipe bombs to a car bomb packed with explosives.'

He paused for a moment and glanced at Dee. 'For those of you that weren't present at the house search, we found ten litre paint tubs he had been storing the explosive in, of which several we're missing.'

'Holy hell!' exclaimed Wood.

'Presumably these are what he placed in the car. We will never know for sure as no evidence of the containers was found after the explosion,' added Buckland. 'However, we did estimate that he would have used around 10 pounds of explosives at the cinema, nearly three times as much at the centre and around 1000 pounds of explosive in the vehicle.'

Everyone around the table fell silent.

'Like I said,' said Mills after a moment. 'Escalation on a disturbing trajectory.'

He took another sip of water from his glass. 'Donovan?'

'Yes Mills?' came the reply.

'Please tell us what you know about the vehicle,' said Mills.

'The previous owner of the car was a Mr Lewis. Extremely helpful gentleman,' replied Donovan. 'Darby gave him a fake name and never registered as the new keeper of the vehicle, which is why the chassis number recovered from the scene led us to Lewis.'

'What alias did Darby use?' Mills asked.

'Robert Smith,' came the reply.

'Figures. He's the frontman and longest serving member of The Cure isn't he? Darby's favourite band,' grumbled Mills.

'I also went ahead and checked Mr Lewis movements at the time of the bombing just to be certain he wasn't involved whist our sketch artist was with him,' Donovan continued. 'According to his bank transactions he was treating his wife to a meal at that ridiculously expensive bistro restaurant in the bay having sold the car.'

'Nice!' said Jons.

'As you can all see from the picture on the board by the sketch artist based on Mr Lewis description, I'm fairly confident we can say it's Darby,' Donovan added.

'No doubt about that,' added Wood.

'Don't forget we also have the parts of the vehicle Darby left in his garage as further evidence,' said Buckland. 'They also match the make and model of the car he used.'

'Great work!' said Mills. He turned round again to survey the case board. 'Justin?'

'Yes Mills?'

'It's your turn.'

'Right,' said Justin. 'Do I need to stand up?' 'Not if you don't want too,' Mills replied with a friendly smile.

'Ok,' said Justin, remaining seated. 'So, the subsequent charity shop footage confirms that Joe Darby purchased the baseball cap he is seen wearing on the CCTV screen captures we already had. He also bought the backpack that very same visit, as well as the coat he used at the cinema, the high vis vest, and a radio-controlled car. He conveniently paid in cash. You can clearly see his face as he is walking towards the exit with his new purchases!'

'Again, sloppy and out of character like leaving the receipt in his car boot,' said Dee.

'I think he was under the presumption that the shop may have not had any CCTV,' replied Mills. 'Otherwise, you're right, it doesn't fit.'

'It could also just be a simple matter of human error,' added Buckland.

'Have you come to any conclusions as to why he used the same clothes more than once?' Wood asked.

'My guess would be that it is far easier masquerading as one than several other people,' said Dee.

'He most likely bought the toy car whilst working out the easiest method to trigger his devices' added Rhys. 'A lot of bombs are triggered remotely using that set up.'

"Hello Rhys,' said Mills. "I'd forgotten you guys were here.'

'There's no real footage from the car park or the cinema though I'm afraid,' Justin continued.

'No matter,' said Mills. 'Did you find anything on his computer?'

'Nothing suspicious no. Just work-related emails and a hard-drive full of resources and spreadsheets he uses for the courses he teaches at the university.'

'Doesn't surprise me,' said Dee.

'He probably walked into the local library and paid to print the bomb details, pictures and all those copies of his manifesto which include a website address. Incidentally, I found the site being hosted on the library's servers,' added Justin.

'So, we have clearly established that Darby had both the means and the opportunity to do this,' said Mills.

'What about the motive?' asked Wood. 'Do you have any idea what possibly motivated him to do this?'

'Only theories based on what we have found,' replied Mills. 'All those photocopied sheets. The Wasted Youth. And the language…'

'Higher educated delinquents I believe was on them somewhere,' said Dee.

'Yes, it was,' replied Mills. 'We have definitely identified that students were his target. During our consultations with William, Rhys, and Buckland over the last few days, we have been continually surprised that none of the devices have contained any shrapnel. They said at the very beginning that this may be indicative that his motivation was not out to commit mass murder but make a statement, and now that finally makes sense.'

Mills pointed at the copy of the Wasted Youth leaflet pinned on the board.

'I think that he wanted to use these in conjunction with the bombings but bottled it.'

'So, you think he meant to deliberately leave them at the scene?' asked Rhys.

'Yes. But he thought better of it,' said Mills. 'Let's not forget that prior to the 999 call from his friend's wife, the only defining characteristic in allowing us to be able to link the same person to all the devices was how they were manufactured.'

'But I thought this was all about his message?' said Wood. 'Ending the wasted youth to use his words.'

'It still is,' said Dee. 'Accept rather than being so bold, he would have released his paper anonymously to the press claiming responsibility afterwards.'

'You mean like Jack the Ripper?' added William.

'There's no evidence that it was the Ripper who sent them those messages,' said Buckland. 'But it's a good analogy.'

'That's if we hadn't caught him first,' said Mills. 'He's clearly dedicated to the cause at whatever cost, particularly when we look at the escalation of his crimes.'

'So do you think he will confess to complete his so-called mission having now been caught?' asked Buckland.

'I don't know,' said Mills.

'Best of luck guys,' said Jons.

'Thank you,' Mills replied. 'And thank you all for your assistance in this case.'

He paused and looked around the room. 'We have only reached this position thanks to everyone in this rooms continued hard work and dedication over what has been a surreal few days. Dismissed.'

## 30.

'He's all ready for you,' said Neil as Mills and Dee arrived outside the door of the interview room. 'Grants in there with him.'

Mills acknowledged him silently by nodding before opening the door and entering the room, holding it for Dee as she followed him. She sat down and immediately began to unwrap a new disc which she fed into the recorder before starting it.

'This interview is being audibly recorded should it be tended in evidence before court,' said Mills. 'Interview room one. I am DCI Colin Mills. This is DI Kate Dee. At the end of the interview, you will be given a notice with information about what will happen to the disc and how you may have access to it. Do you understand?'

He looked up from the document in front of him.

'Yes,' came the reply.

'Please state your full name and date of birth.'

'Joseph Darby. Thirty first, seventh, nineteen fifty-eight.'

'You do not have to say anything, but it may harm your defence if you do not mention when questioned something which you may later rely on in court. Anything you do say may be given in evidence. Do you require any legal advice? This interview can be delayed if necessary.'

'I don't think that will be necessary,' Joe responded. 'I'm not about to waste my money on a solicitor. I have alibis for my whereabouts when every incident took place.'

Mills and Dee looked at each other.

'I was shopping the night of the cinema bombing, and when the bomb went off in the bay, I was visiting my parents. I was in my office marking papers when the bomb in the bar exploded, and I was drinking with my university colleagues before being seen by two of my students on the way home the night of the car park atrocity.'

'Did that sound rehearsed to you Colin?' Dee asked her colleague.

'Absolutely,' Mills replied. 'We shall look into that if you can give us the relevant names, please. However, based on our evidence we know you had ample time to plant the devices and be clear of the area well before you timed them to detonate.'

'That's not presuming you weren't planning to use anymore devices,' added Dee. 'We know you had more of the explosive in your possession.'

To both the detectives surprise, Joe did not reply.

'What would you say to Malcolm James, who is still suffering as a result from his wrongful arrest based on you planting false evidence?' Mills asked.

Joe remained silent.

'You were playing on the social prejudices against his religion, weren't you?' said Mills. 'It's ok. We know that now.'

'Joe. I'll be honest with you,' said Dee. 'If you own up now, we'll say you cooperated with us which is usually taken into consideration by a judge during sentencing.'

'Or you can sit there in silence and face the consequences,' said Mills firmly. 'It's your choice. I'm sure you won't be short of friends on the inside who'd rather you stayed with them a little longer.'

He let the words hang in the air, hoping that the expression on the face opposite him would change.

'We know that you and you alone are responsible for this,' he continued.

'We also know that your fight against the Wasted Youth is not complete,' added Dee.

More silence filled the room.

'Most people would take this opportunity to explain, but clearly you are not interested. I must say I am disappointed based on how we started,' said Mills, before sitting back in his chair. 'Do you really have nothing to say?'

He gave Joe a moment to respond and turned to look at Dee. It was clear from the expression on her face that they were both thinking the same thing.

'This is a waste of our time,' said Mills. 'Any further questions Detective?'

'No, I don't think so,' Dee replied. 'I am more than happy with the evidence we have against Mr Darby.'

'As am I,' said Mills. "Joseph Darby, you are charged with murder, which is contrary to common law. You did plant improvised explosive devices at the city's cinema, centre, and a central bar. You also planted a vehicle based improvised explosive device in a city car park to kill. You do not have to say anything, but it may harm your defence if you do not mention when questioned something which you later rely on in court. Anything you do say may be given in evidence. You will remain in police custody until you are taken to court for your hearing. Do you have anything to say?'

Joe shook his head.

'We need a verbal response please,' Mills prompted.

'No,' said Joe, his voice just above a whisper.

'Our interview is now finished. It's three thirteen pm. I am switching off the tape recorder.'

\*\*\*

After the conclusion of the interview, Mills had remained downstairs. Dee was currently sat on top of her desk attempting to untangle her telephone wire from itself.

'I've just had to tell Mrs Darby that her husband has been formally charged,' she said, replacing the phone receiver and straightening out the telephone cord.

'How did she take it?' Wood asked, stirring his cup of coffee as he walked towards Dee's desk.

'She didn't say much, but that's not really surprising, is it? It'll take a few hours before I think the reality of the situation really sinks in. Thankfully her friend is still with her. Poor woman.'

'Where's Mills?' asked Wood.

'Chaperoning Darby back to his cell before drafting his statement. He knows there's a high chance he'll get bullied into another press conference, but he's digging his heels in.'

'Poor guy,' said Wood, taking a loud slurp of coffee.

'It was his idea for me to let Darby's wife know about the conviction before it appears everywhere. Hopefully we have bought her some time,' said Dee.

'Well, I'm certainly not a media mole if that's what your implying,' Wood replied with a grin.

'I never said a word,' said Dee smiling at him before failing to stifle the start of a yawn. 'Is there any coffee left?'

***

Claire had finished speaking to Joe's colleagues at the university. She replaced the phone receiver back onto its body mounted to the kitchen wall.

'I feel sick,' she said. 'Everything else before this still hasn't seemed real.'

'Then let's go and do something,' replied Holly. 'Shall we go for a walk in the park? It might help clear your head.'

'No, no' said Claire solemnly. 'I need to phone Faye. I'm worried I'll keep putting it off and putting it off and she'll end up hearing it on the news or over the radio.'

'If she hasn't already,' said Holly.

'Either way, it's better coming from me,' said Claire glancing at her watch. 'If I call now her husband will also be home. I don't want to drop this on her when she's alone. I'm worried what might happen.'

'Do you two get on?' asked Holly.

'Famously,' replied Claire without a moment's hesitation. 'One of the reasons I've weathered the storm with Joe over the last few months is because of Faye. She is wonderful and I'd miss her terribly.'

'Make use of your mobile's speakerphone rather than your house phone, and do it sat down!' exclaimed Holly. She moved one of the kitchen bar stools out from under the counter and motioned for Claire to come and sit.

'Thank you, sweetheart,' said Claire.

She sat herself down on the stool before placing her phone on the worktop in front of her. She scrolled through the names saved on the device before initiating the call and activating its speakerphone. It seemed to ring forever.

'They've gone out, haven't they?' said Claire as she looked at Holly. 'Unconsciously sparing themselves the life changing news I am about to bestow upon them.'

'Maybe,' replied Holly. 'But it hasn't rung as long as you think it has.'

Claire became increasingly aware of her breathing as she waited for a voice to answer at the other end. She was just about to hang up when her call was answered.

'Hello?' said the voice at the end of the line.

'Hello Faye. It's me Claire.'

'Hello Claire, dear,' Faye replied. 'My son finally remembered to ask you to call me, did he?'

'Something like that,' said Claire. She paused to try and gather her thoughts, not anticipating that Faye was about to launch into a rapid monologue.

'I've been thinking about getting you and Joseph bicycles for your upcoming wedding anniversary. Me and Mark have seen hundreds of them over the last few days, and if the inner city gets any more pedestrianised you won't be able to drive a car anywhere near it in a few months. Plus, you can never get too much exercise these days dear. It's all about leaving your working life in a decent shape so you can enjoy your free time in retirement. Unlike my first husband, Joseph's poor father. He was too exhausted to see retirement, let alone enjoy it. And...'

There was no answer from the other end of the phone. Usually, Claire would be punctuating the conversation. It was then that Faye heard crying.

'Claire dear, don't cry. I never meant to upset you. It was just an idea I had.'

She heard her daughter in law take a few deep breaths through her tears, trying to control her emotions. Holly stood herself behind Claire and started to gently rub her back.

'What on earth is the matter?' Faye asked.

'Is Mark with you?' said Claire, managing to get the question out by running the words altogether before taking another series of breaths.

'Yes, he's here. Mark!'

In the distance they heard a muffled voice.

'Coming. No need to shout!'

Holly quickly walked over and grabbed a box of tissues from on top of the fridge. She took one and handed it to Claire, before placing the box by the phone and returning to her position.

'Ok, were both hear now dear. Please tell us what my son has done to upset you so much?' said Faye.

Holly looked at Claire. To her surprise she was smiling whilst repeatedly trying to wipe her tears.

'How did you know it was him?' Claire asked.

'A mother's intuition dear,' Faye replied. 'Plus, those we are closest to have the power to cut us the deepest.'

On hearing this, Claire lost control of her sobs again. Holly put her arm around her best friend, anxious to stop her from falling from her position on the stool.

'Whatever has happened, it doesn't change anything between us, do you understand dear?' said Faye. 'I will always love you, and you are welcome here at our home anytime.'

Claire then heard Mark in the background.

'Absolutely,' he said. 'I'll always need you to help me out with this one sweetheart!'

Claire took another giant breath. Thankfully the words came.

'Joe was the bomber.'

She took another deep breath as her body shivered.

There was silence at the other end of the phone.

'I'm sorry dear,' said Faye. 'What did you say?'

Claire screwed up her face. It was bad enough having had to say that sentence once, but to repeat it was something else. When would this relentless nightmare give her some rest bite?

She glanced at Holly, who looked at her and nodded before hugging her tighter and squeezing her hand.

'Joe was the bomber. He's been charged with murder,' Claire said, sounding almost ethereal this time.

As was to be expected, Claire and Holly were met with a barrage of questions from her mother in-law.

'Why?' said Faye, raising her voice slightly. 'How? I don't understand dear. He was here two days ago having tea with us. He'd never disgrace his father like this.'

'Joseph!' exclaimed Mark.

Claire looked at Holly. They could both hear the anger in his voice.

'There must be some mistake?' said Faye, her voice starting to waver.

'No, I'm afraid there's been no mistake,' said Claire. 'The evidence was in our house, right under my nose.' She could hear Faye beginning to cry now, which in turn set her off again. 'It's all my fault!' she exclaimed. 'I'm so sorry.'

She turned and wrapped her arms around Holly, who preceded to continue to rub her back.

The next reply came from Mark.

'Hello Claire. It's Mark,' he said. 'Faye has left the room.'

'It's Ok,' said Claire, turning herself back towards the phone.

'No, it's not,' said Mark. 'How could he do this to you and his mother? Let alone the people he has hurt and the lives he has destroyed. And he sat in this room across from me and his mother knowing what he was doing and pretended to be normal? I am disgusted. I am...'

He stopped at the sound of Claire's sobbing again. 'Forgive my outburst,' he said. 'What do you need from me?'

Mark came from an older generation, adopting a pragmatic approach no matter what life threw at you.

'Look after Faye,' said Claire.

'And what about you?' said Mark. 'Who is looking after you?'

'I have had my best friend by my side for the last few days,' replied Claire. 'She's right here.'

'Hello Mark,' said Holly into the phone.

'Hi there,' replied Mark. 'Thank you for looking out for Claire. I know that guilt and shame are now washing over Faye. She knew something wasn't quite right with Joe when he visited the other day. We even talked about it that evening. She will also be trying to work out what affect she as a mother had on her son for him to do such a terrible thing.'

'None,' said Claire. 'Absolutely nothing.'

'We all know that,' replied Mark. 'But Faye must now go through the gauntlet of emotions for her to accept it herself, just like you are sweetheart. I must say, how you are handling yourself is quite remarkable. I am very proud of you.'

'Thank you.' said Claire through her tears.

'I'll phone you later,' said Mark. 'I must go and check on Faye. Take care. We love you.'

Claire heard Mark hang up the phone. She turned her body and crumpled into her best friend weeping, burying her head between them both.

Holly then started to cry.

'That Bastard!' she exclaimed.

***

Dan was covering one of Joes lectures when a figure appeared at the door.

It lingered for a minute, waiting for Dan to come to a natural pause in his monologue before interrupting.

'We can see you!' Dan said in the figure's direction.

There was a snigger of muffled laughter amongst the students.

'You're a little late, but better late than never my friend. Quick, come in and take a seat up front.'

To Dan's surprise, it was Peter who opened the door. He could see from his expression that he was not in the right frame of mind for humour.

'Can I see you for a second Dan?' Peter asked.

'Sure thing,' he replied.

He looked up and addressed the many faces now staring at him from their seats in the lecture theatre.

'One sec folks. Be right back.'

Jay and Layton were sat at the back of the lecture hall when Jay's phone went off.

'For god's sake!' he exclaimed. 'I told them I was actually attending my lectures today.'

He reached into his pocket and took out his phone.

'Who is it?' Layton asked.

'My Mother,' Jay answered. 'Weird.'

He unlocked his phone and read the message. 'Jesus!' he exclaimed.

'What? What?' Layton asked.

'According to the news, someone has been charged in connection to the bombings.'

'Jay, you don't think it's Darby, do you?' said Layton.

They both paused in the thought and looked at each other.

Dan re-entered the room. His students were used to seeing Dan relaxed, smiling, and constantly using humour. Other students who weren't in the social science department and didn't know that he was a lecturer would often mistake him for a mature student, but his usual demeanour had completely vanished. He looked rigid and pale.

'Sir? what's the matter?' asked Ben Daniels, one of the students sat in the first row. 'You're as white as a sheet!'

'Just so you are all aware, Joseph Darby no longer teaches at this university.'

He paused, trying to contain his emotions. 'He was the bomber…'

Dan's legs then gave way and he collapsed back into the chair behind him.

There was a collective gasp from the students in the lecture theatre. Then came the screaming and hysterical crying in sections, those having lost close friends being hit by another wave of emotions too fast to process before the shouting started.

'How could he!'

'They ought to execute him!'

'I knew it!' exclaimed Layton from the back of the room.

Dan couldn't respond to his students. He was sat staring at the floor, frozen in disbelief.

# 31.

Judge Lee Barnett looked out to a packed courtroom. The public gallery was filled to the brim with press, anxious family members of the diseased, and people who intended to recount the event to all who gave them the opportunity. How many of the jury would be fishing for book deals in the near future? In a trail lasting five days, it had only taken them only eight hours to deliver its verdict. Guilty.

To everyone's surprise, Claire had attended every day throughout the trial supported by either Holly or Mark. Claire and Mark had both insisted that Faye remain at home despite her repeated protest. Eventually they had reached a compromise. Claire would update her on the day in court via phone on the days Mark hadn't attended. Today would be one of those days. Mark was at home support his wife on what would be one of the hardest days of her life.

Judge Barnet's job today was to sentence Joe. As an experienced judge, he had presided over several murder trials in his time, but none that seemed to carry the weight and emotion of this one. He looked up from his notes on the bench in front of him and addressed the court.

'Joseph Darby. Please stand.'

Joe stood up and stared blankly ahead.

'Two world Wars, and countless others have been and are still being fought for personal freedom,' Barnett said looking at him. 'We are given the gift of youth to find our place in the world, but you took from your intended victims the chance to find theirs as well as that of countless others you simply labelled and remorselessly dismissed as we heard during evidence.'

He paused to survey the court. Several people were now crying and being comforted by those next to them. Joe shuffled his feet in the dock as the judge continued.

'Your actions were that of a coward as shown in the way you meticulously planned and deceived others. The pain and suffering caused by your actions is irreparable. In light of this, it is only fair that you receive a sentence that reflects the magnitude of the crimes for which you have been convicted. I hereby sentence you to life imprisonment without parole.'

Cries rang out from the viewers gallery, reverberating around the otherwise silent court room.

'Take him down.'

Everyone watched as one of the two dock officers stationed nearest Joe placed his hands behind his back and handcuffed him. He was then led to the door which was unlocked by the other security officer before he disappeared from view on his way back to the holding cells below.

'All rise,' said the Bailiff.

Everyone stood as Barnett exited the courtroom.

'It's over,' whispered Holly into Claire's ear, watching as people began to make their way out of the courtroom. Below them, the prosecution team were all exchanging handshakes and gathering documents from their bench. 'Are you ready to go?' she asked, standing up.

'I'm not sure I can,' replied Claire, looking over at her. Holly could see the concern in her eyes.

'That's ok,' Holly replied, sitting back down in the seat next to her. 'Take as long as you need.

# EPILOGUE.

'Joseph Darby is like a shard of glass,' said Claire, sitting opposite her councillor Wendy Sayer on a pale grey sofa. 'You think you've got everything until you cut yourself again a few days later.'

She sighed and glanced around the room. It was minimally furnished. Only a single armchair was positioned opposite the sofa. On one of two windowsills beneath large windows sat a vase full of artificial flowers and a set of small leather-bound books.

'That's an interesting analogy to use Claire,' Wendy replied, looking up from her notes.

'Care you elaborate on that? Why are you feeling like that?'

Claire paused to gather her thoughts.

'After my husband was sent to prison, I thought that would have been the end, but it wasn't.'

'Why? What has happened?' Wendy asked sensitively.

'Well to start with, I gave up work in a place I loved,' Claire said solemnly. 'Granted I was a mess. I couldn't draw a straight line with a ruler. So much of university reminds me of him. The guilt I felt knowing that my husband was responsible for the deaths of so many of the students. Just the idea of returning ended up giving me a panic attack.'

'Once a brain has been affected by trauma under any circumstances it sees potential threat everywhere' Wendy replied. 'It's been reconditioned to spot threat even if there is none. You guilt is being caused by the way you are judging yourself irrationally. I would also suggest your harbouring feelings of shame, embarrassed by your husbands' actions. Did you contribute in any way to his crimes in which he has been convicted?'

Claire shook her head.

'It's your sense of empathy that is making you feel responsible,' continued Wendy. 'It will take some time to work through these things, but eventually you will reach a form of acceptance that no longer holds yourself jointly accountable. We have various medications and forms of cognitive behaviour therapy such as we are doing now at our disposal to help you.'

Claire looked at her sceptically.

'It may not feel significant, but you've already taken the biggest step by accepting the need for help.'

'I wish my mother-in-law would accept some help," said Claire. "The amount of stress he's caused her.'

'In what ways are you referring to?' Wendy asked. She was keen to keep Claire talking openly now she seemed to be engaged.

'She looks frail,' said Claire, staring into her lap. 'After Joe's conviction she had a cooking accident. Burned her hand. This is a lady who would regularly host dinner parties for five friends forgetting to put on her oven gloves. Her husband Mark found her crying with her hand in the sink and food all over the kitchen floor.'

'Like yourself she has endured a traumatic experience,' Wendy replied. 'She is probably carrying a significant amount of guilt and shame herself based on the actions of her son.'

'But of all the people I've known, she is the last person who deserves this. Including me,' replied Claire. 'The last time I visited there was an unopened pile of letters from her friends on her writing desk in the living room. They've all been sending them to each other for forty years. I probably haven't helped matters distancing myself from her. I just cannot find the words right now.'

'You both need time to heal,' said Wendy. 'Everyone's healing process is different in both time and methodology.'

'I wish I could just climb inside the airing cupboard and close the door sometimes like I did as a child,' said Claire.

'That's your need for security,' replied Wendy.

'It's amazing what I can remember from my childhood if I concentrate,' Claire continued. 'The taste and feel of an orthodontist's mould for example. In fact, the other day I saw my childhood self in dream.'

'What were you doing?' asked Wendy.

'Drinking strawberry milkshakes in a cafe my grandparents would always take me to when I visited them during the school summer holidays,' replied Claire.

'Can you remember what you were talking about?' said Wendy.

'Something about a bad argument, but I don't remember who it was with, or what it was about.'

'It's a widely held belief that dreams such as yours is a sign that you need to make peace with the past,' said Wendy. 'You have to work through your feelings and understand those that make you vulnerable.'

'Hmm hmmm,' sighed Claire, staring at the flowers on the windowsill.

'Returning to your original shard of glass remark earlier if we may,' said Wendy, anxious to keep the conversation moving. 'What else has happened to reinforce your way of thinking?'

'We had, or should I say I had a framed copy of a famous Irish blessing up in the dining room. May the road rise to meet you. May the wind be at your back. Are you familiar with it?'

'Yes. I believe I am,' replied Wendy. 'It's ending talks about God holding you in his palm if I'm not mistaken?'

'That's the one,' said Claire, adjusting herself in her chair. 'I really do admire your style of furnishing,' she added, looking around the room. 'Smart. Minimal and practical. I like it.'

'It serves its purpose,' Wendy replied. 'My home is nothing like this. But we digress and must focus. You were saying about the Irish blessing?'

'Yes,' replied Claire. 'We bought that to remember our first trip on an aeroplane together. As you've no doubt worked out for yourself, we travelled to Ireland. Dublin to be precise. My great grandparents are from Irish descent. Have you been?'

'No,' Wendy replied. 'But I have read works by Oscar Wilde and James Joyce. The portraits of both Dorian Grey and the artist as a young man being my favourites.'

'It's a beautiful city. We toured the Guinness storehouse, watched elephants bathing at the Zoo, and I marvelled at the centuries old flags that hang in St Patrick's Cathedral. Having thoroughly enjoyed our experience we decided to purchase the blessing as a souvenir.'

'And now the object just reminds you of your husband and everything he's done, rather than what it represented when you initially purchased it together doesn't it?' said Wendy.

'Yes. Only it gets worse,' said Claire. 'The other day I was sick of looking at it, so I took it down, only to be greeted by a sizeable spot of faded wallpaper where it used to hang. I put it back up. It was exasperating!'

'May I suggest repurposing the frame as an alternative solution?' said Wendy.

Claire turned and gazed at the windowsill again for a moment.

'You know, I think I will,' she said. 'Thank you'.

'Pleasure,' said Wendy with a smile.

'But the shard of glass that really hurt the most occurred the other morning,' Claire continued. 'As I shut my front door behind me, I was faced with the word Monster graffitied all over it. Why do people still think I had any part to play in this? He's ruined me just as much as everyone else. I'm destined to remain as Joseph Darby's clueless wife, forever wondering when that association is going to smack me over the head again.'

'It's easier to label or direct a negative emotion at someone else. No doubt they have a perceived expectation of who you are based on your relationship to him,' said Wendy. 'What's interesting is that you are doing something similar, guessing that everyone else will see you the same way as this one person responsible for defacing your front door.'

'Maybe,' said Claire. 'But it's still an extremely deep cut.'

'You present as a very self-aware person Claire,' said Wendy. 'With the right help and time as we have already discussed, I know you have the strength to overcome this. You've already overcome so much already.'

'You know it's funny,' said Claire. 'I remember being stood in the shower conducting mock interviews with myself as a teen.'

'Do you know why you used to find yourself doing this?' Wendy asked, making a note.

'I always wanted to sing. Joan Jet, Heart, and Blonde posters were all over my bedroom walls.'

'Maybe we could try employing a similar technique again,' said Wendy.

Claire looked at her quizzically.

'I thought what we are doing right now was the only technique?' she replied.

'Oh no. This is only one method,' said Wendy. 'A lot of my patients find their own individual practices that they stumble upon just as beneficial as these sessions. The question is, are you open and willing to try anything?'

Claire looked down at the floor, up at the ceiling, and then straight at Wendy.

'Deal!" she said confidently. 'Anything to be rid of him!'

***

Joe was travelling in cubicle nine of a police transport vehicle, his surname written on a whiteboard the other side of the door. He was being moved by the prison service after an attempt on his life. A fellow inmate who it was later revealed to be related to one of the students Joe had killed had attempted to stab him using a toothbrush he had whittled into a point at the tip. Despite this attempt on his life, trying to appeal his conviction would be a fruitless waste of his now limited resources.

As a maximum-security inmate, he was not allowed to work in prison. How should he spend his time? After briefly contemplating writing to his parents and wife, he had decided to numb himself to his new surroundings and maintain absolute focus on the campaign that had led to him being there. In his mind, he wouldn't have to wait long until he started receiving letters of thanks and support for his cause. His crimes and name were now infamous, the Wasted youth manifesto forever to be recycled and studied for generations.

He had paid no attention to the speed of the vehicle throughout his journey but had noticed that they had now been stationary for some time. Joe listened intently as an officer started to open the van's doors.

***

The sun had already begun to set when people started arriving at the park.

Shortly after the harrowing ordeal of having to bury their son, Liam and Kelly Mason, along with student representatives, had decided to arrange a candlelight vigil for victims and their families. This was to be the first official event of the newly registered Shaun Mason Memorial Trust. Having been the first of the Mason family to be able to go to university, Liam and Kelly had decided to set up an organisation in his name to help with the growing cost of higher education.

'Thank you so much,' said Kelly to Tara Hicks, the president of the student's union.

'No, thank you,' Tara replied, rearranging the candles on the table in front of them. 'Shaun would be so proud of you.'

Mingling amongst those that were now stood in front of them was Malcolm James, recognisable to all thanks to the media's reporting of events. He was with his wife and son Samuel, as well as Taz, Saddiq, Adil and several other members of their mosque. At one point, Malcolm became overwhelmed by the amount of people that had come up to him apologising for his arrest. He took himself off briefly before returning to his wife.

'Are you sure you're OK?' Nadia asked him.

'Yes,' Malcolm replied. 'Tonight serves a greater purpose.'

Mills and Dee were stood in front of a placard that been erected opposite the parks war memorial statue, reading the various massages that had already been left. Pictures had also been stuck to it of the victims with their peers and families, the smiles on everyone's faces a stark reminder of the life altering events that had occurred. At the nearby table, candles were being handed out. A collection bucket had also started to circulate.

'Do you think the university and these people will ever recover from this?' Dee asked Mills.

'Yes,' he replied. 'But it will take time. And not just here. There were students from all over the country and internationally.'

'I always forget that,' replied Dee.

'And I hope that the media don't recycle their focus on Darby,' continued Mills. 'Hopefully no one has a duplicate copy of his manifesto either.'

'Did you hear about his transfer?' Dee asked.

'Yes,' replied Mills. 'Doesn't seem fair, does it? Protecting a monster.'

'My biggest concern is still his wife,' said Dee. 'Do you know if she's here tonight?'

'I don't think so,' replied Mills. 'After all her husband is responsible for all this.'

'Shame,' replied Dee. 'She's a victim too.'

Peter Rowan was stood talking to several parents when Dan Silver approached him.

'Where's the bar Pete?' Dan asked. 'I could use a drink right about now.'

'I was just saying to some of the parents that I can't shake the feeling of guilt,' replied Peter. 'We should have known something was happening when he asked us out for that drink.'

'Nothing but an alibi,' replied Dan sighing.

'Exactly,' said Peter. 'We teach hundreds of students about student behaviour every year, and yet we failed to see it in one of our own when it mattered most. I'm thinking of resigning Dan, I really am.'

'Don't you dare!' snapped Dan. 'We need you now more than ever.'

Mills and Dee spotted Rhys and William in the crowd and started to walk towards them.

'Good evening,' said William as they approached, offering his hand to Mills.

'Have you seen?' asked Rhys. 'Malcolm James and his family are here.'

'Really?' said Dee.

'Yes,' replied William. 'They have just collected their candles from the table.'

'Please excuse me for a moment,' said Mills.

Leaving Dee with their colleges, Mills walked off in the direction of Malcolm and his entourage.

'So, what's next for you two then?' she asked. 'Enjoying a well-earned rest?'

William and Rhys both laughed.

'Unlikely,' said William. 'Apparently there's a shortage of people with our expertise in the army, but I only intend to work in consultation if anything comes up.'

'I'd like to try teaching,' said Rhys, 'There's an ignorance surrounding war and conflict, especially amongst young people. That happened to their grandparent's generation, so its significance is lost. Every year the poppy appeal brings in diminished profits, and it's time that changed.'

Samuel was the first one to spot Mills approaching through the crowd.

'Dad' he said, pulling on his father's jacket. Malcolm turned.

'Detective Mills,' he said, holding out his hand.

Mills offered Malcom his hand and the two exchanged a firm handshake.

'Thank you for apprehending the real bomber and helping to clear my name,' Malcolm said. 'I could live with a blemish on my personal reputation, but the thought of it affecting my family, community and livelihood was almost too much to comprehend during those hours in custody.'

'You're welcome,' replied Mills. 'Darby thought he was smart enough to avoid detection. Granted it may have taken us a little longer to find him had it not been for his wife and her friend, but we would have. I must say, I think I speak for several of the people here in admiring your decision to attend this evening.'

Malcolm smiled at the detective.

'Tonight, is a show of solidarity,' he said. 'Please know that I don't hold any blame towards you or your colleagues for what happened, you were just doing your jobs. I am also grateful for you upholding what you said you would do upon my release. With the passage of time, Joe Darby's name will become a distant memory, but we people shall endure. No matter where we come from or what we believe, we are one.'

Mills smiled at him before looking up at the evening stars above the glow of candlelight.

'Amen.'